The Magnificent Death of Mira Meadows

ANJ Press

THE MAGNIFICENT DEATH OF MIRA MEADOWS
ANJ Press, First edition. JUNE 2022.
Copyright © 2022 Nadia Jovie.
Written by Nadia Jovie.

Cover design by Books Covered
Map by MistyBeee

for my darling
should we meet again
I will be a bird
you will be the wind

TARTARUS
VIOLET ISLAND
NORDAVIA
OLD-YORK
NEW BELGIUM
LAURIUM
MAGNIFICO
EMERALD
VERITY
THUNDER ISLAND
N
ISLE OF DRAGONS
ASPHODAVIA

1

Death

M ira hadn't expected to die that day. It happened in a moment as quick as a breath, or a kiss, or the detonation of a bomb.

It was an unwanted moment, to be sure, but there are times when unwanted doesn't mean unneeded.

There are other times it does.

In the end, these happenings happen all the same, and death can't be undone, unless you are lucky, or very unlucky.

Six hours and eleven minutes before dying:
Wedding dress shopping isn't inherently dangerous, though one could argue planning for the future is always risky.

Mira Meadows and her cousin Sara, the bride-to-be, were free from their grueling schedule at the hospital and had intended to sleep in that morning. Unfortunately, the endless mandatory overtime had left its mark. They woke at five forty-seven and six twenty-two, respectively.

"If we were good coworkers," Mira said as she got into Sara's car, "we'd be helping the rest of the nurses on the picket line right now."

"Do you have a need to help someone?" Sara slipped on a pair of sunglasses. "Try helping yourself."

Mira suppressed a smile. She'd expected as much from Sara, but she felt like it needed to be said.

It was the perfect day for striking, after all. The heat of the Richmond summer hadn't yet made itself known, the air still crisp and breathable, and the sun was intermittently blocked by passing white, bulbous clouds.

Ever committed to self-preservation, Sara would argue the weather was another reason to seize the day – for themselves – and truth be told, Mira was excited to have a chance to wear her new tank top. She'd gotten it online and paid extra for expedited shipping. It had the cutest headphone-wearing dog on the front, and a fluffy tail on the back.

Sara said it was grotesque.

"You were just complaining we haven't gotten a raise in four years," Mira countered.

"Yeah, and that's not going to change." Sara put the car into drive, zipping down the street. "What's the point of angering the administrators? You know goading the owners is never wise."

"They're not our owners. You just want to go shopping."

"That's beside the point." Sara cut into traffic, earning the blast of a car horn behind them. She stuck her hand out of the window and gave a peace sign. "You'll see. The nurses will fold faster than it would take for us to drive there."

Maybe she was right. Things never changed. At least, not for the better.

Mira looked out at the cute little bungalows and cottages lining the street. The home prices had doubled since she'd moved to Richmond.

She couldn't afford it then, and she couldn't afford it now. Missing a few days of work wouldn't change that, and neither would an overdue two percent raise.

On the other hand, it hadn't helped Mira's finances when Sara "Look Out for Yourself" Meadows had moved out of their apartment to live with her boyfriend – now fiancé – of three months.

Sara was happy, though, and Mira had no interest in spoiling it. She would keep saving, find a new roommate, and eventually things would work out.

Five hours and two minutes before dying:
The bridal shop had one dressing room, and it was attended by a woman with a permanent scowl and bedazzled shoulder pads. Mira wasn't sure what had come first – the wrinkles in her face or the addiction to sparkle.

Mira sat on a velvet pink pouf outside the dressing room's curtain and watched the woman trudge back and forth between the sea of dresses.

After considerable commotion, Sara emerged from the dressing room, tightly bound at the knees by a lace and pearl studded mermaid gown. Her shuffle to the pedestal in front of the mirrors was enough to make up Mira's opinion on the dress.

"How's my butt look?" Sara asked.

Mira flashed a thumbs up. "Tremendous."

Sara turned around, her face pinched. "That's not a helpful comment."

"Then you should probably be doing this with someone else."

"No." Sara turned back to face the mirror, running her fingers along the netted neckline, her forefinger lingering on a small pearl dangling near her collarbone. "I appreciate the honesty. If you ever set a date for your wedding, I'll be happy to return the courtesy."

"We will. Eventually." Mira paused. Her boyfriend Robbie – er, fiancé – lived on the other side of the country, finishing his fellowship. It worked fine for them. They'd both grown comfortable with what they had, and she wasn't a romantic like Sara. Plus, she wasn't big on planning or details. There was no need to rush. "We have time."

Sara lifted an eyebrow in response. She knew goading the universe was unwise, but she decided not to say anything.

Three hours and sixteen minutes before dying:
"Aren't you a little big for ice cream?"

Mira looked up from her cone. She didn't recognize the guy, and she couldn't quite interpret the smile on his face. Her eyes drifted down, scanning the Hawaiian button-up shirt, the protruding belly, and the sandal with white socks combination.

Was he leering? Or was he an innocent tourist? Someone's unattended, ill-mannered husband?

The sweat pooling at the tip of his nose was distracting, and while at six feet tall, Mira expected comments about her height, erring on the side of friendliness had never worked for her.

It seemed like people always felt the urge to walk up to her and say something. It was often one of the same three questions – how tall are you, do you play basketball, do you play volleyball?

The accusation she was "too big" for ice cream was insulting, but at least it was original.

Mira's mom had always been a firm believer that people approached her daughter because she was a beautiful, irresistible goddess with a cascading red mane of hair and "expensively straightened teeth." She used to say the Christian thing to do was answer politely and excuse herself if she didn't want to talk.

But her mom was three hundred miles away.

"I could say the same for you," she said, nodding toward his belly before turning and taking five steps in the other direction.

Sara emerged from the ice cream shop at that moment, the door clattering shut behind her. "All right, I got you your snack. Are you ready to keep going?"

The man was unmoved, now licking his ice cream cone seemingly *at* them.

She'd made the right decision. "I need to call the hospital first."

"No." Sara let out a groan. "They'll ask you to come in and work."

"I'm not going to cross the picket line." Mira pulled out her phone and dialed. "I need to see if my patient was discharged."

"Why?"

"I have his dog."

"I am not letting you put that dirty mutt in my car! I just vacuumed, Mira."

It was ringing. And ringing, and ringing. "Relax. I gave him a bath."

"The dog or the patient?"

Mira laughed and a familiar voice answered her call – the unit secretary. "Hey, it's Mira. How's my guy?"

"Oh, hey. He's good. They sent him out last night."

"Excellent."

"We're not good, though. Admissions didn't slow at all. We're falling apart."

Sara, within earshot of the call, mouthed, "Told you so."

"I'll be back soon, I'm sure," Mira said before hanging up.

One hour and forty-four minutes before dying:
Harold's dog was sound asleep on Mira's couch. The little mutt technically wasn't allowed on the couch, but when no one was home, who could stop her? The old girl was smart enough to put that together, and Mira knew scolding would have no effect. Instead, she woke her with a head scratch and soaked in the excited tail wags.

Harold was a frequent flyer in their hospital, his homelessness and diabetes ever at odds. The first time he'd refused admission because he had no one to care for his dog, Mira volunteered to take the old girl in. She was only thirty pounds – nothing for Sara to get upset about – and Mira missed having a dog. Her own dog had passed away two years ago, and she still couldn't talk about him without tearing up.

"Keep her from licking the windows this time!" Sara called over her shoulder. "Where is Harold anyway?"

Mira sat in the back of the small sedan, having thrown the piles of clothes that had been draped over the backseat onto the floor.

"He usually hangs out in front of the 7-Eleven, or near the homeless shelter."

"Just what I wanted for my magical day of wedding dress shopping. A trip to the homeless shelter."

The dog snuggled in, resting her chin on Mira's thigh and closing her eyes. She paid no attention to Sara's rants, and Mira followed her lead.

They found Harold a block from the homeless shelter, sitting on the corner in what looked like a new pair of pants.

Sara pulled up and put on her flashers – the universal sign for "I know I'm in the way, but I'm not moving."

Mira rolled down her window. "Special delivery!"

Harold's expression brightened and a smile spread across his face. He was missing his two front teeth, which Mira thought gave him a sort of endearing appearance, though Sara disagreed.

"There's my girl," he said, standing and walking to the car.

Sarah turned to Mira and whispered "Ew."

"He means the dog," Mira murmured before opening her door.

The little mutt leapt from the car and into her owner's arms, her tail shaking the entirety of her body.

"Thanks for keeping an eye on her." He was grinning now, the dog plastering the side of his face with her tongue.

"You're welcome," Mira said. "How about you take your insulin so you don't end up in my ICU again?"

He waved a hand. "Yeah, yeah. The good Lord will take me when it's my time."

"Uh huh. And how many toes will you have left when you finally get to meet him?"

He laughed, scooping the little dog into his arms and walking back to his sleeping bag. He reached under and held up a small plastic bag. "I've got the insulin. I'll do what they said."

Mira nodded. "Good."

Sara watched this exchange with a flat expression. "Are you ready to go?"

Mira reached into the car and pulled out a duffel bag containing dog food and a small stuffed dragon. "She carried the dragon right into my place."

"She doesn't go anywhere without it. It's her good luck charm." He paused, breaking his downward gaze to look up at Mira. His smile faded. "I'm worried about you. You don't look long for this world. Maybe she knew you need it more than she does."

The sentiment was sweet, but Mira was not going to take a homeless dog's favorite toy. "I'll be fine. You two take care."

Once they'd pulled away, Sara started her usual scolding. "If you're not careful, the hospital will find out about this and turn it into some feel-good story they'll take credit for on the news."

"Harold would never go on the news. He says camera lenses zap your energy and plant dark seeds in your soul."

"Hm." Sara made a turn into their second bridal shop of the day. "He's not wrong there."

Fifty-two minutes before dying:
Sara was on her fourth dress when they got the call. The strike had been broken, and while negotiation results were unclear, it

sounded like administrators had agreed to a one-time three percent raise, but nothing to address the unsafe nurse-to-patient ratios or lack of staff.

"Told you." Sara smirked at her reflection in the mirror as the massive, strapless ballgown tried to escape her grasp.

Eleven seconds before dying:

The crosswalk turned to **WALK** and Mira readied herself for the third and final shop of the day.

"How about this time you go in and say you need the quickie package?" She turned, grinning, when she didn't get a response. "Ask what's available to ship in three weeks and we can save some – "

One second before dying:

The truck had been a splurge, a special order: diamond white paint with metallic flecks of pink, oversized golden rims, an LED light bar, and a tastefully lifted body. The owner told herself she deserved it when she bought it, and that's what she told herself when she made the payments. Coincidentally, that was what she told herself when she'd picked up a second Starbucks that morning, too.

She had no idea that a vehicle traveling at thirty-two miles per hour has a twenty-five percent chance of killing a pedestrian, and increasing the speed by ten miles per hour bumps that risk to fifty percent.

If she'd known that, she might not have increased her speed to thirty-nine in an attempt to beat the yellow light, and when that failed, forty-three to escape the red.

In the end, it was the lifted body that did the trick, striking Mira precisely in her chest and stopping her heart on impact.

2

Dark matter

In another world within a different universe lies an island covered in mounds and mountains of blindingly white sand. A sun rises and sets there, as it does anywhere else that hosts life, though there is no freshwater, vegetation, or discoveries to be made other than bleached bones and hunks of glass that appear and disappear with the blowing of the winds.

At its fiercest, the wind is deafening, disorienting, and wild, with unpredictable sandstorms whipping up a darkness that can last for days. In the moment just before Mira's heart was stopped by a real-life Barbie's Dream Truck, the wind had quieted to a whisper. The sand merely danced an inch from the surface, giving a fuzzy but manageable view of the landscape.

Inside the nearest sand valley sat a carriage pulled by two mules. The stark black sides contrasted beautifully with the white desert, though the brass bars on the windows did nothing to keep the sand from blowing in.

"Please," called a man's voice from inside. "I don't want to go back. I'll do anything."

Evander looked out onto the horizon. He wasn't a handsome man, with elongated ears and a too-small nose – a difficult look for a nose to achieve – but his larger-than-average face balanced it in a non-threatening sort of way.

His appearance had never held him back, as his vanity lay else-where, and paired with a set of glasses, he managed a rather book-ish, wise appearance. His once-sandy brown hair had faded nearly entirely to white, only adding to his chosen charm.

The desert was calm and clear – the perfect time to act. Evander turned to his two men and nodded. "Send him out. "

They moved toward the carriage and pulled the small copper-lined door open. The two people inside cowered in the corners as Evander's men grabbed a set of arms and threw the first person to the ground.

"Don't be afraid," Evander said, looking down at the man. "If you're meant to stay, you'll stay."

The man looked up at him, his jaw quivering, his shirt in tatters, torn at the shoulder and stained yellow at the seams.

Evander reached out a hand and brushed the torn cloth aside, exposing the glowing lightning bolt on the left side of the man's chest. It had nearly completely faded, only a faint whisper of the brilliance it once had. There was no time to waste.

"Go." Evander pulled him up by the shirt and pushed him out, toward the next sand dune. "Walk with your head high and meet your fate. Be brave."

The man stumbled forward, dragging his feet and leaving long trails behind him in the sand.

Evander looked at his men and rolled his eyes. If he were ever to die, he would do it with more dignity. Not because he believed in fate, but because ugly or not, there was nothing more impor-tant than appearances, no matter which universe you found your-self in.

Evander knew it well enough. When he had been on earth, it was his job to say things like, "The universe is everything," and to try to teach eighteen-year-old simpletons about the billions of galaxies in existence.

His life as a physicist had yielded no true answers, as he had asked no questions and pursued no leads. He got by whispering phrases like "the universe is less compact today than it was yesterday" and "Earth is a fragile blip in the history of time."

The last statement, at least, had made an impact on him. That fragility was not cause for awe, but for exploitation.

He looked at the foaming grey sky above them. Thunder rumbled around, flashes of light pulsing in the clouds.

The man had turned around to face him. "Please," he yelled. "I'll do anything."

Evander smiled and waved his hand. "Keep going. This could be your destiny."

Another phrase he used to use. It seemed to motivate people. Why, he didn't know.

The man walked on, growing smaller in the sea of white.

Evander decided that next time they needed to bring brighter clothes so he could watch without having to squint. He always thought of it when they were there, but the idea went out of his head as soon as he left the island.

The sky morphed from a smoky overhang to a blanket of soot and coal. Evander's shadow grew longer, and the rumbling grew closer.

His heart raced. This was it. The moment he loved most. He could feel the hair standing up on his arms, but alas, since his own lightning bolt had faded years ago, he was at no risk for a strike.

He took a pair of copper and silver goggles out of his pocket, the round lenses shaded dark, and pulled them over his eyes just as a shock of light illuminated the sky.

The bolt was jagged and elegant, striking the man and holding for just a moment before dropping him to the ground.

Amazing.

It had worked, and the spoils would come later. That was what Evander cared about most. He was untroubled by magic or mechanics, and had never understood his scientist colleagues who toiled for decades, investigating seemingly meaningless minutiae. While their findings could be revolutionary, they could also be entirely useless.

Evander didn't waste time on useless things, and the richness of his life was all he needed to assure himself he was living the right way.

Yet in this one peculiar instance, with its statistically improbable outcome, Evander's faith in himself would prevent the discovery of what – or whom – was at the other end of that particular lightning bolt until it was far too late.

3

The other side

A crack of thunder loud enough to wake the dead echoed through the trees.

Mira opened her eyes and stared at the sea of branches above her. The air smelled of evergreen and fresh, like the time she and Sara had discovered tequila when they were seventeen and woke up sprawled under the Christmas tree.

She took a deep breath and savored the memory before raising herself up and looking around. Everything around her was Christmas trees!

How lovely. The one nearest to her had a strip of bark missing down the center of the trunk. She ran her fingers along it, her mind pleasantly drifting. If only she didn't have heartburn...

One hand went to rub her chest, and the other to absentmindedly pick dry pine needles out of her hair. Something stuck to her hand and she pulled it away to study it.

Sap. Amber, freckled with pebbles and dirt.

How odd.

Mira pressed her hand into the cool, soft ground in an attempt to wipe the sap away. She succeeded only in coating her hand in dirt.

The soil was so pleasantly cold to the touch, though, that it seemed like a good idea to lay her cheek against it again for a few more minutes, just a little longer before she had to get up for work...

She'd dozed off when the sound of a distant scream jolted her eyes open and sharpened her senses. Mira sat up and strained to listen.

Was it a bird? A child?

Mira heard it again, and this time she forced herself to stand, steadying herself on a tree branch.

There was nothing but the chirps of birds for a moment, but then she heard something – something human. It was more of a groan than a cry this time, and it made Mira's heart rate take off. Someone was in trouble, and without exploring the idea of who it might be or where she was, Mira set off to find them.

The trees were easy enough to walk between until she hit a thick patch of undergrowth and shrubs. Mira pressed through, pausing only to break branches caught in her sappy hair.

It was no more than twenty feet of distance, but it took her a frustrating five minutes to free herself from the thorny branches and stumble knee-first onto a dirt road at the edge of the forest.

On the other side of the road was a rolling, green field. A lopsided barn stood straight ahead, the wood slats faded in some parts and entirely missing in others.

The sound was coming from inside, she was sure of it now. It had evolved into hysterical crying. Mira strode forward, so focused on her task that she walked directly into an overturned car.

Or at least she thought it was a car. She took a step back and looked at the thing. It had tires, though they were thin, like bicycle tires, and set askew at an unnatural angle. One had snapped off entirely and laid uselessly at the side of the car's body. The paint was flat black, chipped around the mangled parts, and she could recognize a door and at least one headlight. The canvas canopy had crushed inwards, and Mira was able to easily lift it and toss it out of the way.

No one was inside the antique-looking thing. She would have thought it was a decoration or an abandoned project, but steam was hissing from the front, giving it an altogether too alive appearance.

An idea tugged at the back of her mind, quietly, non-urgently, like the wisp of a memory. She stared at the car, trying to grasp what her mind was trying to connect, but it was like trying to catch smoke with her hands.

She looked up from the mess of metal and again her thoughts were overtaken by the sound of intense suffering within the barn.

Mira walked around the hissing car and tugged at the barn door. It was heavy and awkward to move, but she was feeling more alert and managed to heave it open with two pulls.

"Hello?" she called out.

The crying abruptly stopped. She squinted, unable to make out any human or animal form in the darkness. The only light streamed in through the missing boards on the walls, with dust dancing in the beams.

She walked clumsily, catching her feet on mounds of hay and overturned buckets until her eyes adjusted to the darkness. From what she could see, the barn wasn't large, with a passthrough hallway connecting doors in the front and back, and three gated stalls on either side. It wouldn't be too hard to find whatever was making the noise.

Mira started her search by peering into the stalls on the right side of the barn. After finding only bits of broken pitchforks and wheelbarrows, she moved to the left side.

The first stall was the only one with its door pulled shut. Mira stood on her tip toes to peer inside, finding a dark, huddled mass in the corner.

"I'm here to help," Mira said, pulling on the door to the stall.

With the door open, there was enough light for Mira to see a woman on the ground. She was sitting on a mound of blood-soaked hay, clutching her knees.

The woman looked up and a quiet sob escaped the hand she'd put over her mouth. Her eyes were small and puffy, and her long, chestnut hair was plastered to her forehead with sweat and blood.

"Are you hurt?" Mira asked, kneeling a few feet away. "I'm a nurse, my name is Mira. Can you tell me what happened?"

"Please leave me alone." The woman's lavender dress was hiked up to her knees, and now Mira could clearly see the blood was fresh. She inched closer and the woman flinched, both blood-stained hands darting to her abdomen.

Oh. She was pregnant, and quite obviously so.

Mira retreated and softened her voice. "What's your name?"

A few sniffles, then "Arianna."

"Okay Arianna, I'm going to find help. You're doing great, and you're going to be okay."

She opened her mouth, hyperventilating as tears spilled from her eyes.

Had she been in that mangled car? Surely it had no air bags, because it looked like it'd been driven out of the 1930's.

Arianna had lost a lot of blood. If she had to guess, Mira would bet she had a placental abruption from the trauma. She'd seen at least a dozen when she'd worked in the ER. If she didn't act quickly, she risked losing both mom and baby.

Mira reached into her back pocket for her phone, only to find it empty. She tried her other pockets. Nothing.

"Have you called for help?" Mira asked. "Do you have a phone?"

She shook her head.

"How far along are you?"

Arianna wiped a tear away with her shoulder. "Sixteen moons."

Okay, maybe she'd had one blow to the belly and one to the head.

"Hang tight. We're going to get an ambulance and get you to the hospital."

"No!" Arianna reached forward and grabbed Mira by the wrist. "I can't go to the hospital. My brother went to get help."

No hospital. Sure. She could just bleed to death in this barn. "I'm going to find help – "

"No." Arianna cut her off. "Mick should be here soon." Her grip weakened and her eyelids fluttered, once, twice, then a last time before closing shut.

"Crap." Mira leaned forward and tapped Arianna on both sides of her face. "Hey, hey. Wake up!"

Arianna didn't respond, and Mira rubbed on her sternum, trying to rouse her.

Arianna's eyes opened for a moment before closing again.

Not good. Mira stood up and screamed. "We need help! Someone call 911!"

She ran out of the stall, through the barn and onto the road. "Help!"

There was not a soul nearby, and nothing but silence in response.

She could run down the road, but which way? Where was the nearest house, or car, or anything?

It didn't matter. She started to sprint, kicking up dust behind her, and she made it twenty feet past the barn when her lungs filled with fire. It felt like her chest was being squished and she doubled over, coughing and gagged for air.

Ridiculous. She wasn't in great shape, but she could move when she needed to. Was this panic?

No, Mira didn't panic. Not because of a little blood. She forced herself to keep going, still wheezing when she tripped, fell, and slammed her forearms into the dirt.

What was going on with her today? She struggled to stand, but it seemed like the world was spinning around her. She stumbled to the ground again, and with her face in the dirt this time, she took a few deep breaths before commanding herself to focus.

Breathe – one, two three.

Voices. Mira looked up, still dizzy but at least oriented, and realized they were coming from behind the barn.

Maybe that brother wasn't so useless after all. Mira got up slowly and half ran, half shuffled to the back of the barn. A man came into view first, his black suit jacket hanging open, exposing the blood-splattered shirt beneath.

Their eyes met and she stopped.

"What do you want?" he asked.

It wasn't the bloody clothing Mira found chilling. It was his eyes, ice blue and zeroed in on her. "I need help." She motioned to the barn. "There's an injured woman inside. We need to get her to the hospital. Can you call 911?"

He said nothing and walked off, opening the back door of the barn with one swift pull before disappearing inside. A woman followed him closely, her face obscured by the thick, purple hood of her coat.

They'd ignored her. Great.

Mira took a few steps, reaching the threshold of the doorway. The woman's coat swished around the corner and into Arianna's stall.

Was that a coat? Or was it a robe? It was too hot to wear a coat, and too bizarre to wear a robe. Who were these people?

Mira felt a nudge on her shoulder and she turned, letting out a little gasp. A horse had snuck up behind her somehow, thrusting his velvety black snout into her shoulder before proceeding to rub his neck on her.

"Not now, buddy," she muttered, patting him on the nose and walking into the barn.

Mira finally felt like she could breathe again, and the world had stopped being out of balance. It didn't matter what Arianna said, or what these people were wearing, or that a horse wanted to use her as a scratching post. She knew what needed to be done. This was what she was trained to do.

"We need to call an ambulance," she said firmly. "She's lost consciousness and she doesn't have much time."

Neither the man nor the robed woman acknowledged her, instead focusing on Arianna.

The woman had lowered her hood and knelt down, placing her hands on Arianna's stomach.

"We have to get her out of here *now!*" Mira grabbed at the man's shoulder, but he flicked his arm and sent her toppling to the ground.

The air went out of her lungs, and she struggled to raise herself up. Once on her knees, Mira turned to face Arianna and a light caught her eye. It looked as though the robed woman's hands were emitting a faint yellow glow.

Mira crawled forward, mesmerized.

At first, she thought it was an illusion – perhaps a lantern, or a cell phone trick – but no, the woman's skin illuminated the small space, casting shadows and brightening Arianna's ghostly white cheeks.

Her hands started to shake ever so slightly and the vibration rippled, sending hay dancing and Mira's ears buzzing.

Arianna's eyes fluttered open and she smiled. "Mickey. You made it."

"I did." His voice was deep, like before, but much softer than when he'd addressed Mira. He knelt down and took her hand. "Just relax now."

The glow grew brighter and the buzzing intensified.

Clearly, Mira was hallucinating. She must have hit her head. Perhaps she'd been in that car, too, with many-mooned Arianna.

The vaguest memory of lights filled her mind, and she closed her eyes, trying to make sense of it.

Headlights, headlights. When had she seen headlights? Not like the one on the car out front. Bigger, rectangular, with bug wings on them...

A tiny cry ripped her from her thoughts and Mira opened her eyes. The color had returned to Arianna's cheeks, and she was smiling down at an infant in her arms, his red tomato face pinched, his mouth open as it emitted a steady stream of complaints.

The woman rose from Arianna's side, the glow from her hands gone. She turned, casting her gaze upon Mira, and even in the darkness Mira could see the woman's eyes shone brilliantly, a deep violet color, like an amethyst under a jeweler's light.

She had felt odd before – weak, or sick, perhaps a little crazy – but for the first time, the thought occurred to her that she must be dreaming.

4

Captain Crunch

The violet-eyed woman flashed a smile as she walked by. Mick, stooped next to Arianna, murmured in low tones before standing. He walked out of the stall, motioning for Mira to follow.

She was too stunned to resist so she stood, dusting her knees off and walking behind him.

When they reached the barn's back door, he stopped and turned toward her. He was close enough now that she could see the details of his face. There was a smooth, white scar at the top of his cheekbone, thin and straight as though sliced by a blade. There were other scars, smaller and hollow looking, that broke his smooth, stubble-free skin. She would have guessed he was younger than she was, if not for the wrinkles at the corner of his eyes and the shining, purple skin beneath them.

"Do you always sleep in trees?"

Mira tilted her head. "What?"

He pointed to her hair and Mira reached up, finding flakes of leaves and a pine needle.

She ran her fingers through, trying to comb out the mess. "I don't remember how that got there." A bug with dash of white on its back dropped to the ground. She stared at the white marking. It reminded her of something, a memory still dancing just outside of her consciousness.

"Good." He nodded. "How about you forget what you saw, then?"

She was still stuck on the bug. "Was I in the car with Arianna?"

He stared at her, his expression unchanged and unreadable. "I expect you'll be asleep again soon." He turned his back to her and walked outside.

Mira was at the cusp of a smoky memory, as if she could only take a deep breath, she'd catch it.

She ran after him. "I need to know – "

She stopped. The violet-eyed woman was sitting on the back of the pushy horse. Mira had failed to notice how enormous the animal was before, his shoulder clear above her head. His coat shimmered in the sunlight, his body entirely black except for the silver-tipped wings he had tucked at his sides.

She'd failed to notice those, too.

He extended the wings outwards, stretching, before cantering past the barn, into the grassy field, and taking off into the sky.

A weakness filled her chest and spread to her limbs. Her legs were too heavy to stand any longer. She staggered backward, leaning against the wall of the barn before sliding down and plopping into a pile of hay.

Her eyes closed and her head rolled to the side before she jerked awake once, twice, then lost the battle and drifted off to sleep.

• • •

She was awakened by a jab just beneath her left collarbone.

"Ow!" Mira sat up, covering the stinging area of her chest with her hand.

"Wake up, little Traveler."

Mira stood, still clutching at the bare skin above her tank top, and steadied herself against the barn until her eyes were level with the man's. "Don't touch me."

"Oh, not so little, are you?" The man let out a small laugh, the ends of his meticulously curled mustache dancing at his lips. "You're the fourth one this week, you know."

"Fourth what?" She pulled her hand away and looked down at the offending area. A streak of her skin was giving off heat, but stranger than that was how it looked – jagged, with a dull white glow.

Mira strained, trying to get a better view. The skin surrounding it was red and inflamed, and the streak itself was complicated, splintering into branches like the dendrites on a neuron.

"You've discovered your bolt," the man said, poking it again.

An electric shock ran through her, not as painful as before, but uncomfortable, like she'd hit her funny bone.

Mira gritted her teeth and glared at him. Her skin felt like it had been burned. Had he done it?

What kind of a sicko brands a sleeping woman? He looked like a sicko, with his tall blue hat and matching woolen pants. His ocean blue jacket was piped with gold along the edges, and medals hung from his chest.

It was meant to make him look official, surely, but Mira thought he looked like he belonged on a children's cereal box.

"We received reports of a lightning bolt near here," he continued. "Where did you land?"

Mick emerged from the open stall door and answered for her. "She hit our car, Constable Ferdinand."

"Is that so?" He raised an eyebrow and peered into the barn. "Who else witnessed this?"

"My sister, Arianna."

Ferdinand stomped past Mira and into the barn. Within seconds, he'd retreated back outside. "I see our Traveler wasn't the only birth today?"

Traveler. What was that about? Mira looked down at her chest again. The bolt, as he'd called it, was still glowing.

Mick nodded and pulled the barn door shut behind him. "Luckily there was no real harm done when she landed."

"That's interesting." Ferdinand pulled a kerchief from his pocket and dabbed at the sweat on his forehead. "Are you sure it was the bolt? The damage to your car looked like it was caused by magic to me."

Mira's eyes darted to Ferdinand. Did he say magic?

"Quite sure." Mick nodded toward the road.

A second man, in an outfit similar to Ferdinand's but with a much smaller hat, approached them.

"No one else was nearby at the time, sir."

"Ah." Ferdinand looked at Mira. "What do you call yourself, girl?"

Her first instinct was to lie, but she was too sluggish to think of a name. After a moment of searching, she admitted, "Mira."

"Did you see any magic here, Mira?"

She narrowed her eyes. "Magic?"

Ferdinand turned to his companion and let out a sigh. "They're often slow and confused when they're first born. Some may not realize they've died for some time, but at least it keeps them agreeable."

The man nodded, brow furrowed and eyes focused on Mira.

Ferdinand took a step closer to her. "Yes, magic. Anything abnormal, or stunning, or frightening?"

Mira shifted her weight. That hay wasn't as soft as it looked and her tailbone was aching. "No."

Ferdinand leaned in, his breath hot and sour. "Nothing out of the ordinary at all?"

She flitted her eyes to the side, over his shoulder, pretending to think. She could see Mick locked on her, his stare unbroken and unblinking.

Though she felt off, Mira still had her instincts. Mick was waiting to see if she'd narc about the glowing hands, or the pegasus horse, or the baby that shouldn't have popped out in a matter of seconds.

Though Mira had no idea if what she'd seen was real or dreamt, she knew one thing – she was not a narc.

"Nothing unusual."

"Are you certain? This is important. If anything magical occurred, I need to know." He smiled, his bright white teeth only inches from her face. "It's for your safety."

Of course it was. "I haven't seen a thing, except for the magic of childbirth."

"Still loopy, I see." His smile fell and he backed away. "Fine. Come with me. I'll get you to the Traveler Center."

"Thank you, but I'm not traveling anywhere." She felt more stable than before, enough that she might be able to run away if she needed to. "I've got to get to work."

"Work?" Ferdinand scoffed. "Mira, my dear. You are dead."

5

Pontos

T he mind has an arsenal of tools for reacting to unpleasant information. There's anger, which can smolder and obscure truth for hours, years, or even a lifetime. Another option is to induce a state of shock, common with trauma and surprises. Bargaining and justification can both soften the initial blow, and when all else fails, denial is an excellent fallback.

The heart, however, works differently than the mind. Despite often being the first to recognize an impending reality, it doesn't bluster, or yell, or react at all.

Hearts speak softly, their warnings as quiet as the pluck of a single harp string. Some people refer to the heart's calls as intuition, branding it too vague to be trusted. Others think of it as instinct, something innate and primal.

In still other cases, it can be seen as a hard-earned skill through years of, say, looking at a patient in a hospital bed and knowing death is about to strike, despite having no evidence to support that fact.

Mira had worked her way through nursing school, taking evening classes and picking up shifts at all other hours of the day. She had spent years in the ER, then on a trauma team, and finally in the ICU. Like many seasoned nurses, Mira could sense death not only in the piles of scans and lab values, but in the empty space between, in the absence of fact where words do no justice.

Death has a whisper. Sometimes it echoes for weeks prior, and other times, it gives only a moment's notice.

But to the well-trained heart, there is always a warning.

Even as her mind protested, ready to deflect or insist she was in a dream, Mira's heart knew. There was no explanation needed.

"Dead," she said flatly.

"Yes, yes, but don't fall to pieces just yet," Ferdinand said. "I don't like tears. They're quite defeatist."

"Yes," Mick added. "Keep your distress to yourself."

Ferdinand shot him a look. "Best of luck to you, to Arianna, and to the child. Come now, Mira, the Traveler Center will get you righted. They'll help you get back to your wretched world, if you so prefer."

Her world. "Get back?"

"To your other life." He waved a hand. "Your other body, if it's in good enough form."

She stared at him, waiting for a flood of memories to help her make sense of what he was saying.

Nothing came. It had to be a dream, right?

Ferdinand turned away from her and his man followed. "Are you ready, then?" They took large strides toward the road, leaving Mira standing there, dumbfounded. "You can either accept my help now, or find your own way on foot later. "

Neither of those choices appealed to her, but Mira wanted to know more about this wretched world, even if she didn't fully believe it was real yet. "I'm coming."

A car was waiting for them, different from Mick and Arianna's car. The color was far more vibrant, with gleaming forest green paint, and there was delicate white detailing over the rims and doors. The roof was solid metal instead of flimsy canvas, and there wasn't a single dent in the entire body.

It had four doors, compared to the destroyed car's two, and Ferdinand's man opened one of the back doors for her. She had the brief thought that this was a bad idea, but she didn't feel particularly threatened by either of these men, so she slipped into the backseat without protest.

The interior of the car was even more elaborate than the exterior. It was surprising they didn't make her sit on a towel or something. The shorts she was wearing – the ones she remembered picking out to take Sara dress shopping in – were caked in mud and dust. Her legs didn't look much better. She considered trying to keep them off of the seat, but the caramel leather felt too pleasantly smooth and cool against her skin.

Everything had gold trim, from the windows to the seat cushions to all of the buttons and dials on the dashboard of the car. The steering wheel looked like it was made of solid gold, which seemed problematic, as it had been sitting in direct sunlight.

Ferdinand held the wheel by its only shaded spot before turning a small crank several times and bringing the car to life. It sputtered and spit, steam rising from the hood before jerking forward.

The car puttered along, all the while sounding like a lid atop a boiling pot of water; the ride was bouncy, sharp, and loud. No one spoke to her, and Mira was able to stare out of the window at everything they passed.

It took several minutes of driving down the deserted road before anything interesting appeared. First it was rows of small wooden houses, still interspersed between fields, but with signs of life. Then there were great swaths of tents, some covering entire fields, with smoke rising between the peaks, campfires in full midday swing.

They drove on and the dirt road turned solid and rocky, then into cobblestone as the buildings grew larger and more imposing. The initial homes were single level, all wood, with dark stain applied to the exteriors. The further they drove, the more complex the houses became – two stories, with levels of solid brick and colorful purple and pink paints.

Still further on, she saw buildings made entirely of stone, either white or sand colored, with several stories and grand windows.

By the time they reached what looked like a verifiable town, they were no longer the only ones on the road. They passed several horse-drawn carriages – some simple, with closed tops and black paint, while others were ornate and open to the sky. Women in elaborate tufted dresses rode along, hiding beneath their spinning white umbrellas.

On the other end of the spectrum were carts loaded with hay and barrels, pulled by much slower donkeys and driven by sleepy farmers.

Small stands crowded the edges of the streets, selling everything from flowers to kerchiefs to produce. One man had a stand dedicated to spoons of every size, and he called to them, waving a wooden spoon the size of her head.

Ferdinand and his man talked in front, yelling over the clattering of the car and paying her no attention. Mira was glad for it. She was fascinated by the people walking the streets and their strange clothing, the women in their long dresses and the men in linen shirts and billowy pants. Ferdinand was still the most absurd looking, if only for the fact that his clothes were completely inappropriate for the heat.

The car stopped and Mira remembered she was supposed to be going somewhere.

"Right then, Mira, this is where I leave you. Head inside and they'll take care of you."

She peered out of the window, spotting a wooden three-story building with **Traveler Center** painted on the door. It was in better shape than some of the houses she'd seen out in the farmland, but it wasn't as nice as the surrounding buildings. The wood was painted white, chipped and peeling in places, and the windows were cloudy with dirt.

"Thank you for the ride." She reached for a door handle, only to find there was none. She patted the door like a blind squirrel.

"There's a button," Ferdinand said before letting out a huff. "Don't you see it?"

She felt around until she found it, a small pea-sized lump of metal. The moment she pushed it, the door sprung open. "Er, got it. Thanks again."

As soon as she was out of the car, the door shut and Ferdinand drove off without another word.

Mira stared at the building as life went on behind her – horses clacking by, people yelling about this or that price, and children screaming as they ran, weaving through the chaos.

There was no use in gawking. She straightened her shoulders and walked to the front door, opening it with the slightest push.

Inside, it was dark, lit only by indirect sunlight from the windows and candles hanging from the walls. It smelled musty, and Mira suspected the smell was deep within the stiff red carpet beneath her feet.

The large room she'd entered reminded her of a hotel reception area, with a small desk on the far wall and an overstuffed couch in the center.

"Hello?" she called out. "Is anyone home?"

The wall behind the desk cracked open, revealing a door that had blended seamlessly with the wallpaper. A man emerged with a wide smile on his face. "Hi there!"

"Hi. I'm Mira. I was brought here by Ferdinand."

"Hello Mira, I'm Herbert. It's nice to meet you." He dropped a large, leatherbound book on the desk and split it open. "Is that a bolt I see?"

She looked down at her chest, the glow of the bolt even more prominent than it had been when she was outside. The mark was hard to ignore now. It didn't look like a brand or a scar. It was something entirely strange.

"I'll be honest. I don't know what's going on."

He nodded, jotting something down with a feather quill. "Of course. What do you think is happening?"

"I think," she said slowly, "I've lost my mind."

"Let me get you something to drink." He disappeared behind the hidden door.

More used to the darkness now, Mira could see the cutout in the red and yellow wallpaper where the door had hidden. The paper peeled at the edges. It looked as though it weren't meant to be yellow, but had aged into it.

Herbert reappeared with a glass of water and walked around the desk. "Let's take a seat and we can have a talk."

That seemed reasonable, and the peacefulness of the room made the thought of relaxing appealing. She turned and plopped onto the plump pink couch. The coarse fabric irritated her skin immediately, but it felt so nice for her legs to take a break from standing that she didn't much care.

He handed her the water before taking a seat next to her. "This will help you feel better."

Mira took a sip. It was cold and soothing to her dry throat. The taste, too, was incredible – slightly sweet and refreshing. It had the slightest hint of cucumbers, and shortcake, and summer.

She downed the contents of the glass, then handed it back to him.

"Excuse me," she said, a burp rising in her chest. "That was delicious."

"I'm glad you enjoyed it. I added a bit of kykeon to help you remember."

Mira opened her mouth to ask a question, but instead broke into a yawn.

No!

She couldn't go falling asleep every time she was about to get answers. She tried to stand from the couch, but her legs didn't respond, and her eyes drifted shut, sending her back into the cushions.

Asleep *again*.

At least this time, her nap appeared to be brief, lasting all of thirty seconds in her mind's eye.

Mira was crossing the street back in Richmond, turning to tease Sara when she saw it: the white truck, dead in front of her, the driver's face obstructed by a pair of large pink sunglasses.

The truck's shining grill and headlights, the *headlights* she'd seen in that moment, so close she could make out the wings of the bugs splattered across the plastic.

Mira jolted awake. Herbert sat next to her on the couch, watching.

"Did that help?" he asked.

She put a hand on the couch to stabilize herself. "I was hit by a truck."

"Were you?" He leaned closer, mouth straight and serious. "What is a truck?"

"It's like a car, but bigger." She covered her gaping mouth with her other hand and looked down at her legs. "But I'm not hurt at all."

It had to be a dream, then. In dreams she could breathe underwater, and it never struck her as odd until she woke up. She just needed to wake up.

Herbert stared at her, saying nothing.

Mira looked at the bolt on her chest and delicately ran her fingers over it. It buzzed beneath her touch, vibrating ever so slightly. Her heart leapt in the tiniest of flutters.

"How do I wake up?"

"You are awake, Mira."

That couldn't be right. She rubbed her eyes. "Did the truck kill me?"

"Perhaps."

"What does that mean?"

"This can be difficult." Herbert smiled and clasped his hands together. "What happened is this: you were at the point of death, and in that moment, you were lucky enough to be brought here instead. You are a Traveler, Mira."

"Is this heaven?" Mira paused. "Or is it hell?"

He laughed. "You're not in hell. You're in our world, Pontos."

"Pontos." Mira closed her eyes for a moment too long, and the sound of the truck's impact flashed into her mind, the cracking of ribs, and Sara's screams behind her.

She opened her eyes. "Why am I in Pontos?"

"The bolt selected you," Herbert said, shrugging and standing up. "There is no why."

"You said I was at the point of death. So I'm not dead?"

He nodded. "As long as the bolt on your chest shines light, you have a chance to return. Your old life and your old body are frozen in time, waiting for you."

"My old body," she repeated.

"Yes. We have seen Travelers return to your world, only to reappear here when their old bodies have ultimately not survived."

Right. Her old body. If this was a dream, her brain was giving her a way to wake up.

Her legs felt a little stronger, and Mira got up from the couch. "I'd like to go back now, please."

He stood, placing his hand on her shoulder and smiling knowingly. "Of course. Tomorrow we have a teacher coming for you and the rest of the new Travelers. She'll tell you how to get back."

"Will my bolt last to tomorrow?"

"It doesn't disappear that quickly." He paused. "Though they have been losing light faster the last few years."

She raised an eyebrow. Maybe it wasn't so much a dream as it was a hallucination of an oxygen-deprived brian. "How much faster?"

"The teacher will explain tomorrow. As long as your body in the other world can survive the truck attack, you can return."

Mira nodded. That was all she wanted. She wanted to live – if she was, in fact, dead.

The truck wasn't an issue. Sara was right there; she would do everything to help her. She'd stop the bleeding, get her to the hospital, start CPR.

If Mira was dead, or half-dead, Sara would fix her.

Standing was getting difficult again. "Tomorrow."

"Yes. Tomorrow." He smiled. "How about a meal and a bath before you retire?"

It was the least absurd suggestion she'd heard all day. "Sure. Why not."

6

Cohesiveness

A knock at the door roused her from a dream the next morning. Mira opened her eyes, half expecting it to be Sara yelling at her for missing the bridal shower, or the bachelorette party, or some other sacred wedding event.

Instead, she faced the unsettling realization that she was still in the same bed where she'd fallen asleep the night before – a stiff cot wrapped in rough linen, a too-short blanket, and a flat pillow that smelled of wet wool.

Was she dreaming within a dream? Or was this a world where a rushed wedding was no longer her biggest problem?

She took a deep breath. One step at a time. "Come in," she called out.

The heavy wooden door creaked open, and the face of a woman peeked through. "I'm sorry to wake you, but class is going to start soon."

Mira nodded. She could barely remember eating dinner or getting to bed the night before, but she did remember the importance of this class. "Thank you."

"I'm Alice, by the way." She slipped inside, closing the door behind her. She looked a little older than Mira, perhaps in her forties, with large brown eyes and tightly wound black curls. There wasn't a hint of grey in her hair, which made Mira doubt her age, and not a single wrinkle on her tawny-brown skin. "You're Mira, right?"

She nodded. It seemed rude to stay in bed, but Mira wasn't wearing any pants, and her mud-splattered shorts were on the floor halfway across the room. She didn't want to subject this stranger to her half-naked body.

Alice stepped forward with a cloth bundle in her hands. "I remember how tired I was the first few days. I figured you were still asleep when you missed breakfast." She handed the bundle to Mira. "Are you hungry?"

"I am, thanks." Mira unwrapped a corner to find three slices of bread and a hunk of cheese. It was the same thing she'd had for dinner the night prior, save a spoonful of jam.

"It gets better. I've been here eight days and I almost feel normal." Alice smiled, her teeth straight and white. "I'll let you get to it. Class is downstairs. They said it should start in about ten minutes."

Mira thanked her again and waited until Alice disappeared to devour the food. Before, she'd felt nauseated and weak, but now it felt like she needed to eat an entire loaf of bread.

She finished everything in under two minutes and washed it down with water from the jug next to her cot – plain water this time, nothing sweet-tasting that would put her to sleep. She needed to be awake for this class.

After a quick trip to the communal bathroom and a half-hearted attempt to scrape the larger chunks of dirt off her shorts and tank top, Mira made her way downstairs. She followed the voices through the hallway and to the front room opposite Herbert's reception area.

She'd entirely missed the existence of this room the day before, but her senses were much sharper today. She was determined not to miss anything.

The walls in the small room had the same drab wallpaper as the reception area, but there were so many paintings it was hard to see it.

Every painting was of a person, and the sizes ranged from tiny portraits, smaller than the palm of her hand, to some that were nearly life-sized. A silver placard on the wall read "Our Travelers."

In the center of the room sat a rectangular table. Alice was seated, along with two men, facing the far wall. There was a chalkboard in front of them, along with a small speaker's podium. Mira took the last seat next to Alice at the far end of the table.

"You made it!" Alice looked far more put together than Mira. Her clothes were clean and mud-free, and even her breath smelled fresh. "I asked Herbert for something to take notes with. Here, there was just enough for everyone."

Alice slid a sheet of yellow paper across to her, along with a long feather quill.

"I've got two ink wells, too. We can share."

Mira smiled and thanked her. She had the unpleasantly familiar feeling of being a student – the feeling of being unprepared.

School had always been a secondary task for Mira, something done in the evenings or on weekends, or after a twelve-turned-fifteen hour shift.

This would be different, though. She would be a good student. She apparently had to be, to get back to her mangled, truck-attacked body.

Mira leaned forward, waving at the two men seated at the other end of the table. "Hey there. I'm Mira."

The one nearest to her had a round, jolly face with red cheeks and a soft belly. He smiled warmly. "Slava."

"Nice to meet you."

He jerked a thumb to the man seated to his right. "This is Samuel. Or Manuel. I'm not sure, and his English is worse than mine."

Samuel turned to look at her, a flat expression on his face. She waved, and he nodded back.

Mira was about to ask a question when a woman in a floor-length, creamsicle-orange gown walked in and marched to the chalkboard.

"Excellent! You're all here. We can get started." She clapped her hands together and smiled brightly. The orange dress contrasted with her tan skin and shining green eyes. "I'll be your instructor today. My name is Miss Brown and I'm so excited to welcome you!"

Mira frowned, glancing over to see if Alice was as put off by this woman's enthusiasm as Mira was, but Alice paid her no attention. She was carefully writing "Miss Brown" at the top of her paper.

It wasn't just the enthusiasm. It was the dress, too. What was going on there? Sure, it looked nice on her, but wasn't she a bit overdone? It was silk, with tiny beads of white sewn in to look like lace. Was that normal teacher wear? Or was it a function of her soon-to-fail REM sleep, or brain death?

No one else was dressed up. Slava was wearing jeans and a black t-shirt. Samuel was in a navy tracksuit.

Miss Brown snapped her fingers and a map unfurled at the front of the room, covering the chalkboard. "As you may or may not know, you've entered the world of Pontos. You were lucky enough to land in our country, Asphodavia, specifically on this island here." She pointed to an island labeled *Nordavia*. "You're in the Traveler Center for the city of Laurium, and every major city in Asphodavia has a center just like this. We are lucky to have nine out of every ten travelers land on an Asphodavian island. We are so happy to have you!"

Mira looked at the map, reading off city names. *New Belgium, Old York*. Did Travelers name all of these places?

"As you can see, Asphodavia is a country of islands. We have over twenty islands we call home, and that number increases every year as people around our world compete to join our ranks."

Compete to join their ranks. Mira had never known countries to behave that way. The words rolled around in her head, but she couldn't make sense of them.

She had yet to take any notes, but Alice was diligently copying everything down. Mira leaned forward, seeing that Slava had written only his name on top of his paper, and Samuel was busy sketching a butterfly.

Miss Brown snapped her fingers and the map rolled away. "While you're here, touched by the bolt of life, your old body is on hold. We are happy to help you get back to that life, if you so wish."

Mira straightened, quill in hand.

"You may also choose to stay here in Pontos. Both of these options require successful integration into Asphodavian society with positive scores on your record."

That seemed important. Mira wrote **Integration** at the top of her sheet.

"Integration is granted by The Council of Truth, also known as The Council. To successfully integrate, you will be scored on three important factors: episcope trials, lawfulness, and cohesiveness. All of these will be tallied in your record for final evaluation."

"What is episcope?" asked Slava.

"Please raise your hand if you have a question," Miss Brown said sweetly.

Slava didn't miss a beat before raising his hand, and Miss Brown nodded at him.

"What is episcope?" he asked again.

"That is an excellent question. I have one here." She spun, grabbing a nightstand-height table from behind her and dragging it across the floor with a cringe-inducing squeal.

Sitting on top was a small wooden box with a lens the size of a saucer on one side. Miss Brown pulled a one-inch red vial from her pocket and plopped it into the back of the box. When she turned the metal crank on the side and the episcope jumped to life, a beam of light shot onto the opposite wall.

"What you're seeing is a memory from a Traveler just like you."

They watched the image on the wall, a clear, crisp video of a man and woman at the beach. Their voices, slightly flattened and metallic, emerged from the episcope.

Miss Brown stopped cranking, and the image disappeared. "You are to supply a memory every morning when you awaken. The process is easy and painless, and the more memories you supply, the more scenes the local episcope committee will have to choose from in determining your character."

Slava raised his hand and waited a moment to be called on. "What if my memories will not be in English?"

"You will have to supply the translations," Miss Brown said.

"Too bad," Slava muttered under his breath. "I thought it would translate for Samuel so we could find what he is thinking."

Mira stifled a laugh and Miss Brown locked onto her, never breaking her manic smile. "No talking, please. Each of your episcope trials will be broadcast to the community, and the committee will assign a score, filed in your record along with scores for your ongoing lawfulness and cohesiveness."

"How do we get a good episcope score?" Mira asked.

Miss Brown stared at her, her green eyes fixated and her smile stiff.

"Oh, sorry." Mira raised her hand and waited to be called on before repeating herself.

"That is an excellent question. I was just getting there." She turned to write on the chalkboard. "Here in Asphodavia, we follow the three F's: Fairness, Fidelity, and Felicitousness."

Mira wrote furiously, stumped by both the spelling and the meaning of *felicitousness*.

"If your memories show how you can abide by the three F's, you will receive high scores on your episcope trials."

Alice raised her hand and waited until she was called on. "I'm sorry, I had a question about cohesiveness."

"Go on."

"What is cohesiveness?"

Miss Brown let out a breath, turning and swooshing her large dress behind her. She looked like an angry princess.

But like any good princess, she never broke her smile. "I was going to address that later, but I suppose I can talk about it now. Cohesiveness has to do with how well you fit into Asphodavian society. This means understanding and employing our customs, and being sure not to offend others. Also, if you're lucky enough to marry an Asphodavian, your cohesiveness is greatly bolstered."

Mira added *Marry someone?* under **Cohesiveness**. Sara would've loved that. Mira's fiancé, Robbie, however, would not.

Slava's hand shot into the air. "Is it true a man can marry a man?"

Miss Brown nodded vigorously. "Oh yes, our world is much more fair than your world."

He sat back, hands clasped over his belly. "Very nice, Miss Teacher."

She smiled and resumed speaking, her tone methodic and practiced. "The sum total scores from your episcope trials, lawfulness, and cohesiveness will be filed in your permanent record and sent to the Council on Magnifico Island. If you are approved for integration, you will officially become an Asphodavian citizen."

Mira scribbled furiously, frustrated by how sloppy her handwriting was when using a feather, but pleased with her notes overall on the situation. So far, she somewhat understood what integration was – scores the episcope thing, following the law, and being cohesive. All of that went into her record, which went to a Council.

Oh, and her memories had to show her following some F's, which she didn't yet understand, but she would later.

Simple enough. Sort of.

"Once integrated, you will undergo a record review once a year like all other citizens. This ensures citizens maintain standards of lawfulness and cohesiveness.

"Failure to maintain these standards at any point may result in reeducation, jail time, or exile to the Isle of Dragons."

Mira stopped writing. She didn't know where to fit "dragons" onto her sheet. Was that a metaphor for something? Or just a poorly named place?

She raised her hand to ask a question, which Miss Brown ignored. "Once you have integrated, you can submit an application to make the dangerous journey to Thunder Island, where the lightning may choose to take you back to your world, if your bolt has not faded."

Slava spoke. "We have to be hit by lightning to go back to the old life?"

"Yes," Miss Brown said.

He puffed out his cheeks. "How many bad points will send us to the dragons?"

"I am getting there," Miss Brown said, snapping a quill between her hands. She tossed it aside and cleared her throat.

Slava raised his hand, waving it at her.

She stared for a moment before pointing at him. "Yes."

"Are the dragons real?"

"One question at a time," she muttered under her breath. "Yes, the dragons are very real. Don't worry about them now. Worry about your scores. The points for a passing score vary from year to year, and you should know the most serious crimes, and the easiest way to lose points, have to do with magic." She paused, as though waiting for them to react.

They stared at her, silent.

Did she think magic was more shocking than the bomb she'd just dropped about dragons?

She went on. "Yes, dear Travelers. We have magic in our world, far more advanced than anything in your world. While you may see enchanting alchemy used around town, keep in mind that magic is extremely dangerous. Anyone who wishes to use magic must be approved to do so by the Council and purchase a license. All magic is kept in the Hall of Magic on Magnifico Island, and stealing magic, or using unapproved magic, results in immediate banishment to the Isle of Dragons."

That was clear enough. Magic equaled death by dragons – that is, if dragons were real, and if this world was real, and if she wasn't just experiencing hypoxia.

To be safe, Mira wrote it all down, then shot a glance over at Alice's paper. Her notes were much longer and more meticulously organized, which was good, because Mira's notes had quickly devolved into a jumble of important-sounding words and phrases.

Miss Brown clapped her hands together five times, startling even Samuel. "This is vitally important! If you remember one thing from today, remember this.

"Over half of the Travelers who arrive in our world develop a magical skill known as a marking. It is against Council law to conceal a marking. As soon as you believe you may have magic within you, you must alert your committee and your Traveler

Center representative, Herbert. Hiding magic is dangerous to yourself and others."

Mira wrote this down in its entirety. For all the talk of cohesiveness and being F'ed, magic was what made Miss Brown clap at them like they were a flock of unruly children.

Whatever Mira had seen with Mick was real. It was magic, and her instinct to keep her mouth shut had been right.

"Any questions?" Miss Brown stood in front of them, her hands clasped in front of her sparkling bosom.

Mira raised her hand, and this time she wasn't ignored. "How long will it be before our bolts fade?"

"There is no way to tell. Both the bolt, and the lightning connected to it, are mysterious. They are a magic no one can tame, as wild as the dragons that fly over the southern isle. In the past, bolts lasted years, but recently we've seen them disappear in as little as three months. So be on your best behavior!"

Mira wrote **THREE MONTHS** on her paper and circled it. That was all she needed to know.

7

Denial and all her friends

Miss Brown was in a hurry to leave and told them to send any further questions via mail. When she slipped away, they were left at the table to discuss what they'd learned.

"I wish we could get a list of laws," Alice said wearily, eyeing her notes, which filled both the front and back of her sheet. "Maybe we'll get that later."

"It is easy enough," Slava said. "Rules are always the same, no? Do not cause trouble, do not ask too many questions."

"You were pushing it with the questions," Mira said.

Slava laughed. "I'm already in trouble, then."

"I'll do whatever they want me to do," Mira said. "I just need to get back."

"I had a heart attack. I maybe can't go back." Slava let out a sigh. "It was not the first. This body feels much better – fresh, new. Herbert said our new bodies are without sickness."

"You're not going to try to go home?"

He shrugged, leaning back and resting his hands on his belly. "We will see."

Each to his own. Mira knew what she wanted. She was overdue to wake up from this nightmare. "What about you, Alice?"

Alice carefully folded her note sheet before slipping it into her pocket. "I had cancer. My daughters already saw me suffer enough. I'm not planning on making them go through it again."

Oh. Mira hadn't expected that. If this was all in her head, her brain was going all out on the backstory. "I am so sorry."

Alice looked up, a weak smile on her face. "Don't be. I had a lot of time to say goodbye, and I'm grateful for that. I'm grateful for this, too, whatever it'll be."

"Very good for being cohesive," Slava said. "Ten points for you, Alice." He laughed, and everyone joined in, including Samuel.

Mira stopped laughing. Poor Samuel didn't stand a chance. What hope did he have to integrate if he couldn't communicate? It would be months before he learned the language, and by then, his bolt would be gone.

Hopefully he didn't have anyone waiting for him.

"Why can't we go back without integrating?" Mira asked. "They could save themselves a lot of trouble."

Alice turned to her, a pensive look on her face. "Miss Brown said it was dangerous to go to Thunder Island. They must not want to take the risk of helping us get there if we're not someone they've deemed...worthwhile? I don't know."

Slava let out a grunt. "I don't know, but I am sure we will find out."

. . .

After an hour of debating the meaning of the F's, Herbert appeared and announced lunch was ready. They filed down the narrow hallway to the back of the building and into the dining room.

Mira had been slipping in and out of consciousness between bites of food the night prior, but now she could appreciate the space. It had the same drab wallpaper as the rest of the house, but with the benefit of a large, sunny window. There were two long tables with off-white tablecloths covered in doilies, and an assortment of mismatched chairs, benches, and stools.

Herbert ran back and forth, eagerly fetching bowls and silver-ware, quite proud of what he'd put together. "We had a donation from a local farmer, so there is chicken in this stew." He dropped the black pot onto one of the tables with a clunk. "Enjoy!"

It tasted like chicken and carrots, which wasn't bad, but rather plain. When they were done eating, Herbert sat down at the table with a small stack of cards in his hand.

"Now that you've been to class, I can give you your work assignments. These will help with your integration." He peeled the top card off. "Alice, we have you in the library. They requested someone to help with updating and organizing."

She smiled. "I'd like that very much."

"Slava, the winemaker in town offered to take you on as an apprentice."

Slava took the card and nodded. "What a dream."

Herbert smiled. "Samuel, we are sending you to work with a baker."

Samuel accepted the card and Mira leaned to sneak a glance at it. All it had was a picture of a loaf of bread and an address. He looked up at Herbert and nodded.

So far he was doing all right communicating, at least.

"And last, but not least, Mira."

She sat up straight and reminded herself to smile. "Yes?"

"I didn't think I'd be able to get you an assignment in time, but Constable Ferdinand stopped by this morning and offered to take you on. You must have made quite an impression."

She felt a small panic in her chest, like she used to after a night of drinking when someone told her she'd done something "funny."

Mira had behaved nicely, hadn't she? "Is the constable on the episcope committee, by chance?"

"He is not," Herbert said. "But make no mistake, the consta-ble is an important man. He's in charge of keeping records for all

Travelers and citizens in Laurium, and the records for all of the surrounding villages."

Aha. Mira would love a chance to get into those records. Would she be able to look at her own? Could she suck up to Ferdinand enough to get that sort of access?

Herbert held up the card. "The constable told me to stress to you, however, that his work is dangerous. He maintains lawfulness in the city. Do not feel pressured to take this assignment if you are afraid."

Mira reached for the card. "I would be honored."

"Wonderful!" Herbert beamed at them. "Your employers offer a wage of two tallies per day. Some of that will go to renting clothing, and the rest to renting your room. I do apologize. These rates are set by the committee, and currently it is two tallies a week to rent a set of pants and a shirt, and twenty tallies a week to rent your room."

Slava held up a hand. "The math does not add up."

"Ah!" Herbert nodded. "Our weeks are longer than in your world – fourteen days. Most Travelers work the usual thirteen, but some work every day to get ahead."

Mira frowned and made a mental note to find out how long her three-month bolt would actually last.

"I see." Slava turned to Alice and Mira. "Too much work is not good for the soul, you know."

Herbert let out a laugh. "Yes, excellent point. The rest of the day is yours. I will see you after dinner to give you a dose of kykeon. It will help get your dreams going, and tomorrow morning you can submit your first memory."

Another night in this place. Did she actually have to do all of this crap to wake up? The thought made her feel nauseated.

Instead of thinking about it, she spent the rest of the day with Alice, copying notes, talking about the F's, and trying to will herself to dream felicitous memories.

8

Our Goddess Hecate

The next morning, Mira had no memory of what she'd dreamt, but she dutifully reported to Herbert's office to provide a memory for her first episcope trial.

When she arrived, he placed what looked like a large metal helmet atop her head before securing a strap beneath her chin. The helmet had a series of tubes, lights, and wires connected by shining copper metal. Herbert flicked a switch, stuck a small glass vial to her arm, and asked her to sit still.

Mira watched as the vial filled with blood. There was no needle, and she felt no pain.

If only they had that on Earth.

Once the vial was full with what Mira estimated was no more than fifteen milliliters of blood, Herbert removed the helmet and sent her off to breakfast.

Mira stopped by the dining hall and grabbed a piece of bread on her way out. She wanted to be early to make a good impression on Ferdinand. Even if he wasn't on the episcope committee, he seemed to have enough power that he mattered. More power than Mira had, at least.

Sucking up would be hard, but she had to do it. Sara had always been skilled in cozying up to important people. Mira felt like she'd watched her enough over the years to implement the techniques. If she could smile, resist making snarky comments, and be generally agreeable, it should go well.

She walked out of the Traveler Center and into the bright morning sun. She hadn't gone outside since the day she had arrived, and she was quickly reminded how overwhelming the streets of Laurium were.

She was surrounded by shouting, people, and overflowing stands, with carriages weaving between and kicking up dust. Mira stayed focused, following the directions she'd written on the back of her assignment card.

It was four blocks to the town square, a postcard-cute open area with a fountain and even more commotion. The constable's office was one street over, and just as Mira reached it, a shopkeeper called to her, yelling he had the best prices on shoe rentals in town.

Mira normally ignored anyone who spoke to her in the street, but now she was so afraid of being labeled incohesive that she forced herself to respond. "Thank you! I may be back later!"

He blew a kiss. "I'll take you anytime!"

Ugh. She failed to keep smiling and instead turned to face the constable's building.

It was far grander than the Traveler Center, built entirely of white stone, with designs etched into the surface. The windows were two stories tall with cleanly painted black borders, and the front doors matched, the black paint glinting in the sunlight. A gold sign read "Laurium Constable Headquarters."

Mira took a deep breath and opened the door. Inside was a large foyer with a sparkling crystal chandelier hanging above and a dark wooden desk to the side.

A man dressed in the Ferdinand-blues stood behind the desk. "Can I help you?"

"Yes, hi. I'm Mira Meadows, and I'm looking for Constable Ferdinand."

The man looked down at the sheet in front of him. "This way."

Mira followed him down the hallway, past gold-framed paintings and gold-dipped statues, and into a room with plush blue carpet. There were men working at desks, at least a dozen she could see, and a glass-boxed office toward the back of the room.

"He's expecting you. Go ahead."

Mira forced a smile. "Thank you!"

The door to Ferdinand's office was open. Mira approached and knocked loudly on the doorframe.

His eyes shot up. "Ah, Mira. Have a seat."

She did as she was told, her smile frozen. "Thank you so much for taking me on."

He waved a hand. "Of course. Even I need to do my part in helping the Traveler community." He sat back, weaving his fingers together and resting them on his desk. "What did you think of Miss Brown?"

Her first test. Would Ferdinand like someone like Miss Brown, or would he look down on her? How likely was she to cry defeatist tears?

"She had a wonderful lesson on Asphodavia," Mira said.

A smile spread across his face. "She is one of the most skilled teachers Magnifico has to offer. And beautiful, too."

"Oh yes, she was lovely. So intelligent." Mira's cheeks stung, but she kept smiling.

"Indeed." He shuffled a pile of papers from one side of his desk to the next. "I'd hoped to take you along to handle complaints today, but I can't take you dressed like that."

Mira looked down at her outfit. She'd managed to clean the dirt off, but her funky dog tank top stuck out like a sore thumb amongst the long dresses of the other Asphodavians. "I'm sorry. I'll rent a new outfit as soon as I can and – "

"Of course, it isn't your fault you have nothing. I am an understanding man, Mira." He stood from his desk, motioning her to follow. "For now, I'll have you staff the complaints desk. It'll give my deputies time to do more important things."

She followed him back out to the entry room, and he shooed the deputy away from the desk. "Can you read, Mira?"

"Yes, sir."

His lip curled up ever so slightly. *Sir* had been good choice.

"And write?"

She nodded.

"Very good. When someone comes in with a complaint, have them fill out this document." He pointed to a stack of papers. "If they can't write, you may do it for them. Easy enough, yes?"

"Yes. Thank you, sir." She picked up the stack of papers, and in an attempt to straighten the pile, dropped them all over the table.

He winced before turning and walking out the front door.

Okay, not perfect, but not bad. She wasn't Sara, after all, and she was new to dealing with the feeling of her insides dying while brown-nosing.

Mira fixed up the papers and stood tall, waiting for her first complaint.

Her waiting stretched into an hour, watching the grand clock on the wall. Then she watched for another hour, then another.

No one entered the building except for employees, and they barely cast her a glance, except one man who seemed to be staring at her chest.

Was it the tank top? Or the bolt?

Maybe it was risqué to have her lightning bolt out in the open like that? She'd rent a new outfit as soon as she could.

After six and a half hours of waiting, someone finally walked through the door – a man dressed in the most fabulous outfit she'd seen yet. He wore slipper-like shoes with a heel and a vest of delicate white lace over gleaming yellow fabric. His pants were yellow, too, with ruffles at the pockets. He looked like something out of a movie about Marie Antoinette, if the costume designer had been on drugs.

"Hi! Can I help you?" she asked.

He took one look at her and let out a gasp. "You're a new Traveler, aren't you? Alice?"

She shook her head. "Mira."

He leaned onto the desk, resting his head on his hands. "Did you ever speak to Helen Keller?"

"Ah, no. She died long before I was born."

He tapped a long finger on his chin. "Of course."

"Plus she was deaf," Mira added. "And blind."

"Not here, she wasn't," he said, flashing a smile.

Oh, duh. She let out a laugh. "Right."

"Helen was a fierce figure in our antiwar movement." He dropped his voice. "A raging socialist, you know."

"You have socialists here?" Mira asked.

"Of course not. What about Zhou Yang? "

"Doesn't ring a bell."

He smiled. "No, I'm sorry. I meant Peter Lalor."

She scrunched her eyebrows. "Never heard of him."

"Hm." He studied her, looking her up and down. "Where did you say you were from?"

Mira wasn't sure how much to tell him. Did she need to be nice to him? Was he dressed like that because he was important like Miss Brown? Or was he just...eccentric?

Trying to be like Sara was exhausting. She decided not answering would be rude either way. "I'm from West Virginia, but I've been living in Virginia for some time."

He frowned. "In North America?"

Interesting. He seemed to know some things. "Yes."

"How about Aaron Burr? He was a thorn in the side of Thomas Jefferson, I believe, trying to overtake his rule."

"That was also long before my time," Mira said with a smile. How old did this guy think she was?

"But the right country?"

"Yes, I was from the –"

He clapped his hands together. "Madam C.J. Walker!"

She shifted her weight. They were starting to get stares from Ferdinand's employees. "No."

"Oh, come now, she was a brown-eyed millionaire. A woman, too."

Mira shrugged. "Sorry."

"Wait!" He slapped his hand on the table. "What about Gabriel Narutowicz? Herman Hesse? Malcom X?"

"Malcom X. I've read his autobiography."

"Fascinating. You can't talk about that here, you know."

Mira paused. "Wait, did he –"

"And are you sure," the man spoke over her, loudly, tone wild, "that you didn't see a three-faced woman when you passed into our world?"

Mira stood, mouth agape. It was hard enough for her to try to be polite in a normal conversation, let alone when she was being knocked around like this.

Ferdinand appeared at her side. "Leave the poor girl alone with that nonsense, John."

"It's a simple question, Constable," he cooed, leaning forward. "Whether or not our goddess Hecate escorted her through worlds. Perhaps you saw the dogs at her side?"

She shook her head.

"Too bad. You should stop by and see me some time, Mira. We can discuss your world. And mine."

"What could you possibly know about her world?" Ferdinand said with a scoff.

"Respectfully, Constable, there are some who believe that long ago, our world was populated entirely by Travelers. It would explain our languages overlapping, and our Goddess Hecate escorted a select few animals and – "

"Nonsense!" Ferdinand's face scrunched into a scowl. "Do you have a complaint to report, or are you here to waste my time?"

John took a dramatic step back and crossed his arms. "Do you know, I forgot what it was! I'll have to come back."

Ferdinand waved a hand. "Off with you, then."

John took a step away from the desk, then paused. "Mira, you should know The Hecate Society is a friend to all Travelers."

He walked off without another word and Ferdinand turned to Mira. "You're free to make your own choices, of course, but I would advise you to stay away from that man and everyone in that damned Hecate Society. Very incohesive."

"Of course, sir."

"Good. Associating with kooks is a fail-safe way to get negative marks on your record."

"Yes, sir. I'll be sure to avoid him." She paused. "I am so interested in records, Constable. After learning about them, they seem fascinating."

"Well, yes, they can be."

"An entire history of a person's life – their good deeds. I wish we had something like that in our world."

His expression softened and he reached a hand to twist at his mustache. "Yes, well, perhaps another time I can show you how we maintain them."

"That is *such* an important job." Mira was going for the gold. The more her words made her feel like dying inside, the harder she smiled. "I would love to see them."

"It's good to take an interest in your work," he said, nodding approvingly. "Once you're situated, there will be plenty to show you."

"Wonderful."

Ferdinand tipped his hat and walked off without another word.

Mira felt giddy. She might've out-Sara'd Sara. And though she'd laid it on pretty thick, Ferdinand didn't seem to notice. He'd basked in it, like a bird taking a bath in the sun.

It was a shame John of the Hecate Society was off limits, though. He actually seemed like he'd be fun.

Too bad. She wasn't here to have fun. She was here to...well, get out of here.

Mira moved to re-tidy her stack of empty complaints and spotted a small card sitting on top. She picked it up and studied it – a drawing of three-headed woman, a dog at either side.

Hecate, was it? She flipped it over to find a hand-written address.

Hm. Maybe Ferdinand didn't need to know *everything*. She'd hang onto this, just in case.

9

The episcope

It wasn't until the end of her first week manning the complaint desk that Mira was able to rent some new clothes.

Herbert's selection was unexciting – a closet of tan linen pants and shirts – but Mira was happy to see them. She paid four tallies to rent two outfits and ran up to her room to change.

She was studying herself in the bathroom mirror when Alice walked in wearing a long, floral summer dress.

Mira pointed at her, mouth hanging open. "What is that?"

"My new dress!" She spun, the skirt opening elegantly and encircling her. "The ladies at the library gave me a few hand-me-downs today."

Mira looked down at her monotone prison outfit, then back at Alice. "They *gave* you clothes? Ferdinand doesn't give me anything. He even took away the stool I was sitting on at work because he thought it looked too informal."

"Such an interesting man." Alice grabbed Mira by the hand. "Come on, I got three outfits and I was planning on sharing them with you."

"No, it's okay," Mira said glumly, trying to tie the string of her pants tighter. The waist was far too large, gaping in the back, while the thigh area was skin tight. "I doubt anything will fit me. I'm too tall."

Alice frowned. "The pants might be short, but I've got a cute top I think you'll like. Come on. You can wear it for the episcope trial tomorrow."

That wasn't a bad idea, considering she'd been running around town in a skimpy, dog-themed tank top and short shorts all week.

Mira followed Alice to her room and, as expected, the pants and dress were too small, but a light blue top fit perfectly and managed to hide her bolt.

"Are you sure you don't mind me borrowing it?" Mira asked. The material was so soft that it made her rented linen jumpsuit feel like burlap in comparison.

"Of course not! What's mine is yours." She smiled. "We need to look our best for tomorrow."

"That's the truth. I wish I knew what memories they were going to use."

"I'm sure they'll find something good," Alice said. "You must have so many great scenes of you saving lives as a nurse."

"And cleaning up diarrhea, yes."

Alice laughed. "Oh stop. You'll do great."

Mira wished she had Alice's confidence. Maybe the top would help.

• • •

The first episcope trial was held in the grassy yard behind the Traveler Center. It was surprisingly large for the cramped town block, and they all got there early to scope it out. The only one missing was Samuel. Normally, after work, they'd see him back here through the windows, working on the garden Herbert had helped him plant. It was odd he wasn't using his day off to tend to it.

"He probably has no idea he's supposed to be here," Mira said.

Slava agreed. "Too bad for him."

"Maybe I should go and look for him?" Alice asked, biting her lip.

"No." Slava waved a hand. "He will find his way."

"It looks like the episcope committee is filing in," Mira added in a hushed voice. "We should stay put."

Alice wasn't satisfied with this, but she didn't protest.

The five committee members took their seats at the table near the front. They were dressed in matching black robes – two women and three men.

Herbert had set up a burlap screen atop a small stage, complete with a wobbling podium. He'd tried to decorate the committee table with a doily tablecloth, and Mira decided the number of doilies he had said something about his character, but she couldn't decide exactly what.

The committee didn't seem to mind, sipping on tea and talking amongst themselves as though they didn't have a trouble in the world.

"They look nice," Alice whispered.

Slava pulled a flask out of his pocket and took a swig. "They are not the ones on trial."

"Right." Mira was tempted to grab Slava's flask, but decided against it. She needed her wits about her. "Hide that, Slava. You can't forget your F's."

Slava snorted a laugh, and even Alice cracked a smile.

There were only enough chairs for twenty people, and the three of them sat in the front row, directly in front of the stage. The rest of the seats filled quickly, and more people poured into the grassy yard, boisterous and lively.

Mira kept turning around to look at their audience. Herbert had said hundreds of townspeople came to the trials, packing the field shoulder-to-shoulder, often choosing their favorite Travelers to cheer for and taking bets on when markings would appear.

That was fun for them, but not so much for Mira. Was she supposed to win them over, too? Or just the committee? Was it possible to do both?

The field filled quickly, and as the sun began to set, glass jars silently floated in above their heads, unsupported except by some sort of magic, and filled with what Mira thought were lightning bugs.

Herbert stepped up on the stage and pulled a dented tin can from the podium, tapping it three times. It too floated up, hovering a few inches beneath his mouth.

"Hello, and welcome to the first episcope trial for our newest batch of Travelers!"

Applause broke out, along with a few whoops and hollers. Mira looked over her shoulder before quickly turning around. She hated crowds. They could too easily turn into mobs.

"I'd like to extend a welcome to the committee. Thank you for taking the time to come in today."

A few claps.

Herbert looked down at the card in his hand, his face lighting into a bright smile. "Our first Traveler tonight is a lovely woman reborn at the age of thirty-three who goes by the name of Mira Meadows. Mira, if you'd like to come up and introduce yourself."

The crowd broke into quiet applause and she froze, eyes wide. Mira wasn't prepared to talk about herself. She thought her memories would do the talking.

Alice nudged her. "Go ahead. You got this."

Mira felt herself pushed out of the seat, turning to see Slava's large hand as the culprit. He winked at her, and she walked forward, taking the stairs to the stage, her legs heavy and numb.

Herbert shook her hand and directed her in front of the podium. "Just talk in there," he whispered.

She nodded, lining up with the can and turning toward the crowd. The stage had a powerful light focused in, glowing hot enough to make her uncomfortably warm. She stared into the crowd, and despite the field being lit only by lighting bugs, she could see every face in front of her, looking up, full of expectation.

"Hi everyone." She forced a smile. "I'm Mira Meadows, and I arrived here a couple of days ago."

A few laughs echoed and someone yelled, "How'd you die?"

Oh, right. That was important. She leaned forward, getting closer to the can. "I was hit by a car."

Murmurs in the crowd. She tried to think of something else to say, something charming, but her mind had gone entirely blank.

Herbert stepped in. "Thank you, Mira. If we could have the first memory, please?"

A man started cranking the episcope and Herbert pulled her aside, out of the way of the beam of light, as the screen came to life. The image was vibrant and clear, showing the mall of her childhood.

It looked so *real*. Everything was dated just as it had been – the yellow-white floor tiles, the harsh lighting, the hair-sprayed coifs of passersby. It was unbelievable.

Eleven-year-old Mira came into view, her unruly red hair hanging in front of her face, entirely covering one of her eyes. Behind her was a clear glass counter, brightly lit and filled with jewelry.

A potbellied security guard knelt in front of her. "Now, young lady, if you don't start being straight with me, I'm going to have to call the police."

She peered up at him from behind her hair, her lips pressed in a firm line.

"All right." He stood, shaking his head. "I guess they'll get answers out of you down at the station."

"Please, wait." A man stepped next to Mira, his oversized 1980's glasses slipping down his nose. "My niece is a troubled girl. Ever since her father died, she's been acting out."

The security guard frowned, turning his eyes back to Mira. "Are you missing your daddy, girl?"

Mira looked up at her uncle. He nodded encouragingly, and she took a breath. "Yes."

The guard hesitated before putting a hand on her shoulder. "I know how tough it is to lose someone you love, especially so young, but you can't go stealing things. Do you know what kind of trouble you'll end up in? And for what, a bracelet?" He shook his head. "Don't let me catch you stealing again, you understand?"

Little Mira nodded, eyes wide, and the screen went blank.

So much for lawfulness. Why had she dreamt about that stupid day?

Herbert gave Mira a small push forward, and she stumbled, catching herself on the uneven podium.

An older man on the committee spoke first. "Can you explain what we just saw?"

Ha. If only it were that easy. "That was me when I was eleven or twelve, I think. I went shopping with my Uncle Wesley."

"And you decided to steal something from the shop?"

She shook her head. "My uncle told me to. He said my family needed money, and I could help them if I took a few things from the store."

The man stared at her for a beat before writing something down on the paper in front of him.

Mira spoke again. "I was young. I didn't understand how he was manipulating me."

"Your father – he had died?" asked one of the female committee members.

"No, he was alive. Wesley lied about that. My dad was his brother, and he trusted Wesley completely. Everyone did." She paused. How to explain Wesley? How much time did she have? "Wesley was a sociopath. He had no conscience, and he used people."

"He used you quite effectively, it seems."

Murmurs from the crowd.

Mira's face was starting to feel hot. It would only be a few seconds before her cheeks lit up bright red. The curse of being so pale. "Only when I was young. I didn't fall for it once I understood who he was."

This was not a good look. Yet how could they understand Wesley from that one brief snapshot? He'd fooled people his entire life. He employed a harmless nerd persona, complete with a middle hair part, goofy glasses, and an overexcited manner of speaking. It was all an act, of course. He was a master, and he could pontificate with the best of them.

No one suspected him of any wrongdoing. No one believed allegations made against him – whether they came from his colleagues, his students, or his wife. They believed *him*, always. He was the victim, no matter what the situation, especially when it came to his cruel wife keeping his only child away from him – Sara.

Her heart ached for Sara. She would be able to explain this scene away. It was one of the few skills she'd learned from her father.

The old man nodded. "Let's see another, shall we?"

Mira forced a smile and stepped out of the way. It couldn't get worse than that.

The man in charge of the episcope started to crank, and a beautiful church filled the screen, its ornate baroque architecture and stained glass a stark contrast to the mall.

When was the last time she'd been in a church? Unless... *oh no.*

A dozen kids sat straight across, filling two rows of stiff wooden pews. They whispered and giggled as a nun walked to the front.

"Class, Father Mascull is coming to speak to you. You will be quiet and listen respectfully." She bulged her eyes at them, showing how serious she was.

Young Mira was sat in the second row, her arms firmly crossed, her face flat. She was not laughing with the other children. She was in an active brood.

The priest, his back as crooked as a question mark, slowly made his way to the front, then stared at the kids until silence washed over the room.

"Hello, children."

There were a few mumbles in response.

He narrowed his eyes. "Is this how you greet me? I said hello."

"Hello, Father," the group called back in a sing-song tone.

He grunted, shuffling closer. "I have been a priest for forty-four years, and I'm disappointed by what I see. Do you know why?"

No answers.

He continued. "Every Sunday I see less and less people at Mass."

"Fewer people," Mira muttered under her breath.

Father Mascull locked his eyes on her. "What was that?"

She cleared her throat. "Nothing, Father."

"I asked you a question. What did you say?"

She stared up at him. "I said 'fewer' people, Father."

His nostrils flared. "Did you?"

"I'm sorry," she added with a shrug. "Less is the wrong word."

"Come up here, girl."

She stood, the other children shifting so she could get by. Mira still struggled with her long, knobby gazelle legs, but soon made it to the front. She was almost as tall as the priest.

"Do you think you're smarter than me?" he asked.

She responded without hesitation. "No."

"No, Father," he said sternly.

She looked down at her shoes. "No, Father."

He leaned back. "Then why do you think you're allowed to speak out like that?"

She shrugged, keeping her eyes down and twisting the bottom of her shirt between her fingers.

The priest pulled a handkerchief from his pocket and blew his nose, still picking in his nostrils when he spoke again. "I didn't see you at Mass this Sunday."

Mira kept her head down. "I had to help my uncle. With shopping."

"Helping your uncle is more important than listening to God?"

Mira didn't respond.

"Answer me, girl. Do you think your uncle will keep you out of hell?"

She shrugged. "Maybe."

There was a giggle, quickly hushed, from the other children.

Mira looked at them and smiled.

"Your uncle can't help you. All sinners go to hell. Confess your sins. Tell us what you've done. Go ahead."

A smile danced at the corner of her lips. "You first."

The children erupted in laughter, and the priest looked down at her, his lip curled, before brushing a hand over her chest and grabbing her by the shoulder.

Mira pulled away, breaking his grasp easily. "Don't!"

The laughter was gone from her eyes.

The priest raised his hand again, this time floating above his head before planting a swift slap across her cheek.

The class gasped, and without missing a beat, Mira pulled her arm back and slapped him as hard as she could.

The memory ended, and the screen went dark.

Mira should not have borrowed Alice's shirt. The armpits were drenched in sweat, and it would likely never recover.

The younger woman committee member stared at her, a pensive look fixed on her face. "Tell us, Mira. Were you a violent child?"

Mira stepped up to the tin can again. "No, I wasn't, and I still am not a violent person."

"Why did you feel the need to harm such a frail man? Was that your father?"

A rumble of laughter rolled through the crowd, and Mira took a cautious glance at them. The sea of faces in the audience didn't look like the committee – they weren't tense or concerned. They were smiling.

Mira didn't know what to say. She didn't expect to have to speak for her childhood self. She opened her mouth, struggling to get any words to come out. "No, he was not my father, and he wasn't a frail old man, he – "

"He looked quite decrepit," the woman countered, shaking her head. "Did you harm him?"

"No, not at all." She let out a sigh. "He held a position of power in the church, and he was known to take advantage of those beneath him."

The committee member raised an eyebrow. "And?"

Mira looked out at the crowd, hoping for inspiration. There was a low buzz of voices, and someone hollered something unintelligible.

"And..." Mira couldn't come up with anything. The crowd seemed to be on her side, though. That was good, right? "And he started it."

The field erupted into laughter, and Mira flashed a smile at Alice before looking back to the committee.

They were not laughing. All five of them had their heads down, writing, pausing only to whisper to one another.

"Thank you, Mira," Herbert said after a moment, taking over her place at the podium.

She descended the stairs, grateful her seat was close and she didn't have to look anyone else in the eye.

"You did great up there," Alice whispered, grabbing her hand and giving it a squeeze.

Slava leaned over. "You will do better the next time."

"Yeah." Mira nodded. "Next time."

10

The magical carpet

Somewhere between the stage and her seat, the magical carpet of denial Mira had been riding took off and flew away, abruptly dumping her on the cold, hard ground.

She wasn't in a dream. She wasn't hallucinating, or trapped in her mind as it made up progressively more complicated people and situations.

This was *real.* Asphodavia, the dragons, and the fact that she'd bombed her first episcope trial, surely damaging the record that would determine if she lived or died – it was all ridiculously, horrifyingly real.

Though she'd avoided her reality fantastically until now, denial was no longer an option. She had to face the truth, as miserable as it may be: her life was literally on the line.

Mira grappled with the waves of nausea and panic as she tried to pay attention to Alice's episcope.

The scenes from Alice's life weren't much more flattering than Mira's – one of her rear-ending a car when she turned around to grab her daughter's escaped bottle, then the ensuing argument with the other driver – but they were not as mortifying as Mira's displays of violence.

Slava's scenes showed him in an animated argument with another man. In the first, Slava was young, and in the second, he was middle-aged. In both he was on the brink of screaming at the man, the frustration apparent in his red face.

They weren't speaking English and no one could understand what they were saying, of course, so Slava explained it was his father repeatedly failing at telling the same joke over the course of his lifetime.

"It is supposed to go like this: a carpenter dies and takes a wrong turn, walking into hell. God tells the devil, *You must give him back; he belongs with us.* The devil says, *No, we need him to build for us. We are running out of space.* And God said *If you do not send him, I will sue you!*

"But the devil only laughs, asking God, *Where are you going to find a lawyer?*"

The crowd erupted into laughter and cheers. Even the committee members were laughing.

Apparently dislike for lawyers was ubiquitous.

"My father confused the two all his life," Slava explained coolly. "He said the lawyer died and took a wrong turn to hell. And so we would argue."

The old man, who seemed to be in charge of the committee, wiped tears from his eyes as he wound down from a laugh. "Very good, Slava. You may take a seat. The trials are complete for today."

Mira sat in her chair, arms crossed against her chest, as voices and noise erupted behind them. People pushed forward, rushing to shake Slava's hand and heap him with praise.

No such party came for Mira or Alice, and they slipped back into the Traveler Center unnoticed.

"Well, that was mortifying," Mira said as soon as they were inside.

Alice was as placid as ever. "I'm sure the first one is always rough. It'll get better."

"Yeah. It has to." Mira wanted to add, "Or else we're going to die," but she stopped herself.

Alice didn't want to go back to Earth. She intended for her old body to pass away peacefully, and she had taken this entire integration thing seriously from the start.

It was Mira who was late to the game, Mira who was going to lose her chance to ever see her parents again, or to laugh with Sara about her impromptu wedding, or to finally get her chance to marry Robbie.

Why had she delayed getting married for so long? They could've been happy; they could've had time together. She hadn't seen Robbie in three months – why hadn't they made visiting one another a priority? There were always excuses, always problems. They'd grown apart, falling into a slump of chatting on the phone only a few nights a week.

It was unfortunate, but Mira had walked right into one of humanity's oldest traps. She thought she had more time, despite the fact that all evidence pointed to life being unpredictable, death arriving at random, and time being entirely out of one's control.

For the rest of the night, Mira vacillated between despair and manic hope. She couldn't bear losing her old life. She couldn't bear losing what it was *going* to be.

When Mira finally fell asleep, her mind was made up. She would get back to her life – her real life – no matter the cost.

11

An education

Mira reported to work the next morning and immediately had to endure three of Ferdinand's deputies teasing her for her poor showing at the trials.

"I preferred it when you ignored me," she said, tearing up a sign they'd left on the complaints desk that stated **Beware: elderly attacks**.

"That was before we knew how dangerous you were," said one of the men. "Now we have to keep watch."

She narrowed her eyes. "Are you scared because I'm stronger than you?"

The man laughed. "Yes. We're going to ask Ferdinand for a bit of weakening magic to keep you in check."

She rolled her eyes. "That's not a real thing."

"Isn't it?"

They walked away, leaving Mira to perseverate what it meant for her chances of getting out of this world alive.

She didn't have much time to think, however, because unlike the week prior, she suddenly had dozens of townspeople coming in to make complaints.

Each of them mentioned her episcope trial in one way or another – a few praised her actions with the priest, others encouraged her to lie in the future to better her odds. One woman brought her a slice of cake and patted her on the shoulder. "Don't let them wear you down, girl."

Mira liked her, and the cake.

The day went by much more quickly than usual, even though most of the complaints she recorded were silly, like name calling between neighbors and rumors of unfairness in the market.

She left work feeling better than when she had entered, at least, so that was something new.

On her walk home, she was deep in thought when a horse-drawn black carriage pulled up alongside of her.

"Excuse me," the driver called out. "I've been waiting for you."

She looked up at him, blocking the angled beams of the setting sun with her hand. "You must have me confused with someone else."

"You are Mira Meadows, correct?"

She hesitated, looking over her shoulder. Was this another prank?

The carriage door popped open and a familiarly deep voice emerged. "Come in, Mira. You don't want to tire yourself out walking."

She leaned forward to see Mick sitting inside. He had the same getup as before – a dark three-piece suit, his black hair tidy.

Without realizing it, she took a step back. Mick was even more intimidating than before, which was odd considering last time he'd been covered in blood.

She now knew Asphodavia well enough now to read into the cut of his suit – Mick was wealthy. Confident. The scars on his face did nothing to detract from his striking appearance: his sharp cheekbones, and those blue eyes that always watched her so intensely.

A feeling washed over her she knew she had to resist. She couldn't be pulled in by any of his charms. She didn't have time for it. "That's okay. I enjoy walking."

He leaned toward her. "I'm here to help you with your episcope trials."

"Really?" Mira looked around. Maybe she didn't have time *not* to talk to him. It was as though he'd read her mind...

He extended a hand, and Mira accepted it, climbing inside the carriage.

Mick shut the door and tapped on the roof. The carriage jolted forward, forcing Mira back into her seat. Despite the soft cushions, she was not comfortable, her muscles tense and her shoulders tight.

She took a cautious look around. The inside of the carriage was lined in a luxurious-looking deep blue silk, and the air was cooler than outside.

There was a small shelf next to Mick, and on it balanced two glasses and a crystal decanter with brown liquid, rattling as they went over bumps. To her right was a window, and she could see they were making a turn toward the Traveler Center.

That was good. She didn't appear to be getting kidnapped.

"It was decent, what you did," he said. "Hiding Arianna's birthing magic from Ferdinand."

She locked eyes with him, then looked away. His gaze really was unsettling. "What magic?"

He smiled, only for a second, pulling out a pack of cigarettes and offering her one.

She declined. "How is Arianna doing? And the baby?"

"Fine, both fine." He lit the cigarette and took a puff, staring at her as the smoke filled the space between them.

It smelled like raspberries and reminded her of a hookah bar Sara had once dragged her to.

What a terrible evening they'd had, with Sara being psychically thrown out by a bouncer after she tried to wrestle the microphone away from the band...

"Have they told you how dangerous magic is yet?"

She nodded.

"Told you to report any inkling of a marking?"

"Yes." She paused. "Not that I've had any."

Mick took a long drag of the cigarette. "I wouldn't expect you to tell me. But you shouldn't tell them, either."

She raised an eyebrow. "Why not?"

He sat back, reaching for the crystal decanter. "Magic wasn't always considered dangerous. Travelers used to be free to live normal lives."

"Normal how?"

He didn't respond at first, instead pouring a drink and offering it to her.

Hm. Did she trust him? The way he stared at her made her feel like prey, but she'd already gotten into his carriage. He would probably take it as an insult if she wouldn't drink it.

Also, free booze was free booze. She accepted it and took a sip.

Whiskey! Or something like it. She'd never loved whiskey, but the burn in her throat was welcome.

"Thanks."

He poured himself a glass and balanced it in his empty hand. "When I was young, Travelers could enter and exit the world as they pleased. There were no Traveler Centers, no episcope trials, and no records."

"No records for Travelers?" Mira asked.

"No records for anyone." Mick took a swig of his drink before setting the glass back on the shelf. "Then a Traveler entered our world and managed to rob half the banks in Asphodavia."

Mira looked out the window – another right turn. They seemed to be going in a circle. "That seems problematic."

"For the banks, it was. He was marked. Could pass through walls." Mick flicked the stub of remaining cigarette out of the window. "In the end, it was the news of his robberies that did the most damage."

She stared at him, her mind repeating his words again and again. It was as though he was presenting her with a puzzle, and she felt determined to solve it.

Nothing came to her, though, and she finally asked, "Why?"

"People found out how much money was being stolen when the wealthy went crying to the papers. The result was regular people finding out how much money they didn't have. They were working all hours of the day for a handful of tallies a week. The rich, most of them on Magnifico Island, thought sharing the fact that hundreds of thousands of tallies were stolen from them would turn the Traveler into a villain. It did the opposite."

That was something she couldn't have come up with. Mira smiled. An Asphodavian Dillinger. It could have been Dillinger, actually. "That's pretty funny."

He nodded his head once. "It caused unrest across Asphodavia, and The Council of Truth was formed to handle the threat of Travelers."

Ha. Mira didn't have three pairs of pants to her name, but somehow, she was a threat.

Mick continued. "It was slow at first. Travelers were intercepted upon rebirth and sorted. A law was passed that magic had to be licensed, controlled, and kept by the Council in the Hall of Magic. Travelers were given records. Then Asphodavians tried to help the Travelers, so the rest of us got records, too."

Mira took a gulp of her drink, finishing it and setting the glass down next to Mick's. "We Travelers aren't too popular around here, are we?"

He shook his head. "Asphodavians used to embrace Travelers. We would help them get to Thunder Island, help them return home. In return, Travelers would share their markings, their magic."

Mira leaned forward, feeling slightly dizzy. "Markings can be shared?"

He refilled her glass and handed it to her. "They didn't tell you, did they?"

She really shouldn't take another, but what was the harm? They were driving around in circles, and Mick was being helpful. Maybe he wasn't as mean as he looked.

He held his glass up to hers, and she clinked it, taking the tiniest of sips.

Mick went on. "The Council has control of almost all of the magic in Asphodavia. Travelers are a source of power to them, nothing more. You won't do well in your episcope trials unless it benefits them."

"Hang on." She set the glass down. "I don't follow."

He pulled out another cigarette, lit it, and took a puff. "The episcope committee and The Council will keep you around long enough to see if you develop a marking. If you do, they'll cart you off to drain as much magic as they can. If you don't..."

He sat back and crossed his legs, eyes still focused on her, and shrugged.

Mira mirrored him, crossing her legs and nearly kicking him in the process. "What if I don't have a marking? They'll let me go back?"

"Sometimes," Mick said with a nod, "yes."

"What do you mean sometimes?" It wasn't just the carriage going in circles. He was, too. "I need to get back to my life. My real life."

"You'll have a chance if you don't prove yourself too useful to them. Or too dangerous."

She sat back. They'd made another right turn, this time coming up behind the constable's office.

That was a lot of history Miss Brown had left out, if it were even true. "How many Travelers get to go back?"

"No one knows. If you go around asking too many questions, you'll be flagged by the Disinformation Board of Governance."

Ew. That sounded almost too dystopian to be true, which meant it had to be real. "That sounds unpleasant."

He tapped out his cigarette. "The Council is of the belief that anyone who criticizes them must be brainwashed or mad. They will reeducate you until those thoughts are gone."

She sat back, feeling a little dizzy from the alcohol. Her new body wasn't as tolerant as her old body, and on top of that, this was a lot to take in. It was a lot more complicated than a few F's. "You said you could help me."

Mick nodded. "One of my men can change the memories pulled for your trials."

"Okay." She paused. "What do I have to do in return?"

He leaned forward, locking eyes on her again. "I saw your episcope trial. It seems you have some talents."

She crossed her arms. "You mean slapping the elderly?"

He stared, expression unchanged. "No. You're a skilled thief."

Mira stared back at him. "Hardly. I got caught."

"Was that the last time you stole, then?"

Mira picked up her drink. It didn't matter if she ended up drunk for this interrogation. He had already gotten into her head. "No."

"Right then." He cleared his throat. "You're working in Ferdinand's office. You have access to the town's records."

"Not really." She finished the drink, setting down the glass with a clank. "I stay at the complaints desk. I don't have access to anything."

He shrugged. "The opportunity may arise."

"I'm not stealing records, if that's what you're thinking. That'll get me sent to live with the dragons."

"More like to die with them."

Her heart sank. That was right – people didn't go to live out their lives there. It was a death sentence.

The carriage stopped. They were a block from the Traveler Center at a small, wooded park.

Was Mick going to kill her there if she said no?

He spoke again. "I don't need you to steal them, but I haven't found whoever was responsible for the attack on me and Arianna."

"You told Ferdinand it was my lightning bolt."

"He knew it was a lie." Mick picked up the crystal carafe, gesturing toward her.

Mira shook her head. Two was more than enough.

He poured himself another. "I need to know if there's anything in my or Arianna's records regarding the attack."

"And if I can't find anything?"

"Then you can't find anything," he said, voice low and even.

This was clearly going against lawfulness, and probably also cohesiveness. But if what he'd said was true, her episcope trials would never improve...

Mira was still debating what to say when Mick reached toward her. Despite her reflexes being slowed by the alcohol, she flinched and pulled back.

His intention, however, was not to strike her. He held his hand open, revealing a small, silver-toned coin.

"When you find what I need, turn this over in your hand three times. I'll send a carriage to meet you."

She took it, saying nothing, and studied the flower etched into the metal. Mira was terrible at identifying plants, but it was a pretty, delicate-looking thing.

Mick opened the door and the humid air floated in. "It's best if the Traveler Center doesn't see you leaving my carriage. Have a good evening, Mira."

She wanted to tell him no, or at least that she'd have to think about it, but instead, she clumsily hobbled out of her seat and onto the street without another word.

The door shut behind her and the carriage took off, leaving her alone in the darkness.

12

A consensus against extremism

A crash rang out in the hallway of the Traveler Center, and Alice rushed from her dinner to find Mira laying on the floor, giggling.

"Mira!" Alice knelt down beside her. "Are you okay?"

"The rug got me." She covered her mouth with her hand and dropped her voice to a whisper. "Do I smell like booze?"

Alice leaned in, then immediately pulled back. "Yes. Very much, yes."

Mira pressed a finger to her lips. "We have to be quiet."

"All right, let's go." Alice grabbed Mira by the arm and pulled her up. "You need to get upstairs."

"*You* need to get upstairs."

Alice successfully guided Mira to her room before anyone else saw her. She told her to stay put before returning with a plate of food.

"Eat this, then you can tell me what you've been up to."

Mira made a face. "You're going to yell at me."

"I will not."

Mira let out a heavy sigh and poked at the boiled fish on the plate. "I think I need to lie down."

"Try to eat something first."

Mira did as she was told, shoving mouthfuls of the fish and rice into her mouth until her plate was cleared.

"There." She then fell backwards, almost falling off the edge of the cot. "Look what Mick gave me."

"Is it a tally?" Alice took the coin in her hand. "There's a violet engraved on here. What is this, Mira?"

"How'd you know it was a violet?" She sat up. "How come I don't know any flowers?"

Alice handed the coin back to her. "Violets are important in Asphodavia. I've been reading about them in the library."

"Violets?" Mira laid back down. Sitting up was dizzying.

"They only grow on Violet Island, and not much else can grow there. 'Violet' is a nickname for the purple-eyed people of this world, too."

Mira's mouth popped open. "I met someone with purple eyes when I first met Mick."

"At the car accident?" Alice frowned. "You didn't mention it before."

"She was only there for a little bit." Mira struggled to sit up, keeping her voice low. "She used magic, Alice. She saved Arianna and the baby. I got the feeling she wasn't supposed to, though, and then she disappeared."

Alice let out a *hm*.

"Not disappeared," Mira said, sitting back. "She took off on a flying horse."

Alice narrowed her eyes. "Are you making this up?"

"No, I swear!"

"Because Violets are the only people in Asphodavia who are born with magic. They wanted me to destroy a book that talked about it."

"Why?"

Alice leaned in, dropping her voice to a whisper. "There used to be mobs who went after Violets and tried to siphon their magic. It sounded like torture."

Mira bit her lip. "Did it work? I mean, getting their magic?"

"No. Never. The only way to get magic is from a Traveler."

Mira gasped. "Yeah, that's what Mick said!"

"Why were you hanging out with Mick?"

Mira took a drink of water and steadied herself before repeating everything Mick had told her.

When she was done, Alice stared into space, biting her nail. "You're not going to go after the records, are you?"

Mira shrugged. "Who knows?"

"You can't trust him," she continued. "He left out the detail that Travelers used to be hunted, too. Boats would line the shores of Thunder Island, catching anyone who was trying to get to the lighting. They'd kidnap the Travelers and try to pull magic from them, too."

"Ugh." Mira laid back down. "Magic is the worst."

"You can't get into the records, Mira." Alice leaned over her, pointing at her face. "Promise me you won't go digging for them. You're going to end up in trouble, and for what? Mick is using you."

Mira closed her eyes. The room was spinning too wildly now. "I promise I won't go digging for the records."

"Good."

Mira's breathing picked up, heavy and loud. Alice shook her head, quietly taking Mira's plate and shutting the door behind her.

• • •

Mira fully expected to roll out of bed the next morning with a headache and her usual post-drinking nausea, but miraculously, she felt great.

Slava wasn't the only one – her Asphodavian body was in far better shape than the version frozen back home.

Still. She preferred the old one.

She got to work early, ready for another day of filing complaints and getting unsolicited advice, but Ferdinand was waiting for her at the desk. He had other plans. "It's time for a new task, Mira."

"Oh?" She paused. "I'm sorry, did I do something wrong with the complaints?"

He shook his head, gathering the pile she'd put together the day before. "No, it's not your fault that people are making excuses to see you. They're filing too many complaints, in fact, frivolous as can be. I'll have to spend my day sorting through them."

Mira tried not to smile. There weren't that many. Maybe a dozen? How could it take him all day?

He stomped off across the grand room and to the staircase. "I've got something else for you to do today."

Her heart leapt. It wouldn't be breaking her promise to Alice if Ferdinand *made* her look at the records. "Anything you need, sir."

They climbed to the third floor, making a right off of the staircase and following the lush blue runner. Mira walked quickly behind him, trying not to trip as she peered into every room they passed.

Ferdinand stopped in front of a door labeled **Pillory**.

"Do you know what this is, girl?"

She shook her head. "No sir."

"Excellent. Follow me."

He opened the door and she walked in first. The room was large, at least twenty feet in each direction, and lined with rows and rows of shelves. The shelves were crowded with boxes and stacks of slumping papers.

Ferdinand led her to the far side of the room. Against the windows stood a table at least ten feet long, made of dark, heavy wood. On top were some sort of machines, noisily clacking away.

"These are our pillories," he said, beaming.

"Wow, they're beautiful." Each one, an exact replica of the next, had a wheel the size of her head and a glass box. As the wheel turned, papers dropped into the tray below. A green light buzzed inside the glass box each time a paper started to appear. "What are they?"

"This is how we transmit mail in Asphodavia," he said, reaching for the nearest pillory and withdrawing a sheet. "It's an elegant bit of magic, and any mail office can transmit a letter here in a matter of seconds."

"Amazing!" Mira had the urge to tell him about the internet, but didn't want to burst his bubble with technology from her wretched world.

"I think you're ready to graduate to something a little more challenging, no?"

She looked up at him, a smile plastered on her face. "Oh yes! I'd love to."

"All of the letters must be read and reviewed before they can go to their intended destination." Ferdinand waved her toward a nearby desk. "We must screen each letter using a book that contains a list of problematic and offensive topics."

Mira ran her hand over the cover. It was as long as her entire arm and thicker than a phone book. "How...neat."

"We've fallen behind with the letters. It's been a busy few months." He dropped a stack of papers onto the desk. "Read through these, referencing the book, and pull out any letters that appear offensive, dangerous, or unkind. We must enforce a consensus against extremism," he explained. "The acceptable range of views are in the book, and updates are added to the end of the book each week. The updates cancel out previously acceptable topics, mind you. If you have any questions, don't hesitate to ask. I'll send a deputy up to clarify."

"Thank you. I'm excited to learn more," she said, hating herself and her forced enthusiasm.

Ferdinand turned to leave and Mira took a seat. The first letter was addressed to Mickson Kellet.

"Sir," she said, raising her hand to stop him. "Is this the man I met when I landed?"

Ferdinand turned, looked at the name on the page, and scowled. "Indeed it is, Mira. A nastier man never drew breath – nay, a nastier family. The Kellets are criminals."

She looked up at him, her surprise genuine. She thought Mick was just rich. She didn't realize he was interesting. "Criminals?"

"Nordavia has been plagued by their schemes for generations."

"What have they done, sir?"

"What haven't they done?" He puffed his cheeks out and shook his head. "Mickson murdered his own wife in cold blood."

"What?" Goosebumps rose on her neck. He did sort of have that look about him. "How did he – I mean, why?"

"Who ever knows what goes through that man's head? He brags of it. Can you imagine?" Ferdinand took a deep breath and looked through the window. "One day, we'll stop him."

She resisted the urge to comment, hoping he would say more, but Ferdinand was done with the topic. He turned on his heel and walked out the door. "Best of luck, Mira!"

If Mick were willing to kill his own wife, he wouldn't think twice about killing Mira. She would have to get him what he needed. He seemed more dangerous than Ferdinand.

The first step, though, was still gaining Ferdinand's trust. She settled into the chair and spent a few minutes flipping through the book of rules. It was organized alphabetically, while the stack of papers shoved in the back were completely random.

Some of the offensive topics made sense, like remarks critical of the Council being labeled *incohesiveness*, while others were more nebulous, like "dangerous speech" and "words that could cause discomfort." Apparently, those fell under *felicitousness*, making that particular F only more confusing to Mira.

Any discussion of magic had to be flagged for review, along with any offers to buy or sell products, since renting was the preferred model of Asphodavia. Oddly, any complaints related to a "deficiency of tallies," or what Mira surmised as poverty, were considered high risk for incohesiveness.

Magic and money, the two things that made Asphodavia go 'round.

As silly as it was, she was excited – this was better than standing around all day, and she hoped it would at least lead to some fun gossip.

The first pile had thirty letters, and of those, twenty-five were addressed to Mickson Kellet.

The thought of getting a secret view into his private life made her giddy, but once she got started, she realized that every one of the letters was nothing more than a proposal of marriage.

Some came from men all across the country, offering their daughters' hands in marriage. They suggested family alliances, often including pictures of said daughter with the father scowling in the background.

Mira scoured the book, trying to decide if these letters broke any rules. They were pleasant, free of dangerous speech – unless love was dangerous – and generally amusing.

Still, she set them aside, along with the letters written by lovesick women. These were even better, complete with tortured poetry or sketches of the sender's and Mick's future children.

For a man who had killed his first wife, he certainly had a lot of women willing to take a chance on him. Was it because he was rich? Was it the blue eyes? The conflict between his face being scary yet boyishly handsome?

Or was it like those women who fell in love with death row inmates? They alone could save Mick, find the goodness in his soul...

By the end of the week, Mira had made her way through the three-month backup of letters, getting to the point where the only ones that needed to be addressed were brand new.

"This is marvelous!" Ferdinand said when he came to check on her. "What wonderful work you've done. Now all that's left is to file the offensive letters into the records of the senders and receivers."

"I'd be happy to do that, sir." Mira tried to keep her tone light, but she felt like she'd spoken too quickly, too desperately, and he was already waving her off.

"No, certainly not," he said, shaking his head. "You're too valuable here. I'll leave you to it."

He walked off with a cart piled with letters and shut the door on her.

Mira fought the urge to punch one of the pillories. *All that hard work for nothing.*

She had to return back to the letters and the stupid book. Mira sat down with a huff and flipped the book open to a section titled **Unsafe Speech.**

This was one she'd skipped over before, but as she skimmed it, she realized she'd apparently approved a slew of letters that were considered unsafe.

Maybe that was why Ferdinand wouldn't let her into the records?

It was her fault for skipping that section of the book. After looking through the categories, however, she realized it encompassed everything from disparaging remarks about Travelers to criticisms of justified wars and any comments referring to "different-eyed peoples."

Maybe she'd read it and skipped over it because it made no sense. Either way, she'd have to be more careful. Hopefully Ferdinand wouldn't notice. It wasn't like he'd had the time to read the letters in the first place.

She finished the last batch of the letters and headed out for the evening. A block away from the Traveler Center, a black carriage pulled up beside her and the driver called her name.

"Mr. Kellet is waiting for you."

She looked up at him and shook her head. "I don't have anything yet. Please tell him I'm working on it and – "

The driver ignored her, stepping off of the carriage and opening the door for her. "I must insist."

A flash of panic went through her mind. Had he found out she was reading his letters? Would he kill her for that? Or for not getting into the records?

The driver cleared his throat.

It looked like Mira was about to find out. She stepped inside the carriage, the door snapping shut behind her.

13

Blue Hue

The drive to Mick's would have been pleasant if Mira weren't genuinely afraid of being murdered. Thanks to her frantic mind, it was a short drive, and she arrived at the sprawling estate within minutes.

The house itself was stunning, with beautiful sand-colored stones stacked two stories high. The roof was lined with burnt red clay shingles, and the large windows had vines growing around them.

There were two more buildings in the distance, and fields and meadows as far as she could see. It was the prettiest place Mira had seen since she'd gotten to this world, and it stunned her for a moment.

A large white dog, the size of a German Shepherd, rushed to meet her, barking wildly and tail wagging. She bent down, scratching the animal behind the ears, and the barks quieted to whines.

"Can I count on you for protection, little friend?" she asked.

Her answer came a moment later when Mick walked through the front door. The dog ran to him, leaping and barking with joy.

"Try not to scare our guest, eh?" he said, voice low, scrubbing the dog's neck.

Maybe the women writing those lovesick letters had seen Mick with his dog. He looked different, relaxed, with a genuine smile on his face.

He didn't look frightening at all now, the smile reaching the corners of his eyes.

Mira realized she was staring at him and forced herself to look away, focusing on the dog instead. The goofball had rolled onto his back and at that moment, stuck his paw straight into the air.

A breath caught in her throat. Her dog used to do something like that. He'd roll his eighty-pound body like a ballerina, legs sticking straight up and jowls hanging in an upside-down smile.

It had always made her laugh, and the reminder felt like a fresh jab to the heart.

"Glad you made it," Mick said, standing up.

She offered a weak smile. "Thanks."

Mira was about to explain why she hadn't gotten the records yet, but Mick had already turned and started walking back into the house. "I have something to show you," his deep voice bellowed.

Mira followed, like the dope she was. He led her into a marble-floored foyer, past two grand cascading staircases, and into an expansive hallway with shining dark elm floors. Paintings and bookshelves lined the walls on one side; the other side was made up entirely of windows.

They reached the end of the hallway and Mick opened a door. "After you."

He probably wouldn't murder her here, she decided. He wouldn't want to get blood in his nice house.

Mira stepped into the room, first struck by the bookshelves stretching from ceiling to floor. The room was two stories tall, with a rolling wooden ladder on the bookshelves, each corner absolutely stuffed with leather-bound books.

She looked up, admiring the books, and slowly turned to the center of the room where an empty fireplace stood. There were two stately couches, and two chairs and –

Mira gasped. Tied to one of the chairs was a man, blood pouring from a gash on his face.

She stumbled backward.

"Ah, Mira." Mick appeared behind her and gestured toward the man. "This is a friend of mine. Don't be rude, old friend."

The man looked up at her with his one unbloodied eye. "Hello, Mira."

"Have you met before?" asked Mick, staring at her.

She shook her head. "No."

"Are you sure?"

Mira looked at Mick, then back at the man. She took a deep breath and stepped closer, trying to imagine him without the blood. Finally she said, "I don't recognize him."

"Too bad." He walked forward, untying the man's hands before leaning in and speaking close to his face. "Next time you'll lose the eye. Or your life."

The man scrambled to his feet, muttering a "thank you" before running out of the room.

Her heart pounded in her chest. Was she getting the chair next? Should she run?

"He made a threat against Arianna months ago." Mick said. "I thought he may have been the one who attacked our car."

"Oh?"

"Wasn't him, it seems. Though he confessed to turning in Arianna's husband."

Mira stared at him, unable to speak.

Mick paused. "Did you know Arianna's husband was sentenced to six months of reeducation?"

She shook her head.

"Ah." Mick grunted. "He was overheard criticizing the Asphodavian invasion of another island. Used to be a soldier, but what does he know about war?"

Mick half-smiled, shaking his head, and Mira forced herself to smile back.

He walked to the table next to the couch and poured a drink. "Would you like one?"

She shook her head.

He shrugged, taking a sip and sitting down. "So, tell me. What have you found out this week, Mira Meadows?"

"Ferdinand has me reading letters," she stammered. "I tried to get into the records today, but I wasn't able to – he wouldn't let me. I'm going to make it work, though. I'll get the records somehow."

He nodded slowly, setting his drink down and pulling out a cigarette. "I've seen some of your memories."

"Yeah?"

"You led an interesting life."

She stared at him. This could be the beginning of a threat. How, she wasn't sure, but her mind was desperately trying to predict his next move.

"You had a husband," he continued.

"No," Mira said. "Robbie wasn't my husband. He was my fiancé."

Mick tilted his head. "Fiancé?"

Were there no French people in this world? No croissants? No wonder things were so terrible. "It means we were going to get married, but we weren't married yet."

Mick leaned back, thinking on this. "How did you know he wanted to marry you?"

"He proposed, and he gave me a ring."

He stared at her for a moment. "What kind of ring?"

"One made of gold." She hadn't Traveled with it, because she hadn't been wearing it when she died. It was too big and always felt like it was in the way.

"My grandmother could turn any metal into gold."

She raised her eyebrows. "That's...nice."

"Gold lost much of its value after that. She was a Traveler, my granny. She sold the marking when she should have sold the gold."

"Ah."

He cleared his throat. "Your almost-husband was green-eyed. The committee would rate you favorably if you were married to a green-eyed man. You should say he was your husband."

It didn't seem like he was going to kill her in that moment – maybe her explanation had worked. Now he was back to talking in riddles. "Why do his eyes matter?"

He motioned for her to have a seat, and she stiffly lowered herself onto the couch.

"Have you noticed that every person with power in Asphodavia has green eyes?"

Mira looked down, then back up at him. "No."

"Ferdinand, the committee members, all of them. Green-eyed." He walked over the bookshelf and grabbed a thick brown tome, then took a seat next to her before opening it.

The book filled the space between them, with Mick so close that his leg ever so slightly brushed against hers. "Have a look."

She leaned over, studying the chart on the page labeled "Eye Color Correlation to Intelligence and Other Key Traits."

The first category was green eyes. Under intelligence, it said, "The most intelligent of people. These individuals are fair-minded, capable of complex thought, and the most benevolent of all known beings."

Mira frowned, then followed her finger down to her section. "Blue eyes signal a simple mind. The inability for a person to develop hue to their eyes does not bode well for the development of the rest of their intellect, body, or soul."

She looked up at him, bewildered enough that her fear of being murdered was subsiding. "Is this a joke?"

"No. Most of these books have been destroyed, but until about fifty years ago, this is what the Council taught."

"Taught who?"

He tapped out his cigarette and lifted a shoulder. "Everyone. They enforced laws to keep green eyes separated from the rest of us."

Unbelievable. "What do they say about Violets?"

He turned to the next page and Mira read on. "The presence of any shade of purple in the eye is a mark of madness. Violet-eyed individuals are aggressive, destructive, have slowed intellect, and are known to steal magic."

"Wow." She pulled back. "That's awful."

"It is. And now the Council has changed their story. They claim to be for fairness of all eye colors. They insist we are the ones who are bigoted, not them, and any suggestion otherwise ends up in front of the Disinformation Governance Board." He paused. "Your husband had green eyes, and they would assume you had positive qualities to deserve him."

"Because of his eyes?"

"Because of his eyes."

Mira scoffed. "Joke's on them, then. I don't have any positive qualities."

He set his drink down. "I disagree."

Mick stared at her, and Mira only managed to look back at him for a few seconds before breaking his gaze and standing up. Maybe she understood the letter-writers better than she wanted to admit. "Listen, you don't have to scare me with the chair and the blood. I'll get into the records. I just need a little time."

A half-smile pulled at the edge of his lips. "I didn't bring you here to scare you."

She pointed at the puddle of blood on the floor. "Really? You're going to act like that isn't to scare me?" He said nothing, and she rambled on. "It's fine. I'll do what you want. I'm just – "

"I'm sorry, I didn't expect a little blood to frighten you. You've seen worse in your past life."

He stood and stepped toward her, and this time, Mira managed not to flinch.

Mick reached into his pocket, pulling out a twenty tallie note. "This is from Arianna. She's convinced you were a good luck omen for the birth of her son."

This seemed like a bribe. At the same time, she could use the money, as her reserves were down to two tallies after a night out at the nearby pub with Slava, Samuel, and Alice.

"Unless you don't need it." Mick pulled the tallie note away.

No need to let her pride get in the way. Mira took the note from his hand. "Tell her I said thank you."

He nodded, turning to walk out of the room. "I'll be in touch."

He disappeared through the door, and a moment later a maid came to fetch her.

14

Marked

On the way home, Mira made the decision not to tell Alice she'd caved into Mick's demands. It would only worry her, and really, Mira was doing it for the right reasons.

It was clear Mick knew more about this world than Mira did, and if he could get more beneficial episcope scenes pulled for her, then her chances of getting back to her real life went up exponentially.

It wasn't like Ferdinand knew what she was up to. If she kept sucking up to him, he'd eventually hand her the keys to the records.

Probably.

It was dark when Mira got back to the Traveler Center, and she snuck through the front door quietly. Her plan was to grab a plate of food and sneak up to her room, expertly avoiding Alice and her prying eyes.

It worked perfectly, except for when she opened the door to her room and found Alice sitting on her bed, arms crossed.

"Where have you been?"

Mira flashed a smile. "Getting dinner."

She gasped. "You were with Mick again!"

"Yes, fine. Keep your voice down." Mira shut the door behind her. "At least I'm not drunk this time."

"Did he threaten you?"

"No." She paused. "Not exactly. I thought he did, but now I'm not so sure."

Alice gasped again, covering her mouth with her hands. "Why was there so much blood? And Robbie..."

Her voice trailed off.

Mira set her plate down before taking a seat on the bed.

"Alice," she said slowly, "How did you know about the blood?"

She looked up at Mira, eyes wide, shaking her head and covering her mouth with her hand.

"Talk to me."

Her eyes drifted down. "Why did he tell you to say Robbie was your husband?"

Mira pulled back. "I didn't tell you that."

"Yes, you did, just now."

"No, I didn't."

"Stop messing with me," Alice said, standing up and pacing the small room. "I can't handle it today."

Mira stood and followed her. "I'm not messing with you, Alice. I didn't say any of that."

"Yes, you did!"

"No, because I had fully planned on hiding it from you!" she shot back.

They fell silent.

"Alice..." Mira approached her slowly. "I think something is happening."

"I know." She rubbed her face with her hands and sat back down. "It's been happening all day, but not this badly. It's only gotten clearer as the day went on."

"What has?"

Alice looked up at her. "The thoughts. Your thoughts, and the thoughts of the ladies at the library, and of Herbert."

"Herbert's thoughts. Those must be interesting."

"It's exactly how he speaks," Alice said, shaking her head.

"Still. That sounds overwhelming."

Alice let out a deep breath. "I thought I was losing my mind when I heard the words filtering in. It's quiet at first, and it makes it hard to think. But now, with you..."

"What?"

"It sounded like you were talking. Out loud. That's how clear it was."

"Maybe because you were interrogating me!"

"Maybe." Alice pressed a hand to her forehead. "It's better now."

"Like it went away?" Mira studied her. She didn't look any different, maybe a bit more tired than usual. Maybe Mira's determination to hide everything from Alice was making it worse.

Alice looked up at her, a slight smile on her face. "I didn't know Mick was attractive. I assumed he was old for some reason."

Mira's mouth popped open. "Did you get that from my head?"

"I'm sorry!"

"It's fine, I mean, I just – I think you're marked, Alice. You can't tell anyone about this."

She shook her head. "Mira. It's against the law to hide a marking. You know that. I've been thinking about it all day. I didn't think it was real, but – "

"No." She grabbed her Alice's arm. "You can't tell them. You don't know what they'll do."

"Neither do you!" Alice stood, pacing the room. "I can't go back to my old life, Mira. I need to build a life here. Whatever Mick says – "

"You don't have to trust him, but you should trust me. I've seen some things at the constable's office. Life here isn't as simple as Miss Brown made it out to be."

"What if my marking is dangerous?"

"It's not dangerous. We'll figure it out. Just – please. Don't tell anyone. Not yet."

Alice put a hand over her eyes for a moment. Mira tried to clear her thoughts, as to not overwhelm her, but she couldn't help thinking one thing: *please*.

Alice looked up at her and nodded. "Fine. I'll stay quiet for now."

Mira pulled her in for a hug. They would sort this out, one way or another.

15

Gonzo

Their episcope trial that week started off much the same as the week prior, except as the audience filed in, Mira noticed some of patrons sporting large paintings of Slava with a crown on his head.

"What's that about?" Mira asked him, pointing to one the size of a banner being strung up in the back.

"Ah, that." He laughed. "A few of my friends are calling me the Traveler King."

Alice turned to him. "I wonder how they came up with that."

"Who knows!" he said, putting his hands up and smiling.

Slava knew how to play the game, and Mira admired him for it. She was trying to learn, and hopefully she would be able to before she ran out of time. Her bolt still seemed to be in good condition – nice and bright.

It was Alice she was worried about.

"I guess you should go first, then," Mira said. "Since you're the king."

"Not save the best for last?" he asked.

"No. Warm up the crowd for us." She nodded toward Samuel. "Give the rest of us a chance to survive."

He let out a laugh, his eyes twinkling. It was all a game to him. "Fine. I will tell Herbert. I will be first, to serve my people."

Slava got up and walked to the committee table, leaning against it as he chatted with the members.

When he was called up by Herbert, the crowd cheered. His first memory showed him knocking a guy out with one punch, and they stood captive, silent, as he explained the man had tried to break into his home.

Then the crowd cheered again, chanting his name. The next memory was of him in a jail cell, singing to the guard and getting the other six imprisoned men to join in.

He explained he served a week for punching the man, but it was well worth it because he never had a break-in again. The crowd roared, and even the committee clapped for him.

Slava was a star. It seemed punching was okay, if it was for a good cause. Slapping an old priest was never okay, though.

Mira was called up next, fully regretting her suggestion for Slava to go first. He was an impossible act to follow, and she suspected Mick had not yet pulled any strings to help her.

She got up to the podium and said hello, receiving some applause, but nothing like what Slava had gotten.

The screen lit up and she stepped back, holding her breath.

The memory opened on the face of a seven-month-old puppy. He was panting, his white teeth glistening in the light, his fur slightly puffy around his neck in that puppy way, and his snout perfectly black.

Wesley leaned down and grabbed his collar, dragging him across the kitchen floor.

"Dad!" Sara stepped in, trying to move between Wesley and the puppy, but it was useless. He pushed her away.

"You don't know how to discipline a dog, Sara. Move."

The puppy began barking, then retreated, running into a trash can and knocking it over. Coffee grounds and potato peels spilled to the ground.

"Come here! Now!" Wesley yelled, pointing at the floor in front of him.

The dog looked away and fell silent, tail tucked under his body.

"When I say come, I mean come."

"He's just a puppy," Sara protested.

Wesley pushed past her, approaching the puppy and barking another command. The dog stared at the floor and started to tremble.

"I've had enough with his disobedience." Wesley leaned down, smacking the dog across his nose. "I'm the alpha! Do you understand?"

"Stop it!" Sara said, grabbing him by the arm. "That's not how you train a dog."

"Go and clean up that trash!" he yelled, turning back to the dog and planting a firm kick to its side.

The puppy yelped, and at that moment Mira walked into the kitchen. "Stop it."

Wesley ignored her, but in a moment she was in front of him, thrusting her phone in his face. "Smile, Uncle Wes. You're on camera."

He froze, turning his eyes to her. The rage had disappeared from his face, replaced with a befuddled smile. "Mira, we've really got our hands full with this little guy."

She knelt down, blocking the space between him and the puppy. "People like you shouldn't have pets."

He let out a little laugh, rubbing the back of his neck. "We're trying our best here."

"Maybe you can't handle him."

"Well, you know, we're going to do everything we can, one day at a time, and – "

"You should give him to me."

He fell silent, his flat brown eyes staring into her.

She tucked her phone into her pocket and stared back. "I'll tell my dad he was too much. That you work too much and don't have time for him."

Wesley looked at her, then down at the dog.

She spoke again. "Then I'll erase the video. You have my word."

He smiled, bright and wide. "Yeah. Of course. Let's forget this ever happened."

Without another word, Mira scooped the puppy into her arms and carried his forty-pound body to her car.

The memory ended, and Mira stood for a moment, staring at the blank screen with tears in her eyes.

He had been so beautiful, with his shining black fur and fat puppy paws. His eyes were a shade she'd never seen before or since, like maple syrup touched with honey, glowing with light and soul.

The older man on the committee spoke. "Well, Mira. Do you care to explain?"

She cleared her throat and approached the podium. She needed to think like Slava. "That was my Uncle Wesley. Again."

He smiled. "Yes, we can see that."

She needed to construct a narrative, like Slava always did. Though, unlike Slava's, hers would be true. "My cousin Sara called to tell me her dad had gotten a puppy during a fundraiser. He did it to show off at work, to look like a nice guy.

"They'd only had him a few days when he started to lose his temper with the dog. Sara called me because she didn't know what to do."

The committee member nodded. "I see. Why did he agree to give you the dog? Was your uncle afraid of you?"

"No, he wasn't afraid of me. I was still a kid, and I mostly stayed out of his way. But Sara and I made a plan. I hid and recorded a video of him. I had a record of what he'd done, just like this memory."

A series of murmurs rippled through the crowd, and the committee member told them to quiet.

Mira continued. "He didn't want anyone to see how he behaved, so he gave in to what I wanted."

"You were able to keep the dog?"

"I was." She paused. How could she make this work? How could she recreate what Slava had with the crowd? "When I brought him home, my dad was livid. He told me the dog needed to be gone by the morning."

"Then your plan failed."

She shook her head. "No. I named him Gonzo and had him for the next ten years."

The audience erupted into laughter, as though they had been waiting for something to tip them over the edge.

She wasn't sure if Mick had pulled that memory for her. It could've gone either way, really, but she felt like she'd saved herself.

Mira smiled tentatively, and the committee man laughed and shook his head. "Very well. What do we have next?"

The episcope man began cranking, and Mira stepped out of the way.

"Starting compressions," a nurse called out, steadying herself above the patient's bed. The man was unconscious, his skin thin with liver spots on his face and arms, his mouth hanging open.

Mira popped up, staring at the monitor. "We've got V-fib."

The nurse pumped away, a wisp of hair escaping her ponytail. "Thought so."

Mira grabbed the defibrillator pads and placed them onto the man's chest.

At that moment, Robbie walked in. "What do we have here?"

Mira answered him without looking up. "Ninety-two-year-old man, COPD exacerbation. He was extubated this morning."

Robbie frowned. "Do we have a rhythm?"

The nurse stopped compressions for a moment so Mira could place the last defibrillator pad.

"V-fib," Mira said.

"Have we shocked him yet?"

Mira shot him a glare. "No, but if you'd take your hand off his neck, we could try."

Robbie suppressed a smile, putting his hands up in surrender.

"Charging." Mira motioned for them to move away. "Everybody, stand clear."

She hit the button, and the old man's body contracted, rising a few inches from the bed before dropping down again.

"Should we rotate compressors?" Robbie asked.

"Go ahead and jump right in, doc," Mira said. "They like to run our codes lean here. Just like everything else."

"That's fine," he said, ribs cracking beneath his hands. "You already made me feel right at home."

The memory stopped. Mira walked to the podium, her mind racing. They could see his eyes were green there, right? Could they tell? Was it close enough?

A younger committee member spoke, a man who had been silent until now. "What happened to that man?"

Time to use Mick's advice. "We fell in love and got married," she said firmly.

He cocked his head to the side. "The old man?"

"Oh!" She shook her head. "No, he died."

Laughter filled her ears again, and Mira forced herself not to look too pleased. "We were trying to revive him, but he was too far gone."

"It looked like a valiant effort."

"Yes, that was my job. I was a nurse."

The committee didn't look unhappy with her, but they didn't look pleased, either. They were all staring, quills in hand.

She needed to add more. "The other man, the doctor, was Robbie. My husband. That was the first time we met."

"Your husband? Was he a good man?" the younger woman asked.

"Yes. He was..." The words from the book flashed in her mind, with green-eyed people being the most benevolent of all beings, so of course the only word she could think of was *benevolent*. She managed to come up with something else. "He was wonderful. Really wonderful."

An "aw" rumbled through the audience and Mira turned toward them, nodding and smiling.

"Thank you, Mira. That was illuminating."

She left the stage, feeling much lighter than before, and took her seat. A few hands reached forward to pat her on the shoulders, and she turned and smiled, thanking them.

When she turned back to look at Alice up on the stage, her excitement fizzled.

Alice nearly tripped getting up the stairs, and when she got to the podium, she was breathing heavily. The whites of her eyes were reddened, and her dress hung crookedly off one shoulder.

Mira tried to direct her thoughts to her: *It's okay. Calm down.*

Alice looked around, from the committee to the crowd, then the screen, frantic. "Yes, let's begin," she said, stepping away.

A memory played, showing Alice cradling her newborn daughter, singing softly. They all watched for a few minutes until the screen went dark.

That wasn't so bad, Mira thought. Boring, but nothing bad. Alice could handle it.

Alice stepped to the podium and faced the committee.

"That was my first daughter," she said. "She was born just before my mom died."

The older man opened his mouth to speak, but Alice cut him off. "Yes, she was able to meet her."

Crap.

He stared at her, and Alice took a deep breath before speaking again. "We had two daughters, and they were the greatest joys of my life."

No, no, no. Mira needed to create a distraction. They needed to break the episcope, or set a fire, anything. She jabbed Slava in the ribs.

"Ow!" He turned to her with a scowl. "What is wrong with you?"

"Do something."

He narrowed his eyes. "Do what? She is fine, she – "

"Friends, I think we will end here for the night," the committee man said.

Groans rang out, followed by a chorus of boos.

The committee paid them no attention, huddled together as Alice stood up front, wringing her hands.

The jig was up.

16

Fairness and Friends

Try as she might, Mira could not get to the stage before Alice was whisked away. The loudest, and drunkest, members of the disgruntled audience rushed to the front, some congratulating Mira and Slava on their scenes, while others demanded to know why the show had been cut short.

Slava reassured them it must be some "technical difficulties," then jumped into a story of his own technical problems when his car once broke down in the middle of a bridge.

Mira slipped into the Traveler Center, away from prying eyes, and shut herself in Alice's room.

This was disastrously bad news. If only there was someone she could talk to, someone who could help them.

She had Mick's coin. She could summon him, and try to plead with him for help.

What would he do, though? He wasn't more powerful than the committee, was he?

She and Alice could run off and start over in another city. What were the chances anyone would track them down? She had the twenty tallies from Mick; those could get them far. They'd appear in a new place with new names, and no one would be the wiser.

After two hours of waiting, the door to Alice's room opened. Mira shot up from the bed, her heart pounding in her chest.

Alice peeked through, a smile on her face.

"You're okay!" Mira rushed forward, hugging her.

"I'm fine. I feel a lot better, actually."

"What happened? Tell me everything."

Alice took a seat on the bed. "It was so hard to control, with all of those people around us. I was hearing so many thoughts at once, I thought I was going to pass out."

Mira cringed. "I guess we should have anticipated that."

"It's fine!" Alice waved a hand. "I met with the committee and they were excited! They had so many questions."

"You didn't tell them you've known, right?"

She shook her head. "I told them it happened all of a sudden."

"Good." Mira released her breath. "Now what?"

Alice looked up and smiled. "I'm not sure. They said they'll contact the Council and we'll go from there."

The Council. Ugh.

"I don't like this." Mira took a deep breath. "I think we should run away, Alice. I have money. We can start over and – "

"We're not going to run away!" Alice let out a laugh. "Don't be dramatic. How do you know the Council is all bad?"

Mira glared at her. "Get out of my head!"

"I'm sorry, I didn't mean to! It's just – I don't know, they're being so positive. They're so excited about my marking, they're going to throw a festival to celebrate! It's going to be later this week. We'll all get the day off and – "

"Alice." Mira took her by the hands. "You can't trust them."

"I'm not going to run away." She pulled her hands back. "I'm going to face this, Mira. They're going to help me control it."

Mira tried to keep her thoughts from being too panicked. She thought happy thoughts – Gonzo's face, his puppy breath, his favorite ball.

"And no," Alice added, "I am not going to Mick for help."

Ah. So much for her plan.

. . .

The committee wasted no time in celebrating their discovery. The fair was announced the next morning, to be held in five days' time.

Ferdinand offered to let Mira out of her letter-reading duties a few hours early to get to the fair, but in the end, he forgot himself and let her go only a half hour before her usual time.

Mira rushed back to the Traveler Center and changed into a dress she'd bought from a woman on the street. It had been an odd exchange. The one-eyed woman told her she was only willing to sell it to her because she "liked the dog" from her episcope, and then made Mira swear secrecy about where she'd gotten it.

Only later did Mira find out that selling clothes, as opposed to renting them out, required a license, and she could only guess the one-eyed woman had nothing of the sort.

The dress itself was pretty, a deep violet color, tight at the waist and flaring out from there. It hit just above her knee, which was short for Asphodavia, but it covered her bolt and she was pleased with it. She smiled at her reflection before running up to the next floor.

Slava, Samuel, and Alice were waiting for her.

"Here," Slava said, shoving something into her hand. "I got this for you."

Mira accepted the small, rounded container, holding it in front of her face. "What is it?"

He wagged a finger at her. "Aha, that is the question, isn't it?"

It was no bigger than the palm of her hand, smooth, and made up entirely of hard, waxen leaves. She saw a small spout on the side and righted the container before popping off the lid.

The smell of cinnamon, apples, and alcohol floated to her nose. "Is this...brandy?"

He snapped his fingers. "Yes, my love, an apple brandy for you! Enjoy!"

She laughed. "Did you steal this from work?"

"Steal is such an ugly word." He put his arm around her. "You drink it, and if anyone sees, throw the leaves into the forest. No one will know."

"Thanks Slava." Mira took a sip. The stuff was strong, and not nearly as smooth as what Mick had given her. Still, she appreciated the gesture.

Samuel had long ago finished his, judging from the songs he was trying to sing at Alice.

"Where's yours?" she asked Alice, pulling her aside.

"I left it in my room. They told me alcohol can make it harder to control my marking, so I'll abstain for now."

"Ah. Okay."

"I'm doing a lot better, you know. I've been training every day to control it. I can walk through a crowd, no problem!"

Mira forced a smile. "That's great!"

"Some people came from Magnifico. I met them today, and tomorrow, I'll meet more. They've come for me to practice on them."

Mira stared at her, trying to keep the negative thoughts out of her mind.

It didn't work, and Alice scowled at her. "They're not all bad, you know. They want to help."

Mira let out a sigh. "I hope so."

"Ladies and Samuel," Slava announced, "we need to go or we will miss the party."

They paraded through the Traveler Center and spilled onto the street, the sun rapidly setting and casting a warm glow on everything it touched. Music and laughter carried through the quiet of the night, beckoning them to the next block where the festivities were to begin.

Mira walked arm in arm with Alice, and as their shoes clicked on the cobblestone, a flutter erupted in her stomach. It was like she was ten years old again, going to the county fair with Sara.

They rounded a corner and walked into an explosion of color. Above them floated a glittering tent, covering half of the block and shining down with thousands of warm, twinkling lights. The street itself was blocked off so no carriages could get through, with people filling the space instead.

There were people all around them, children running up and down the street, and performers floating above. Booths lined both sides of the road, some peddling goods or food, others with brightly flashing games. In the distance, Mira saw a queue of people waiting in line for flying horse rides.

"Isn't it something?" Alice said in a quiet voice.

Mira smiled. "It is." She looked at Alice and saw she had tears in her eyes. "What's wrong? Too many people?"

Alice hastily wiped her cheek. "No, nothing like that. I was thinking about how much my girls would've loved this. They're at that age where nothing seems to impress them anymore, but this…"

Mira reached over and squeezed Alice's hand. "Come on. Let's buy something magical."

"Don't waste your money on me! I'm fine."

The tallies from Mick's bribe were burning a hole in her pocket. "We either spend it here or I'll have to waste it renting another prison jumpsuit. I vote here."

Alice rolled her eyes. "Fine."

They walked down the street, losing Slava to his admirers, and peered at the offerings of each booth. Alice had no interest in a riding a flying horse, though she did like looking at the animal, and also claimed she didn't want a snack.

They came across a man making enormous glowing drinks and settled on sharing one. In line, they watched as the man behind the cart concocted a movie-theater-sized drink, glowing green and spitting bubbles five feet into the air.

There was no menu or signage at all, just a man at an empty cart. As they got closer, Mira realized there were only two glasses. The buyer had to finish their drink and hand it back in time for the next person.

He waved them over. "Come ladies, any flavor you can imagine. You tell me, and I'll make it for you."

Alice smiled. "Anything?"

"Do you know what pizza is?" Mira asked.

"Of course I do, but why would you want that?" the man said, scowling at her.

Well! Fizzy drinks were no joke. "What about a margarita?"

"The flavor, yes, but no alcohol. That would be unlawful, as my license doesn't cover it."

Alice smiled at her. "That sounds really nice, actually. A fresh margarita."

Mira nodded. "Perfect. One alcohol-free margarita, please."

The man nodded, throwing a glass into the air and catching it behind his back. "Margarita. You want the regular? The lemon? A prickled pear? A sriracha mango? Kumquat?"

They passed a glance to one another, and Alice said, "The regular."

"Coming up."

He closed his eyes and placed his hand on the glass. Lights erupted at the bottom, flying from side to side, before turning to smoke, then ice, then liquid.

"All right, finish it up over there." He motioned to his left, where the last customer had just downed his drink.

Mira slipped him the half tallie before they stepped aside, taking sips and passing the glass back and forth.

"Do you think he's a Traveler?" Mira asked.

Alice shrugged. "Maybe?"

"How mad do you think he was when he realized he had a magical power, but all he could do was make drinks?"

Alice let out a laugh. "You know, I couldn't drink anything when I was going through chemo. But before that, my husband used to make me margaritas with fresh limes, and it tasted just like this."

"That's so sweet." Mira passed the glass. Maybe it wasn't such a stupid trick.

Once they finished the drink, they went on their way, a bit merrier than before. Their enjoyment was cut short, however, when Alice was called away by one of the committee members.

"I'm sorry," she said. "I'll find you again soon, okay?"

Mira waved her on. "Go. It's your party."

She watched Alice walk away and noticed a man step out of the crowd, following behind her. He was tall, dressed in all black, and seemed to be watching Alice from a distance.

Mira was going to quietly alert Alice to this when the man joined the committee members, shaking hands.

He was one of them, it seemed. To Mira, however, it looked like Alice was being watched.

She debated what to do, imagining how hard it would be to slink around in the shadows, when she felt someone tap on her shoulder.

She turned to see Arianna's smiling face. Her hair was clean and shining, cascading down her shoulders in pretty brown curls, and she was dressed in a low-cut golden gown.

"Mira, how good to see you again!"

"And you!" Mira beamed. She was glad to see Arianna looking so well. "You look lovely."

She waved a hand. "Thank you. Better than last time at least, right?"

"No one was at their best that day."

"Have you seen my brother, by chance?"

Mira shook her head.

"Ah." Arianna frowned. "He's been giving tours."

Mira looked back, but Alice and the committee had disappeared into a building. Dang it. "What kind of tours?"

"Showing off to some business partners who came in from Magnifico." Arianna waved a hand. "It's always business with him."

Naturally. Mira shouldn't read too much into his staring and interest in her memories. He was a businessman. "Ah."

"I'm supposed to meet my future sister, but she's nowhere to be seen either." She strained, looking over Mira's shoulder and into the crowd. "Leona Frum. She's a Fairness Auditor, so we have to be careful what we say," Arianna added with a giggle.

"Say about what?"

"Oh, I'm only joking. It is her job to monitor fairness, but she won't mark our records. Her father is dead set on a match with Mick. She's here to make friends."

"There's an F you don't often hear about – friends."

Arianna threw her head back, laughing. "Come on. Don't stand here like you don't have a friend in the world." Arianna waved her over. "Help me find them."

Mira was slowly realizing that the drink they'd had, which wasn't allowed to have alcohol in it, had had alcohol.

She just needed to not say anything stupid and she'd be fine.

"Unless you were waiting for someone?" Arianna asked.

Mira shook her head. "No. I'm happy to help you."

It would be impossible to follow Alice all night, and further, maybe Arianna could tell her more about what the Council was planning for Alice.

They wove through the crowds, Arianna gabbing on nonstop, as Mira prayed to not end up terribly drunk again.

After half an hour of walking around, Arianna spotted Mick walking out of a building with an elegantly dressed woman.

"Oh," she cooed, "he was showing off our bathhouse."

"You have a bathhouse?"

"Yes, and it's a lot nicer than our betting hall. I doubt Leona would like that. Might get spit on if she wasn't careful." Arianna laughed, waving a hand in the air. "Mickey! Over here!"

He nodded at her and changed course, coming their way. As they got closer, Mira could see that the woman's intricately pinned dark hair. Her red gown dragged behind her, collecting debris from the street. She didn't seem to mind, and her arm was linked through Mick's.

"Evening," Mick said, nodding as he joined them. "Leona, this is my sister, Arianna."

Leona's dark green eyes sparkled and she extended a dainty hand. "Arianna, so lovely to meet you."

Her eyes were unlike anything Mira was used to, so green that they looked unnatural. She tried not to gawk, instead turning her gaze to Mick, only to realize he was staring at her.

Her heart jumped and she looked away.

"This is Mira, one of the new Travelers," Arianna said.

"Well!" Leona's eyes swept down, lingering on Mira's chest, then back up. "How fun."

Was her bolt shining through her dress? While she was thankful it was still quite bright, she hadn't thought to check how it looked under low light and flimsy fabric.

"Mira helped me deliver Nicholas," Arianna added. "She was so helpful. She was a healer in her world."

Leona made a face. "A healer? I thought your world didn't have magic."

"Not a healer, exactly," Mira said. "I was a nurse."

"How special for you," Leona said, smiling.

There was a commotion behind them and Slava came stumbling into their circle. "Mira! Look at you, making friends, even with your grumpy face."

"Hello, Slava."

"Slava!" Arianna turned, opening her arms to him. "I've seen your episcope memories! I feel like we're friends already."

"Of course we are friends!" He opened his arms and hugged her.

Mira detected the slightest cringe on Leona's face.

Heh.

Mira decided she should be polite and introduce them, perhaps earn a hug for Leona as well. "Slava, this is Arianna and Mickson Kellet, and their friend Leona – "

He gasped, putting a hand to his chest. "Kellet? I heard about the most wonderful bathhouse where you are levitated in the air, and the water is around you?"

"That's right," said Arianna, a smile on her lips.

"How would a lonely Traveler get into one of these?"

Arianna dropped her voice. "It takes a half tallie and the password for the week."

"I hear it is a wonderful place for the men to gather." Slava narrowed his eyes. "It is your establishment?"

"It is."

He clapped his hands together. "Excellent. I'm finally meeting the right people."

Everyone laughed, except for Mick. He stood there in his dark suit, smoking a cigarette and looking off into the distance.

Mira couldn't help but notice Mick's body was turned away from Leona, though she was still clinging to his arm. Perhaps she was just another in a long line of potential wives.

It seemed odd Mick would even consider her – she was green-eyed, for one thing, and apparently had a job enforcing fairness. Mick didn't seem to be someone interested in enforcing the rules. Why would he pick *her*, of all people?

She wasn't sure if it was the alcohol or something else, but the questions piled in Mira's mind as she watched Leona talk down her nose to Slava.

After a few minutes, one of Slava's admirers stumbled into the circle, eyes bloodshot and reeking of booze. "Watch out, Slava, we have green-eyeds walking the streets of Laurium. They've come down from their castles in Magnifico to –"

Slava patted him on the back. "Oh, my friend, telling stories again." He flashed a smile before dragging the man off.

A stiff silence fell between them, and Mira peeked at Leona. Her fake smile had faded, and her shoulders were stiff.

Arianna rushed to speak. "The fair has been such fun for the children."

Leona nodded, lips pursed, and delicately touched her hair. "And the drunks."

Oh dear. So *sensitive*.

Something inside Mira urged her to poke at that irritated spot. Normally, she would resist that petty feeling, but the alcohol gave her just enough of a push to speak.

"Magnifico?" She looked at Leona. "Is that where you're from? I'm sorry, I'm so new to everything."

"It is." She straightened her shoulders before diving into her purse before retrieving a vial of lipstick. "My grandparents moved to the island years ago. I studied at the university in Emerald, and now I work in Fairness in Verity."

Mira raised an eyebrow. "Verity?"

"Yes, it's the capitol city of Asphodavia. Really, you should have learned that on your first day here."

She forced a smile. "I must have forgotten."

Leona finished applying the bright red lipstick and stuck it back in her purse. "Of course. There are no universities on Nordavia, so I hardly expect you to know more than how to milk a cow." She laughed at her own joke, casting a side glance to Mick.

Having grown up in West Virginia, Mira was used to cow jokes. She was also used to dealing with the sort of people who made such jokes.

"What's a university?" she asked, doe-eyed.

Leona looked at her, a wrinkle creasing her stiff forehead. "It's a school for advanced education. Do you not have universities in your world?"

"Never heard of one," Mira said, shaking her head. "How interesting."

"Why, that's terrible!" Leona frowned and turned to Mick. "Mickson, we must correct this."

He tapped out his cigarette, a smile on the edge of his lips. "I think it might be too late for Mira."

Arianna shot him a look and he let out a small laugh disguised as a cough.

Leona didn't seem to notice this exchange. "It's never too late." She dropped her voice. "You have to do something to help those less fortunate than yourself, Mickson."

"You must think of others, Mickey," Arianna added, putting a hand to her chest.

Mira could hardly keep herself from bursting out laughing. She bit her lip and tried to think of unfunny things, like her graduation from nursing school. That had been boring. And Leona's dress, dragging dead leaves and horse droppings from the street and sweeping them behind her.

No, that actually was funny.

Leona went on. "We've done it at home. I created a program where we spent time reviewing memories with the Travelers, helping them understand which of their habits are not acceptable in Asphodavia."

"All right," Mick said gruffly. "Something to think about."

Slava had returned, this time without his drunken fan. "If it's held in the bathhouse, I will go."

"Oh you," Leona pointed at him and scrunched her nose. "I'm sure we can find a place to do it. A Traveler University!"

Wait, no. This was not funny. Mira started slowly backing away, but Leona grabbed her by the wrist. "You can be our first student!"

Mira pulled her arm away. "Oh no, that's okay."

"Come now, Mira," Slava said. "You always need help."

"That settles it, then," Leona said. "We'll have our own little university before I go back to Magnifico."

There it was. She had decided to poke where she shouldn't have poked, and now she was paying the price.

She never learned.

Mira forced a smile. "Wonderful. Looking forward to it."

17

Evander Kagan

There was little hope of hearing what the Council might do to Alice with Leona around, and Mira decided she'd done enough damage for the night with her provocation of the Traveler University. As soon as she could, she excused herself and restarted her search for Alice.

It was easy enough to find her, back in the town square and surrounded by official-looking people. Alice was still being tailed by the man in black. It was impossible to get near her, so after a few hours, Mira took herself back to the Traveler Center to wait it out.

At the front door, a man dressed in black stopped her.

"Name?" he asked.

She thought of lying, but decided it wouldn't help. "Mira Meadows."

He pulled a sheet from his pocket and grunted. "Go ahead."

Mira studied his face as she walked past. He wasn't the man she'd thought was following Alice earlier, but he was dressed the same, head-to-toe in black.

Whatever was going on, she didn't like it. She went looking for Herbert and found him in the kitchen preparing dough.

"Mira! How did you enjoy the fair?"

"It was nice." She paused. "Do they always hold a fair when a Traveler discovers a marking?"

"Not always," he said. "Usually, they do them once a year for the most exciting of the markings. Alice must have something special."

"You don't know what she can do?" asked Mira.

"Of course not. Do you?"

Mira shook her head. "I'm curious, but no." She edged around Herbert's work station. "Is there a chance more Travelers could arrive soon? With more exciting markings than Alice's?"

He stopped what he was doing and looked up, thinking. "I would say that's unlikely. I wouldn't expect more Travelers until your bolts fade. Time is still frozen in your world, after all."

"Ah. Right." So that wouldn't help. Mira hoped maybe someone would come along and distract them from Alice. "Who is that man at the door?"

Herbert resumed his dough kneading. "The committee sent him. They don't want anyone getting in who shouldn't be here – you know, markings can attract such fanfare. There's another man at the back door."

Odd. The townspeople didn't even really know about Alice's marking. On the other hand, the Slava fandom had reached obsession level for a few of the townspeople, but the committee had never sent men to protect him.

It was off. It was all off. She turned to leave. "Thanks, Herbert."

"Don't miss breakfast tomorrow!" he called out after her. "I'm making maritozzi!"

"I'll be there."

She walked away, the wheels spinning in her head. To keep out a crowd, they'd need more than two men. But to keep someone inside, two men would work just fine...

Mira walked back to the front door and sat in the darkness of the staircase, watching the guard through the window. He didn't seem particularly attentive, at one point falling asleep, but when

Alice approached, he sprung to life. He greeted her by name before opening the door for her.

Mira waited until the door shut behind her to make herself known. "Psst!"

Alice squinted in the darkness. "Mira? What're you doing up?"

"Worrying."

Alice smiled, reaching a hand forward to pat her on the shoulder. "Can't we worry tomorrow?"

As much as Mira liked seeing Alice happy and relaxed, now wasn't the time to be relaxed. "Let's go to my room."

"All right."

Once upstairs, Mira shut the door and pulled out the sheet of paper with her old class notes. She wrote, "I think they're watching you" in a blank corner.

Alice read it and laughed. "Come on."

Mira pressed a finger to her lips, shaking her head. She wrote on, adding, "There are guards outside, I think to keep you here. You need to run. I can help you. I have tallies."

"Mira," Alice whispered, "You don't have to write all of this, remember?"

"I didn't know if you were feeling up to it!" Mira whispered, though truthfully, she'd forgotten. She passed the quill and paper to Alice and focused her thoughts, repeating, "You have to run. They're trapping you here. This isn't good. I have a bad feeling."

Alice pushed the paper aside. "You're always having bad feelings."

Mira frowned. "This is different," she whispered. "Please, Alice."

She shook her head. "Let's get some sleep. We can talk tomorrow, okay?"

"Fine."

The next morning, Mira didn't get a chance to talk to Alice before three members of the committee stopped by in an excited tizzy.

"The head Council member is coming today. He's just been appointed; I've never gotten a chance to meet him," said the old man. He was dressed normally, or at least normally for Asphodavia, in a gray velvet suit. Mira thought he looked strange, not wearing his usual robe.

It made him look too human, and Mira didn't like it. It was lulling Alice into a false sense of security.

Mira sat at the table, picking at her pastry bun and sending her angry thoughts at Alice.

Alice, however, didn't seem to notice. Either she was ignoring Mira, or she really had gotten skilled at blocking out unwanted thoughts. She got up from the table after having eaten only half of her bun, both guards at her side.

Despite not wanting to break Herbert's heart, Mira didn't finish her breakfast bun, either. She needed to get to work and get information out of Ferdinand about Alice's situation.

She walked to the constable's office in a hurry and went straight back to Ferdinand's office.

"Good morning, Mira. I hope you weren't too festive last night."

"No, sir. I'm not one to party," she lied. So many lies. "I heard the head Council member is coming to town today?"

"Oh yes," he said, his voice deep. "Very serious business indeed."

"Serious?" She took a step forward. "Does the Council always meet newly marked Travelers?"

"No, Mira, they don't have the time for that." Ferdinand sat back and folded his hands on his desk. "For Evander Kagan to come and visit us, something must be very wrong indeed."

Her heart rate picked up. "What's wrong, Constable?"

"You just missed him, in fact. It's unfortunate; I could have introduced you. It was my first time meeting him myself, but he was quite impressed with our operation here. Quite impressed! I could have put in a good word for your integration."

Mira didn't give a damn about her integration right now. "Is Alice in trouble?"

"Not in trouble." He stood, straightening his jacket. "Though from what Evander told me, she's become increasingly unstable because of her marking. It's a shame." He walked to the window, shaking his head. "If you hurry, you can see him off. A wise man, that Evander."

Alice wasn't unstable. If anything, she was *too* stable, and too trusting.

"Come, Mira. He's just setting out now."

She walked to the window, her mind spinning, and looked down at the lavish convertible car across the street. It was the prettiest car she'd seen yet, with shining baby blue paint, white trim, and golden leather seats.

A uniformed man rushed from the driver's seat to open the back door.

Mira squinted. "Is that Evander?" she asked.

"Yes, there he is! An extremely civil man – perhaps he'll stop back for tea later. Perhaps you could change into something nicer."

Ferdinand babbled on, but Mira didn't have the strength to acknowledge him. She was focused on the back of Evander's head, wishing she had Alice's marking so she could hear what the man was thinking.

He spun, as if on cue, and sat into the back of the convertible, smiling widely, wrinkles lining his face.

Mira's heart dropped.

She knew this man. He looked at least thirty years older, despite having left her world only a decade prior. His hair was white now, and his glasses were different.

Still, she would recognize him day or night, nightmare or daydream.

Uncle Wesley.

18

Unsafe statements

S he stumbled back, away from the window, and fell to the ground.

Alice needed to get away *now*.

"What has gotten into you?" Ferdinand shook his head. "You're missing the procession. The Council has the finest cars in all of Asphodavia."

"I'm not feeling well," she said, getting to her feet. "I think I need to go back to the Traveler Center."

"Nonsense. You overindulged last night, I'm sure. Nothing a little hard work can't help you forget." He pointed at the window. "There she goes now. Oh dear, she does not look well."

Mira vaulted to the window. "Where?"

"Just there, in the last car."

Mira caught sight of Alice, her curly hair tossed by the wind of the convertible. "Where are they taking her?"

"To Magnifico, of course."

She could hardly see the back of Alice's head now as she disappeared down the street.

He looked over at her and smiled knowingly. "Don't fear, Mira. Your time will come."

She'd never wanted to punch Ferdinand as much as she did in that moment. If she could knock him out, then she could take his car and chase after the procession. But how would she get to the other island? Were there boats? Flying cars?

"We've got *very* important business today, girl," he said, turning back to his desk and picking up a sheet of paper. "I think you're ready to come along with me to address a complaint."

Mira pressed her forehead against the window. There had to be a way to get Alice back. If only she'd made her run away last night. Why hadn't she insisted on it?

"Mira?" Ferdinand let out a sigh. "Why don't you take a moment and tidy yourself up before we go."

She pulled away from the window to face him. Ferdinand was a head taller than her, and the deputies might even come to his aid. He was too big to punch. "Yes sir."

"We don't have all day. Hurry along! You can use my restroom over there, if you'd like."

He pointed to a door in the corner of the office and she nodded. "Thank you."

The muscles in her legs were stiff with tension as she walked across the office. It was as though she thought keeping all of her muscles taut would help her run when the moment was right.

Except the moment was not right. Not anymore. That moment was last night, or four days ago, before Alice had round-the-clock guards. Before Wesley had heard what she could do, before he'd surely made a scheme to drain her of her magic.

She shut the bathroom door behind her. The thought of Wesley being able to read people's thoughts made her blood run cold. How had he managed to gain so much power in this world?

Mira knew the answer to that. He sought power above all else. Of course he was powerful; there was nothing he wouldn't do.

She let out a grunt and walked over to the sink. It was stupidly ornate, white porcelain with a gold faucet, gold handles, and gold dragons painted around the edges.

Gold, gold, gold. Didn't they ever get sick of covering everything in gold?

Mira bent over, splashing cold water on her face before straightening to look at herself in the gold-rimmed round mirror.

No wonder Ferdinand assumed she'd had a rough night. There were bags under her eyes and her hair was more disheveled than normal. She pulled a white towel from the pile and dabbed at her face, trying to cool her skin and her thoughts, then wetted her hands and straightened out her hair.

She tossed the towel into the golden basket at her side and froze. Next to the basket stood a small table with books and pamphlets scattered in piles. Intermixed with the books were plain brown folders.

Mira got closer to the pile of folders. The first was labeled with a name she didn't recognize – **Archibald Smith**.

She carefully pushed it aside, noting its exact angle, and worked through the pile. The fourth one down was labeled **Arianna Kellet**.

She looked over her shoulder to make sure she'd locked the door before picking it up.

It was thin in her hands, and she opened it to find only a few sheets inside. The top sheet was a page of handwritten notes labeled "Incidents."

The most recent one read, "Childbirth – investigated. Magic negative."

Beneath it was another note. "Traveler discovery – Identified Traveler Mira Meadows, reported car was struck by her landing bolt. Further investigation needed, car appeared to be damaged by magic."

Beneath that, another entry. "Returned to site of car accident, car had been cleared. No remnants of magic found in soil near car. Bolt explanation likely."

Mira frowned. What did that mean?

She flipped the page, but the next notes were unrelated, merely containing snippets of Arianna's letters that were found to be offensive.

"Mira?" Ferdinand called through the door. "I need to tell you what we'll be doing today."

"Coming!" she yelled, shoving Arianna's record back into place. She quickly scanned the other names, not recognizing any of them, and tried to set the pile how it had looked before she'd touched it.

Finally, she had something for Mick. Maybe she could change their old deal and he could help Alice instead. It was worth a shot, and she would figure her integration out later.

She pulled the coin from her pocket and turned it three times. At first she thought it hadn't worked, but then it glowed warm in her palm.

Maybe he'd send a carriage for her at the end of the day. Maybe Alice wouldn't even be off of the island by then...

"I'm feeling refreshed," she said, throwing the bathroom door open. "Sorry for the delay."

He was busy straightening his hat in the mirror. "Never mind that. We have a reeducation to initiate today."

"What's that?"

He turned, his pale green eyes bright. "You shall see, my dear! Follow me."

They walked through the office, past the deputies' desk, and out the front door.

Ferdinand's car was waiting, and this time, Mira got to ride up front. She got in and the car sputtered to life before carrying them off.

They drove in a direction Mira had never been before, away from the town square and the bustle of the many carts and shops. Ferdinand babbled on, telling her the history of the buildings and previous committee members.

Mira murmured enough oh's and ah's to keep him rolling. She had nothing to say, preferring to look out the window. The further they went, the fewer carriages and people they saw, until they were the only ones on the road.

Ferdinand stopped on a street lined with simple brick townhouses. "Here we are!" He hopped from his seat, knocking his hat on the roof on the way out.

Mira didn't share his enthusiasm, though she tried to fake it. "Where are we, sir?"

"This is one of the premier neighborhoods in Laurium," he said. "Each home features a private bathroom *and* a kitchen."

She looked around, nodding. It seemed nice enough, each home almost exactly alike, with red brick walls and shiny black doors. They all had flowers in the windows, alternating pink, yellow, and white.

"It's so quiet," she said. "Where is everyone?"

"Ah, well, yes." He leaned toward the car, using his reflection to fix his hat. "There are only a few residents at present. The homes are listed for rent, though not everyone can afford them."

"I see."

He walked, motioning for her to follow, and went to the door labeled 147, knocking three times. After a moment, there was no answer, and he pounded on the door. "Open up! It's the Constable."

Silence.

He turned to her, shaking his head. "I have the authority to break this door open. It's a solution when they refuse to cooperate." Ferdinand motioned for Mira to step back.

"What if they're not home?" Mira asked.

"Then we will leave a note inside," he said simply, pulling a pen-sized metal rod from his pocket.

He held it up to the door and tapped it on one end. The little rod let out a high-pitched squeal before exploding, blasting the door open.

"Whoa." Mira stepped back. "I'm surprised you'd carry that in your pocket, so close to your...skin."

"Impressive, isn't it?" he said before shoving what was left of it back into his pants.

Mira nodded, surveying the splintered wood and crumbling bricks in the doorway. "Very."

Even without the exploded door, the house didn't appear to be in good shape. She could see a hallway and a staircase ahead of them, the ceiling caving in, yellow and rotted. The staircase was crooked and missing any semblance of a banister.

A man emerged from behind the rubble, arms in the air. "What are you doing, breaking my door like that? Do you know how much it'll cost to have that fixed?"

Ferdinand took a step toward him, almost slipping on a chunk of wood but recovering gracefully. "Archibald Smith?"

"Yeah, and that was Archibald Smith's door that you just destroyed!" he yelled, waving a hand at the scene in front of him.

The man looked familiar. Mira had seen him at her trial, or perhaps at work...

No! She'd seen him at the fair – Slava's drunk friend.

Ferdinand grabbed the man by the arm, pulling him down the steps and onto the sidewalk, nearly toppling Mira in the process. He reached into his bag and pulled out a large, black block of wood. "By the authority vested in me by the Council, you stand accused of making unsafe statements and have been summoned for reeducation."

Ferdinand shoved the box on top the man's hands, trapping them.

"Now, hang on, I haven't done anything!" Archibald protested.

Ferdinand turned to Mira and dropped his voice. "That's what they all say."

He then reached into his back pocket and pulled out what looked like a remote control with far too many buttons, wires, and a glowing light. He pressed one of the buttons, and a moment later what looked like a floating dark sarcophagus zoomed over their heads and lowered itself over Archibald.

"This is insanity!" Archibald yelled. "Stop this! Never a day in my life have I –"

The box opened wide before swallowing him whole.

"Constable!" Mira yelled. "What is that?"

Ferdinand smiled at her knowingly. "Don't be frightened, girl."

The lid snapped shut, and Archibald's cries were silenced. The box floated upwards and away without a sound.

"Well!" Ferdinand clapped his hands together. "How was that for your first complaint?"

She couldn't force a smile, and she couldn't form a convincing lie, either. "Very interesting, Constable."

They drove back to the office, Ferdinand chatting all the while as Mira weighed what she had seen.

It was impossible. Mira wouldn't be able to rescue Alice on her own. Clearly there was too much magic she didn't know about.

What she needed was an ally, a friend. Mick wasn't a friend, exactly, but he was powerful. She made up her mind to steal any record he needed, even if she had to break into the office in the middle of the night to get it.

They pulled up to the office and a deputy ran out to greet them.

"This was hand-delivered for Mira, sir."

She accepted the envelope, pink and scented with honey and roses. "For me?"

"A letter from an admirer?" Ferdinand laughed at his own joke, patting his belly.

Rude.

As soon as she tore the envelope open, some sort of enchanted butterflies fluttered out, hitting her in the face. She swatted them away. Inside was a sheet of light pink paper inviting her to Traveler University.

"It's from Leona," she said. "Leona Frum. She'd liked to host me at a Traveler University."

"Leona Frum!" A smile spread across Ferdinand's face. "You are extremely lucky to have caught her attention."

Mira tucked the letter away. This was the last of her problems. "I won't be able to attend. It starts in the middle of the workday tomorrow."

"Nonsense," Ferdinand said. "You must go, and send her my regards. You must tell her how we handled her complaint today."

"That was her complaint?"

"Oh yes. Whatever Archibald said to her made her feel most unsafe. Tell her he has been taken care of."

Mira clenched her jaw for a second before releasing it. "I'd be happy to."

19

Traveler University

The workday refused to end, and Ferdinand sent her off to tend to new letters. Mira approved all of them without corrections and without reading them. She hoped they all contained language that would make Leona feel unsafe.

As soon as her time was up, she left the constable's office and started her usual walk home, slowly waiting for a carriage to appear.

After an hour, no carriage came for her.

She paced up and down the surrounding blocks, making three trips around the town square. After two hours, she grew sick of waiting and went to the Traveler Center to eat a quick dinner.

As soon as she was done eating, however, she went back outside, walking to the small park where Mick had once dropped her off. She watched every carriage with excitement, only to be passed by each time.

After standing around in the dark for far too long, she gave up and returned to her room. It was possible Mick was busy, or that he'd lost interest in their deal.

She'd have to find a way to get into more records. She'd done enough sucking up to Ferdinand. Now she needed to turn up the charm. Mira could do it, especially if Alice's life depended on it.

The next morning, she left the Traveler Center early, long before she was due to see Leona. Still, no carriage came for her, and she had no choice but to break her waiting with a trip to the university she'd goaded into being.

•   •   •

Traveler University was held at the Three Pigs Pub. The sign outside didn't list the name of the pub, instead having only a drawing of three pigs standing around a trough.

Lovely.

She pulled the heavy door open and, as she stepped inside, a banner shouted "Welcome Travelers" in Leona's voice. Mira stopped in her tracks, staring at it, and a wad of flower petals smacked into the top of her head.

The flowers didn't do anything to improve the smell of the place – stale beer and urine. Nor did it help with the rest of the décor. Everything looked dirty, from the heavy wooden tables and chairs to the peanut-shell covered floors to the yellowed glass windows. The center space was filled with tables, and a bar spanned the back, paint peeling off the surface.

The room had a few doors on the far wall, and no one else seemed to be inside.

"I'll be with you in one moment," Leona called out from a far corner. She was in a booth sitting next to an episcope, along with a loudly complaining Slava.

"People like the jokes," he said.

Leona patted him on the shoulder. "We're looking for a kinder, gentler version of Slava. Do any of the memories we watched show *that* version of Slava?"

He made a face, staring at the table in front of him. "No."

"We'll just have to keep looking, then," Leona said, excusing herself and walking toward Mira. "I am so glad you've made it. Did you bring Samuel?"

Mira shook her head. "No, I'm sorry. I don't know where he is."

She frowned. "That's a shame. I'm sure he'll turn up."

Mira was sure he wouldn't. If he'd gotten out of work, he'd be toiling away at his garden, which had grown an impressive number of potatoes and onions for their stews.

Leona continued. "Slava and I are having a productive session, but we're running a bit over our time. And that's *absolutely* okay, because that's what we're here for, but now I can't give you my full attention."

Mira cleared her throat. "That's all right. If you're busy, I'll just get back to work and –"

"I can take her."

Mick had appeared in the doorway of one of the far rooms, leaning against the frame with his arms crossed. His gravelly voice carried across the quiet pub, sending a chill down her spine.

Leona clapped her hands together. "Thank you, Mick. I'm so glad you could make it."

He nodded. "Happy to."

"You're lucky to get Mickson's help." Leona said with a wink. "He's a busy man."

"I'll take some of Mick's help," Slava yelled from the corner. "Such a beautiful man can help me any time he likes."

Mira caught eyes with Mick and had to quickly look away so they both wouldn't laugh.

Leona stood frozen with a smile on her face, and after a beat, she turned back to Slava. "Let's get back to your memories."

Mira crossed the room, stopping before she reached Mick. "Oh, Leona?"

She looked up. "Yes?"

"Constable Ferdinand wanted you to know we sent Archibald for reeducation yesterday following your complaint."

"Oh, lovely. Thank you!" She smiled again, scrunching her nose, then turned back to Slava.

Narc.

Mira walked into the room and shut the door behind her. It was a small space, perhaps for private meetings, and it had better lighting than the main bar area. An episcope was set up, along with a screen, and a box with her name on it sat at the center table.

"I need to talk to you," she said in a hushed voice.

"I know." Mick took a seat next to the episcope and pulled the box over.

She sat next to him. "I found Arianna's record."

He looked up, eyebrows raised. "These are your memories."

"I don't care about that anymore," she said, waving a hand. "I want to make a new deal with you."

"Oh?" He pulled a vial out of the box, squinted at the label, and stuck it into the episcope.

"Alice is going to be taken to Magnifico."

He sat back, pulling a cigarette out of his pocket. "She's already there."

"I want to get her back."

He pulled a glass lighter from his pocket. It was clear with a flame dancing inside. He removed the cap and a light emerged. "You can't."

Of course he wasn't going to make this easy. "I have to. I saw the head Council guy yesterday. Do you know who he is?"

"Evander?"

"Yeah, whatever fake name he's going by. That man is my Uncle Wesley."

"He's a Traveler?" Mick took a long drag of the cigarette. "That's something."

"Don't be impressed by him, Mick. It's a disaster. He's the most vicious man I've ever known. I don't know what he'll do to Alice. He could – "

"I'll tell you what he'll do. He'll give her a drink of ambrosia, shock her with current, and catch the offshoot of her marking into an aion, which he'll lock away in the Hall of Magic."

Mira rubbed her face with her hands. "And then he'll kill her?"

He made a face, as if weighing this. "No. He'll repeat the process, again and again. She's valuable, with a marking like that. He'll keep her alive as long as he can."

"Do you know what her marking is?"

He nodded. "I do."

"How can I help her? What can I do?"

"There's nothing you can," Mick said. "Except hide any markings you develop. Secure your integration and get back to your life."

"I can't leave Alice with him."

"Alice may have a reprieve – the Council is running out of ambrosia. They can't extract as many markings as they once did."

"What if we – "

He cut her off. "You're missing the point. Do you know anything about Evander Kagan?"

"Yeah, basically everything. He's the worst."

He tapped out his cigarette in an ashtray and leaned forward. "He's in charge of the Council now. He has full control of the largest arsenal of magic in Pontos. All of those changes I told you about? With Travelers and records?"

She nodded.

"Those ideas came from him. He's been working his way up for decades. He's not only a mastermind, Mira, he has the power of the entire country behind him." Mick sat back, setting his stare back on her. "There's nothing you can do."

She let out a huff. "Why didn't you tell me who Evander was sooner?"

"I knew of him, but I've never seen him. He's kept his life private." His voice softened. "You can't challenge him, Mira. You'll only get yourself killed."

Mira's arms and legs felt numb.

"Your memories," he said, pushing the box toward her. "Leona had them delivered from the Center."

She looked up at him. "What if I could steal any record you wanted?"

"That would be helpful, but not with Evander." He pushed the box of memories aside. "What did you see in Arianna's record?"

Mira fidgeted. He wasn't going to be happy with this. "There wasn't much in it. It said she had a non-magical childbirth, and that there was a suspected magical attack on your car."

"That's all?"

She shook her head. "It said they went back to the site of the car accident and determined there was no magic in the soil." She paused, trying to remember the wording. "It said the bolt was likely the cause."

He nodded. "As I thought."

"I didn't get to your record yet," she said. "But I'll get it. I will."

"That's all I need," he said, pulling a flask from his suit jacket. He offered it to her, but she shook her head. "I needed to be sure Ferdinand hadn't ordered the attack."

She paused. "Ferdinand?

"Yes."

The thought of it was absurd. "He's not capable of it. He would've been too giddy when he saw the car blown apart. He could hardly contain himself when we sent Leona's offender away in a flying box."

He caught her eye. "You don't like Leona, do you?"

"I didn't say that."

"You don't have to." He stood, moving into the seat next to her and leaning in.

She tried not to stare at him, but it was too hard. He had the prettiest eyelashes she'd ever seen on a man, so dark and long. They framed his eyes perfectly...

His voice was low. "Much worse will happen to you if you challenge Evander."

She snapped her head toward him. "I don't care."

"You're being emotional. You need to look out for yourself. Alice can't be helped."

Mira scoffed. "You sound like my cousin Sara."

"You've fulfilled your part of our deal," he continued. "How is your bolt?"

She absentmindedly looked down. It was covered by her shirt, but she'd just looked at it this morning, like she did every morning. "Fine."

"Good. Then I can get you to Thunder Island."

Well, that was unexpected. She sat back and crossed her arms. "When?"

"Leona's family is powerful," he said. "Her father is stationed on Violet Island, and he's having difficulty with revolts among the people. He says disinformation is rampant there, causing the people to act out."

"What kind of disinformation?"

"It doesn't matter. Disinformation has nothing to do with it. The people aren't acting out because of things they've heard or read – they've had a drought for three years. They're acting out because their food supplies are running low and their children are starving."

That was heavy. Mira sat back, trying to put some distance between herself and Mick. "Why doesn't Leona's father get them some food, then?"

"The Council, and the people of Magnifico, do not want the people of Violet Island to grow used to handouts."

Oh, the benevolent Council. "Of course they don't."

Mick took another swig from his flask before tucking it away. "What Leona's father *can* do is hold an episcope spectacle to bolster their spirits."

"I don't follow."

"After we're done here, I'm going to show Leona a few of your memories and convince her to send you on a tour of Violet Island."

"A tour?"

He nodded. "They'll put on a spectacle of your most inspiring memories, and by the end, you should have earned enough positive marks on your record to be approved for integration."

That made it sound easy. Too easy. "Why are you doing this for me?"

Mick smiled and leaned closer, stopping inches from her face. She could smell his cologne and see every detail, every scar, every eyelash.

Her heart pounded against her ribcage. Mira no longer dreaded his intense stare, that feeling he was looking through her. At some point, she didn't know when, she had started *looking* for that feeling.

A smile cracked at the left corner of his mouth and he sat back, breaking his gaze. "Because we had a deal."

Mira realized she'd been holding her breath and released it. "It seems like you're going out of your way to help me."

He pulled another cigarette from his pocket. "I have some business on Violet Island, and acting as your chaperone is a good reason for my travel to be approved."

She crossed her arms. There it was. He was using her; nothing more.

But, if what he said was true, this trip might be all she needed to get back to her life.

He pulled the box closer, squinting at the vial labels and picking out a handful from the corner. "I think these are the memories that show your uncle. I'll destroy them, and make sure there aren't any more."

"You can't." She took one of the vials and rolled it in her hand. "It's evidence of who he is. If people knew – "

"It's evidence that will get you killed." He took the vial back, dropping it onto the pile. "I can't let that happen."

She cocked her head to the side. Mira knew she shouldn't push him, but she couldn't help herself. "Since when do you care if I die?"

"It's hard to say." He blinked, his entire expression softening. "And while I'd prefer to keep you alive in this world, you seem determined to get back to that disappointing husband of yours."

Her mouth popped open, and before she could form a response, the door creaked and Leona peeked her head into the room. "Everything going well in here?"

Mick stood, buttoning his suit jacket. "Quite well, yes."

"I knew you'd be a good teacher," Leona said, beaming her blindingly white smile.

Mira stared down at the table, trying to will her cheeks to return to a normal color. She couldn't let Mick see her blush. He couldn't know he had gotten to her, or that Robbie had never looked at her the way he did, or induced a rush anything like what Mick made her feel.

She took a cautious glance at him. His back was turned to her, listening to Leona as she prattled on about Slava's progress.

What did he know about her and Robbie? Why was he hinting he wanted to keep her around in this world?

And worse, why did Mira care what he said?

She was suffering from a little case of infatuation, that was all. Mick did this to women. Mira wasn't the first, and she certainly wouldn't be the last. Handsome men were always dangerous – they were too aware of their charm. Too confident, too arrogant, and fully willing to use their indifference as a force of magnetism and attraction.

She wasn't going to fall for it.

With a few deep breaths, the heat in Mira's face faded. She needed to focus and rescue one of the Wesley-damning memories. Those memories were her last chance to out him to the world, and her last chance to help Alice.

Watching Mick and Leona closely, she darted a hand forward, grabbed a vial, and slipped it into her pocket.

"I had an idea," Mick said, interrupting Leona and turning around. "I'd like to show you some of Mira's memories in private. I think they can help your father with his problems on Violet Island."

"That would be marvelous!" Leona put a hand to her chest. "You are so clever, Mick."

Ugh. Mira had had enough of Leona for the day. "Thank you for your help," she said, standing from her seat and moving toward the door. "Hopefully I can return the favor and my memories aren't too disappointing."

"Oh, you poor thing." Leona put a hand to her chest. "I'm sure I can make *something* out of them!"

Mira smiled. "I'm sure."

She walked out of the room, expertly avoiding Mick's eyes.

20

The secret garden

There was too much going on and Mira had to force herself to focus. The newest dire situation was that Alice wasn't safe. That was her first priority.

Her second priority was her own integration. Really, she told herself, these priorities could run concurrently, especially if Mick was working on a plan to help her.

But since he wouldn't help Alice, she needed to find someone who would. Someone, or a group of someones, who were crazy enough to try.

She followed the address for the Hecate Society and found herself in another empty neighborhood. Instead of tidy brick townhomes, however, it was ten-story buildings built of dark brown stones with balconies cut into the sides.

The only signs of life were from the birds, chirping and flitting about, nests bursting from corners of the balconies. It was still quiet, though, and eerie – even some of the nests looked abandoned.

Mira stood in front of the building labeled 16 and debated what to do. Hecate John's card specified no unit. Was it possible the Hecate Society filled the entire space?

Mira tried the door, only to find it was locked. She pushed on it with more force, leaning in with her shoulder, but it didn't budge.

Terrific.

It was possible John had given her a fake address for the Hecate Society – maybe as a prank, or to lure her away from prying eyes. The thought more annoyed than frightened her.

"Hello!" She pounded on the door with her fist. "Is anyone home?"

She stood, listening, and only heard more birdsong around her. There was no chance she'd gotten the wrong street. She'd borrowed a map from Herbert and followed it exactly.

Thump.

Something smacked into her shoulder. Mira turned around to find nothing and no one in site.

She turned back to the building. "Hello?"

Thwack.

"Ow!" This time it hit her in the front, and she spotted the culprit. It wasn't a person, like she'd expected from the force of the blow, but a small yellow and black bird, peering up at her from the ground.

She knelt down to get a better look. "Watch it, little guy."

It looked up at her and she leaned in, starting at the little thing. Its eyes were flat white, with black zig zags in the irises.

The bird cocked his head, turning one eye toward her. His motions weren't quite right, and he moved his head too smoothly, more like a dog than a bird.

Not that Mira was a bird expert, but something was just...off.

She kept staring until it hopped toward her and pecked at her foot.

"Hey!" She took a step back. "Stop it."

He stopped, hopping backwards before lifting from the ground and hovering in front of her face with the grace of a hummingbird.

She put her hands up. "All right, fine. I'll leave. Enjoy your nest." Mira turned, walking directly into John of the Hecate Society.

"Mira!" He opened his arms. "You've come to see me!"

She took a step back, reeling from the realization that he'd snuck up on her without a sound. "Hi, John. Yes." She cleared her throat. "Is that your bird?"

"Oh, him?" John smiled at the creature hovering next to his ear. "He's not mine. He's magical. Who knows where he came from?"

She stared at him for a beat. "Right."

"What brings you to my side of town today, Mira?" He started slowly walking down the sidewalk, the bird still buzzing alongside him. He was dressed in a similar manner as before, though instead of yellow he was in hot pink, with frills at his wrists and white tights peeking out at the knee of his black pants.

"I was wondering if you could help me with something."

"I would be happy to try."

She hurried her steps to catch up with him. "My friend Alice – another Traveler – developed a marking."

He nodded. "I know of Alice."

"Did you know she was deemed dangerous?"

"Yes, Mira. All valuable Travelers are."

Crap. So what Mick had said was true.

She stopped walking. "What can I do to help her? How can I get her back here, or at least away from Magnifico?"

John squared off with her, and for the first time, he wasn't smiling. "I'm sorry, Mira. Nothing can be done."

"Not even with your goddess? Or more of these birds? Anything?"

He shook his head. "I'm afraid not."

"What do you guys do, then? What's the point of your society?"

He studied her for a moment, and his smile returned. He continued walking and Mira followed him down the deserted street and onto another.

"We consider ourselves friends of all Travelers and Asphodavians."

Mira resisted the urge to say, "Good for you," instead responding with a grunt.

"This puts us at odds with the Council, and even with the local constable, as you saw."

Mira shrugged. "Ferdinand doesn't like anyone."

"He seems to like you." He stopped, and Mira almost ran into him again. "Do you consider him a friend?"

"A friend?" Mira took a deep breath. There was no need to say anything rude, but it was tempting. "He's my employer. One who can influence if I can get back to my real life. He has total power over me, so no, he's not what I consider a friend."

John stared at her, unblinkingly. "Then you understand the plight of the Hecate Society."

"Are you Travelers?"

"Some of us, yes, but many are not. We are people who wish to discuss solutions."

"Not for Alice." She was unable to keep the edge out of her voice.

"No, not for Alice." He shook his head. "Not today, at least. Perhaps tomorrow? Perhaps after we have food on our plates and roofs above our heads. When we can own the things we need instead of renting them at criminal prices. Or when we don't have to fear being labeled dangerous for thinking thoughts not on the approved rolls, or when we can use magic to heal our sick, or when our letters are not scrutinized for disinformation."

Mira looked away. Did John know what she did at the constable's office? There was no way.

Unless that little bird had floated outside of the window and watched her. Or because she couldn't keep the blush off her cheeks, announcing her guilt.

"I'm sorry," she offered weakly. "I started approving all of the letters now. I didn't realize – I didn't know what it meant."

He smiled. "How could you? We're not meant to know the full picture, because then it becomes too clear."

"And that's Hecate?"

He let out a laugh. "Hecate is our protector, yes. She keeps prying eyes away."

They'd arrived at a small lot surrounded by a white knee-high fence. Beyond it was another open parcel, though instead of a fence, the land was covered in tents of varying sizes. Some were large and sturdy-looking, with multiple strips of burlap and waxen leaves on the surface. Others looked no better than a scrap of material held up by two sticks, lopsided and damp.

"This is our garden," he said. "You're welcome to it any time you have a need. Just beyond is where many of our members live. They can't afford the rents of the homes in town."

Ah. That was why there were so many tents and empty homes. People had been priced out.

Mira peered over the fence. The soil was dark and moist, the plants flourishing and green. She could see peppers, blueberries, and onions from where she stood. "It looks lovely."

"That's the thing about gardens." He opened the gate and motioned for her to enter. "To make something beautiful and functional, you must always be fighting. Whether against weeds that hoard the nutrients, or pests that eat at the leaves, or even waters that wash out the roots – you are always fighting."

Mira reached out a hand to touch one of the nearby fruits. It was the size of a lemon, but it had dark purple skin with fuzz like a peach. "Sounds exhausting."

He knelt, picking a handful of plump raspberries and hand-ing them to her. "That's nature, and life. Exhausting but beauti-ful, no?"

She popped one of the raspberries into her mouth and the sweetness was an explosion. It was better than candy: a memory of summers spent camping by the lake – her mom setting out hamburger buns and barking orders, her dad nearly burning off his eyebrows over the grill, and her and Sara giggling into the late hours, Gonzo splashing through the lake and being chased by a flock of aggressive geese...

"You're right," she conceded. "Very beautiful."

He rose from his kneeling position and dusted off his hands. "You're welcome to join us any time, Mira."

A bird landed on the raspberry bush and pecked at one of the berries. Mira was about to shoo it away when John's bird shot forward, hitting the intruder with a direct blow.

She turned to him and smiled. "I'll keep that in mind."

21

Violet Island

Within a week, Mira's trip to Violet Island was approved by the local committee and Constable Ferdinand.

"Keep your wits about you, girl," Ferdinand warned on the eve of her travels. "The violence and thuggery on Violet Island have been out of control for years."

Mira was tempted to ask if this was physical violence or the ever-menacing unsafe words, but she held her tongue. If all went well, this would be the last time she would have to listen to Ferdinand's stupid advice again.

She could be back on Earth and free of Wesley's influence in a matter of days. If it weren't for the guilt, the giddiness would have overwhelmed her.

But Mira had a plan. Sort of.

She had the memory of Wesley that not only showed his true colors, but showed he was a dreaded Traveler. If anything could stop him, this was it.

She wasn't sure how or who would deliver this threat, but she was confident she would figure it out soon enough.

On the morning of her departure, she had breakfast with Slava and Samuel. Slava gave her a going away gift – a bottle of wine – and Samuel gave her a hug, his eyes filled with tears.

"I explained to him that you are leaving us, probably forever," Slava said. "I am happy for you. Get back to your life, Mira."

"Thanks, Slava." She gave him a hug. "Maybe I'll see you up there?"

He shrugged. "Maybe, maybe not? Who knows what the future holds?"

Herbert offered to help her get to the train station and she accepted. They took the public carriage to the edge of town, with Herbert praising everything from the Violet's unique cuisine to the decadence of the train she would be taking.

"Normally they send Travelers on ship, and that can take quite some time, depending on the currents," he told her, unaware of the annoyed looks he was getting from other riders in the carriage. "It's quite remarkable they've chosen to send you via train. It speaks highly of your future, Mira."

It had less to do with her future and more to do with Mick's influence, but the two had become intertwined.

Would Mick give her as emotional a goodbye as Slava and Samuel? Would he give her any sort of goodbye at all?

He didn't seem like a terribly emotional guy. Perhaps that was what attracted all of those other women to him – they thought they alone could break down his walls and soften his heart.

Mira was annoyed that, despite her best efforts, she had the same thoughts. He'd been showing up in her dreams, too, which was mortifying, especially considering how random her episcope memories could be. "I'm excited to see it."

"This train is an *astounding* advance in transportation. Thanks to a Traveler's marking, we had the ability to levitate trains decades ago, but only recently did a Traveler share his design of a turbine engine to complete the picture."

Mira turned away from the window to look at him. "Did you say a turbine engine?"

"Oh yes! It's powered by draconite, which I don't believe you have in your world, but – "

"No. We don't have draconite."

"Ah, well, it's a stone sourced from the Isle of Dragons – a single flake can provide never-ending energy. You'll see how powerful it is when we get to the station. The Traveler who created the invention said it was quite like the turbine engines in your world."

Her heart leapt. *My world*. She could be back there soon. "Can't wait."

Mira turned back to look out of the window. There was some small part of her that was sad to leave. How silly was that?

Maybe she would've enjoyed her time here more had she had accepted it was real, and if she'd known it wouldn't be forever. Would she remember the people she'd met?

The carriage pulled up to the train station and everyone slowly filed out. Some of the other riders had traveled with their arms full of supplies. Once they emptied into the street in front of the station, she realized they were there to sell goods.

"The train is connected to the rail by a seventy-foot chain." Herbert was speaking more rapidly, sensing his time to teach was coming to an end. "The engineer tightens it to lower the train, and releases it to give more space. Sometimes the waves in the sea can reach heights of fifty feet, so it's important they are diligent during the entirety of the rail."

He kept talking, but Mira couldn't focus on what he was saying. She had moved on, captivated by the building ahead of them. There was a grand split staircase at the front, made entirely of shining grey stone. The railings were polished copper leading up into the building, which was capped in a dome of glass, and ornate windows stretched from the ground level onwards. At the corners of the building stood two large, stone statues – one of a dragon, and one of a man, all muscles and strength.

People rushed in and out, and adding to the chaos was a throng of horses, their eyes shielded, walking onto a platform next to the stairs. Mira watched as a man raised gates from the side of the platform and pulled a lever, levitating slowly to deliver the horses to the next level.

Herbert was staring at her, apparently having asked her a question.

"I'm sorry." She flashed a smile. "It's so beautiful; I got distracted."

"Oh yes, this station was built over a hundred years ago. Laurium was the shining jewel of Nordavia," he said. "It was heavily damaged during the Great War, but we've managed to restore much of its glory."

"What war?" asked Mira.

"When we joined Asphodavia."

She narrowed her eyes. "Who was the war against?"

"Asphodavia."

"And then Nordavia...joined them?"

He nodded. "Yes, of course. Asphodavia had won." Herbert looked up and extended an arm. "There, do you see it?"

Mira followed along with her eyes, squinting into the sky. A moment later, she saw what he was pointing at – a tiny black loco-motive breaking through the clouds and charging toward them.

"You'd better get to the platform!" He handed off her bag and let out a sigh. "Best of luck to you, Mira. You'll always have a home in Laurium."

"Thanks, Herbert." She slung the bag over her shoulder and took off, running up the stairs.

Her chaperone, as he'd called himself, was nowhere to be seen.

Maybe it was for the better. He was distracting, and the more time she spent with him, the less she thought about him being a criminal, or cutting that guy's face up, or killing his first wife.

Allegedly killing his wife. Mira wasn't sure if she believed it. On the one hand, the fact that she thought it was possible should be enough for her to steer clear of him.

On the other hand, he might be the only one who had the resources to plant the Wesley memory. He may not be willing to do it until she was back on Earth, but he would at least be capable of it.

She presented her ticket at the gate at the top of the stairs, then passed through onto the platform just as the train made its puffing entrance. Mira stood on the platform, crammed with the other travelers, as it lowered itself jerkily to the rails.

The locomotive looked perfectly normal, black and pouring out steam, except for the large, silver-toned turbines on either side. It stopped rather abruptly, the doors to each red carriage opening in unison, and people poured onboard. Mira used her height to her advantage and shoved her way onto a carriage.

The agent at the door directed her to her seat, three carriages back, and off she went, pleased by what she saw. Apparently the Traveler from her world hadn't brought the entirety of airplane travel to Pontos. The seats were generous, padded and well-spaced, with little tables in between – much more comfortable than the typical turbine-laden plane she was used to.

Mira found her seat and stuffed her bag beneath it, relieved to be free of the jostling crowd. She watched as the rest of the riders walked by, and when the train started again, she was delighted to find no one sitting next to her.

Once they were clear of the station, the train took off from the tracks, rising thirty feet in the air in one stomach-churning leap. Once airborne, the speed picked up and the ground flew beneath them.

They passed over a large, dense forest, then got a few glimpses of the ocean and a smattering of small islands. The most frightening part of the ride came when the train crossed from land to sea. The guiding chain disappeared beneath the water's surface, cutting through like a razor as water spit out on either side.

It felt unsafe to Mira, but the train blasted along, completely unaffected. She stared into the depths of the waves for some time, but when no one else seemed alarmed, she gave up her post and settled into her seat.

They were served a small lunch, and afterward, Mira managed to relax enough to take a cat nap.

An announcement roused her, stating they would soon be arriving in Tartarus on Violet Island. She yawned and stretched out her arms, smacking a hand into someone beside her.

"I'm sorry," she said, turning to see whom she'd struck.

It was Mick, reading a newspaper. He smiled at her, and she scowled back.

He was getting too friendly, and she didn't like it. She didn't like the intensity of his gaze or that she was always wondering what he was thinking hours after they'd parted. She didn't like how he popped up with no warning, and worse, how the sight of him induced a flutter in her chest.

What she especially disliked was the fact that despite knowing he put women under some sort of spell, and clearly seeing how absurd it was, she found herself trapped under it just the same.

Mira had a fiancé back on Earth, and she'd get to see him soon. They'd rekindle their flame, and plan their wedding, and have the life she had always hoped for. There was no need for her to have any sort of feelings about Mick.

He dropped the paper into his lap. "Here I thought I'd find you enjoying the view from your window seat."

She straightened, cracking her back and stretching out her arms. "And here I thought you were supposed to be my chaperone."

"I am." He slightly dipped his head. "At your service."

The train stopped and Mira stood, grabbing her bag from under her seat.

"Leona's father will meet us at the station," Mick said. "He's a Fidelity Officer."

"Fidelity," Mira repeated. "I always forget that one."

"Everyone does, because it doesn't mean anything." He stood, buttoning his suit jacket. "You can't let him be reminded of it."

She nodded. "Got it. Best behavior."

He walked down the aisle and exited through the door, with Mira following closely behind. They traveled down the platform until Mick spotted his target and offered a handshake.

"Mira, this is Gulliver Frum."

"It's a pleasure to finally meet you," the man said, shaking her hand. He had the same unnaturally green eyes as his daughter, and his uniform was the purple version of one of Ferdinand's deputies. "I've had a chance to review some of your memories, and I think the people here will be inspired by them."

Inspired? What the hell had Mick picked out for her? Did she have fidelity in her other life?

She forced a smile. "Thank you. I'm glad to be here."

"Violets don't get many Travelers," he said, offering to take her bag, and she accepted. "So this is even more of a treat."

Another man approached, also purple-suited, and nodded a hello.

"Ah, this is my good friend, Ignatius," Gulliver said. "Mira, he'll be the one showing you around today. People are anxious to meet you."

Mira cast a glance at Mick. He seemed untroubled by this, so she went along with it. "Sounds great."

"Mick and I will drop off your bag at the Traveler Center and you two can start your tour!"

She flashed a smile at Ignatius, and he nodded back.

"This way," he said, leading her down the platform and onto a waiting car.

He opened the back door for her, and she took her seat and readied herself for awkward conversation.

The conversation never came. Ignatius drove silently, his green eyes focused on the road.

Mira didn't mind. It gave her more time to look through the window at the passing city. The roads were dirt here, instead of the stone and gravel of Laurium, and the buildings were far less orderly, some with collapsing roofs or missing bricks.

The people looked the same, though – laughing, carrying on in the streets, yelling about the wares they were peddling. She studied the faces of the people they passed, each one with their own variety of purple eyes. Some were more of a plum, others closer to periwinkle, but all dazzling in their own right.

They started their tour in the city's center, in the middle of a myriad of shops. It seemed there was not a soul in town who hadn't heard about her arrival. She met the town butcher, the town florist, and the local constable with all of his staff.

Ignatius then took her to a school, where the children sang a song for her, their voices causing the glass in the windows to vibrate. Mira tried to focus on the words of the song, and not the fact that none of the children had shoes.

Her tour ended at the crystal-clear waters of a lake. Ignatius, hardly a conversationalist, had more to say about the lake than he had about everything else combined. "We've been trying to restore it to its former glory. However, there have been years of drought on the island."

Mira shook her head. "That's terrible."

"Indeed. The Violets are irresponsible with the water they do have. We are hoping a Traveler arrives with the skill of rain calling. The Violets are quite certain it will save them."

Mira detected a hint of something in his voice.

He quickly moved on. "Your spectacle will be held in two days' time. We've procured an outdoor theater for it. I hope that is acceptable to you."

"Yes, of course."

He nodded. "Good. We expect Violets to come from the neighboring villages, upwards of five hundred people. We don't expect trouble, but if you encounter anything concerning, do not hesitate to alert me. Gulliver and I will deal with it swiftly."

Mira didn't doubt it. She wasn't afraid of these people, though. They treated her like a home-grown Slava, and all she'd done so far was show up. "Thank you."

He started walking toward the car. "We are hoping your appearance will bolster the Violets' spirits. With the drought being particularly bad this year, they have turned their anger onto everyone but themselves."

Mira wasn't sure why the Violets should blame themselves for the drought, but she held her tongue. "I hope I can help."

"If you are successful," he said, taking a deep breath, "I will personally approve your integration and expedite your application to Thunder Island. I believe that's what you were planning?"

Her heart leapt. "Yes, it is."

"Then let's hope your spectacle goes well, for both our sakes."

He opened the driver side door for himself, and Mira let herself into the back.

It was all going according to plan, and the thought made her feel giddy. She slipped a hand into her pocket, running her fingers over the small red vial she'd tucked away. As soon as she was integrated and approved, she'd set the rest of her plan into place.

22

Dragon

A gaggle of five children came into the Traveler Center early the next morning, demanding to know where Mira was. She heard them coming, their laughter and yelling providing enough warning for her to get dressed before they burst through her door.

"We made this for you!" the littlest girl, no older than six, yelled as she thrust a scrap of paper into Mira's hand.

She looked down and studied the drawing – long red hair, two blue dots for eyes, and a glowing bolt on the chest. It was much larger than her real bolt, and it gave off an actual, glowing yellow light. Mira brushed a finger over it. "This is beautiful," she said.

"Cressida added the glow," the girl added, pointing at an older girl in the corner.

Mira looked up from the page. Cressida was the oldest, at least eleven or twelve, the age Mira was when all of her troubles started. "This is incredible, Cressida. I love it."

Cressida smiled briefly, her soft lilac eyes cast down. "Thank you. I've just learned I can do it."

The Violet Island equivalent of Herbert came in. She was a gruff woman, and she took her cooking duties just as seriously as Herbert, if not more. She was carrying a tray of food and set it down before properly yelling at the children. "That's enough of you!" She waved her arms, herding them out the door. "Off to school, now!"

The kids scattered, only to return a moment later.

"Will you come back to see us today?" asked the girl who'd given her the picture.

"I'm not sure. I can try," she said.

"She doesn't have time for that," Cressida said sternly before looking up at Mira. "We'll be at your spectacle tomorrow. I'll be turning the episcope. I get to practice it today."

The mysterious spectacle. Mira still didn't know what Mick had picked out for her. Maybe his plan was to totally embarrass her. It wouldn't be hard to do.

"I'm excited to see you there." Mira picked up the tray, which was overflowing with biscuits and hard-boiled eggs, and offered it to the kids. "Anyone hungry?"

The little one reached forward immediately, only to be smacked away by Cressida.

"It's not for you," she hissed.

"Please." Mira thrust it forward. "I already ate this morning. I can't eat this, too."

Cressida hesitated, then said, "Only if you're sure."

"Very sure."

Eight hands darted onto the tray and the kids ran off, leaving only a single biscuit on the plate. Mira offered it to Cressida, who insisted she wasn't hungry.

"I guess it'll go to waste, then," she said, setting it aside.

Finally, Cressida relented, taking the biscuit. "Thank you, Miss Mira." She paused. "Please don't tell anyone about the bolt I made."

Mira shook her head. "Don't worry. I won't."

Cressida smiled before turning and taking off.

This Traveler Center was much smaller than the one in Laurium, with only one floor and a total of four rooms. Mira took her tray and returned it to the small kitchen before slipping outside to the fenced-in yard that housed the "private" latrine.

She tried to hold her breath when she got inside, but like always, she couldn't last, exiting a minute later coughing and gagging.

Up to this point, she'd managed to have her coughing fits out of sight, but today, a dark-suited figure was leaning against the back of the building, smoking a cigarette and watching her.

After a moment of her struggle he said, "You'll get used to it."

Mira looked up, mortified until she realized who it was.

Mick.

She wiped the tears from her eyes and straightened. "I got a bug in my throat."

"Did you?"

She walked past him and toward the center's back door. "Yes."

"Where are you rushing to?"

She stopped to look at him. "Why? Are you going to send me off with Ignatius again?"

He smirked. "You're angry with me."

"No. I'm just noticing you're not a good chaperone."

He dropped his cigarette to the ground. "Ignatius volunteered to take you around today. Seemed to enjoy your company."

Could have fooled her. "We hardly spoke."

"Must be why he enjoyed it."

"Ha, ha." Mira narrowed her eyes. "He told me he'd approve my integration and application if things go well tomorrow."

"If that's still what you want."

"It is."

"All right." Mick nodded. "With you being on your way out, you don't have much time to repay your debt to me."

She crossed her arms. "Since when do I have a debt to you?"

"I arranged this spectacle to save your good name, didn't I?"

Mira stared at him and silently counted to ten, trying not to let her temper rise.

He was exhausting. If he hadn't directly killed his late wife, he'd at least worn her out.

"You're getting your math mixed up," she finally said. "You owed me initially, because I covered for your blown-up car. Then I got into the record you wanted – "

"I fixed your episcope trial, and brought you here," he countered.

"Then we're even."

A smile danced at the corner of his mouth and Mira's glare intensified.

Mick so rarely smiled, but when he did, it was often because he was teasing her. It was annoying.

At the same time, she did like that smile...

"There is someone I need to see today," he said, "and you being there might help. You don't need to talk to them. It's better if you don't, actually."

One, two, three, four...

"You can meet Dragon."

She uncrossed her arms. "Who's Dragon?"

"Follow me."

He turned, walking through the small grassy yard before reaching the knee-high fence, its gate hanging crooked on its hinges.

Mira stood, staring daggers at his back. How did he know she would follow him?

He didn't turn to look at her, opening the gate and walking on, disappearing from her sight.

As infuriating as he was being, the thought of spending the day with Ignatius made her anxious. If she had managed to make a good impression on him, she didn't want to ruin it.

Spending time with Mick could be a good excuse. And anyone who went by the name Dragon had to be interesting.

Mira followed, as she always did, catching up to him halfway down the dusty street. Ignatius had shuttled her from place to place the day before, so she hadn't had the chance to see much on foot.

She told herself it was good to get out. A few doors down from the Traveler Center were two boarded up buildings.

"What used to be here?" she asked.

Mick cast a glance at the brick building. "That was a bank."

"And that?" She pointed to the A-frame building with a collapsing thatched roof.

"A church." He pressed on, not slowing his pace. "The Council declared it a nest of illicit magic and disinformation."

Mira looked over her shoulder. The building was the largest one on the block. "How do you know all of this?"

He stopped, and she almost ran into him. "Because I was the one who supplied the magic."

Mira was about to ask another question when he turned and kept walking, reaching a two-story wooden building with open barn doors.

"This way," he said, footsteps crunching on the dirt and rock floors.

She walked after him, peering into the stalls as they passed. When he got to the last stall, an enormous black horse trotted forward to greet him, sticking its head above the stall gate.

Mick patted him on the nose, whispering, "Hello, hello, hello." He unlocked the gate and the horse walked out, tossing his head up and stretching.

Mira took a step back. The animal was taller than a Clydesdale, with massive legs and hooves the size of dinner plates. His black fur glistened, and his sleek wings were tucked at his sides.

"Is this Dragon?" she asked.

Mick nodded.

"I think we've met before."

He led the horse by his bridle, through the back of the barn doors and into an open, dusty lot.

"Is he a rental?" Mira asked.

Mick smiled, patting Dragon on the shoulder. "He is not. He was my brother's."

"I didn't know you had a brother."

"I don't anymore."

Mira paused. Had Mick had killed him, too?

"Dragon is a pegasus – smart, strong, and stubborn." Mick led Dragon to a set of freestanding wooden steps. "I've got a saddle for him, but he prefers to fly without it."

Mira raised an eyebrow. "We're flying?"

"Unless you'd prefer to drive with Ignatius."

Dragon shook his mane before flexing and stretching his wings wide. The silver tips were blinding in the sunlight.

"Flying sounds nice."

Mick climbed the steps and slid onto Dragon's back in one swift motion.

He made it look easy. Mira followed, clumsily stepping from the top stair and plopping herself onto Dragon, nearly falling off of his side until Mick caught her by the arm.

He leaned back and dropped his voice. "You'd better hang on."

He took her left hand and wrapped it around his waist, followed by her right hand. Goosebumps erupted down her neck. She didn't want to notice, but she couldn't help it – he was solid, muscular.

Something to hold onto, at least. Mira tightened her grip and leaned forward. He didn't smell terrible, not like the booze and cigarettes she'd expected. He had some sort of cologne, fresh with hints of sandalwood, enough to tempt her to lean closer.

Mick tapped Dragon on the neck two times, and the horse started a bouncy trot. Mira tightened her grip, feeling surprisingly steady with her body pressed against his.

He tapped him again, and Dragon broke into a canter. It looked like they were going to slam into a ten-foot fence less than twenty feet ahead. Mira clutched onto Mick and resisted the urge to close her eyes. At the last moment, Dragon extended his wings, dropping them with one fantastic push, and lifted them into the sky.

She wanted to scream, but when she opened her mouth, nothing came out. Mira looked down, the familiar street disappearing beneath them and growing small, replaced by a stretch of yellow grass and sparse trees.

It was peaceful in the sky, and so quiet. She'd flown in a plane a handful of times, but it was nothing like this. The wind rushed past her ears, and Dragon only had to beat his wings every now and then to keep them afloat. He was gliding. An enormous animal like him, gliding!

After a few minutes, Mira realized that her legs were digging into Dragon's sides. She forced herself to relax, loosening her muscles and lowering her shoulders down from their spot up by her ears. As long as she didn't fall to her death, it was really quite relaxing.

"Where are we going?" she asked.

"To ruin another church."

What a prospect.

Mick leaned forward and Dragon began to descend, flying low over the scraggly treetops. Mira wished they could keep going – suspended in the sky, no one watching them – but soon the trees thinned out and they glided toward a large, open field of pale grass.

Dragon dropped quickly, thundering to the ground with remarkable ease, and Mira let out a breath.

What a ride.

A young boy rushed over to greet them. "Hello, sir!" He grabbed Dragon's bridle and clipped on a lead.

Mick gingerly jumped off Dragon's back and onto the ground. He tossed a coin to the boy before holding a hand up to Mira. "Come on then."

Mira peered down. It looked too high to jump, but if he could do it, then she could, too.

"The grass is enchanted to slow your fall," he added.

"Oh." Mira swung a leg over and eased herself forward. "That's cool." She elected not to use Mick's help, and as she slid down, she gained the momentum of a woman-shaped torpedo, knees buckling when she hit the ground.

The boy laughed, and Mick looked down at her, a bemused smile on his face. Mira glared at them both before stumbling to her feet.

Mick offered her his hand again. "I thought you would let me help you."

"I don't need to be any more in your *debt*," she said, swatting dried grass off her butt. "Where are we going?"

"This way."

They walked through the field, the dry grass crunching beneath their feet, and onto a dirt road.

Mira's curiosity outweighed her annoyance. "What kind of disinformation were the churches spreading?"

"The usual – questioning the necessity of war, advocating that workers should earn enough to live."

"How radical." Mira smiled. It was astonishing how consistent the playbook was, world to world. "Herbert said there was a war in Nordavia years ago?"

"There was. Ambrosia wells were discovered in New Belgium and Old York, and the Nordavians had the foolish hope of nationalizing the profits to improve the lives of their citizens." He pulled a glass orb from his pocket the size of a baseball and tossed it to her.

Mira caught it, barely. "What's this?"

"It's an aion, filled with magic from a Traveler. Ambrosia is needed to extract the magic and trap it inside."

She stared at it. The outside was encased by two gold rings, which Mira assumed was to prevent it from breaking. Inside it looked empty, but just as she was about to look away, a small zap carried from one side to the next.

"Asphodavia decided it was their ambrosia, after all, and welcomed Nordavia through a Great War that lasted six years."

"Yikes." Mira offered the aion back to him.

He shook his head. "Keep it for now."

They walked on until they reached a small farmhouse, crooked but clearly cared for, with flowers bursting from the walkway and vegetables growing from a small patch of dark soil.

Mick walked up to the front door and knocked.

A woman opened the door, her pomegranate eyes widening when she laid eyes on Mick. "How to help, sir?"

"I'm here to speak to your husband."

She shook her head. "He's not here, and I don't know when he'll be back."

Mick nodded, pointing over her shoulder. "I can hear him breathing behind that door."

Mira raised an eyebrow. Either he was bluffing, or he had given himself a marking for super hearing.

That was one Mira would enjoy. It would make eavesdropping so much easier.

The woman shook her head again, but the look on her face gave her away.

He turned to Mira. "The aion."

She pulled it out and placed it in his hand, watching the woman's eyes grow wide.

"Come in," she said, stepping out of the way.

They walked into a small kitchen, a pot boiling on the massive block stove. There was only one door off of the main room, and it opened slowly to reveal an ashen-faced man.

"I didn't expect you, Mr. Kellet."

"I have the marking you've been looking for." He held it up, a zap appearing as he did. "Allows for growth in dry soil. I imagine it could help many families here."

He nodded, casting a glance at his wife before looking back at Mick. "Yes, sir. We can't seem to raise enough tallies for something like that."

Mira let out a sigh, and everyone looked at her. "Sorry," she muttered.

The fact that this marking was out there and the almighty Council hadn't used it to spare these people from starving to death was beyond disgusting.

"I apologize for my friend," Mick said. "She's a Traveler. You may have heard about her. She can read thoughts."

Mira turned to him, but the hard look he shot back was enough to silence her.

"I have heard, yes sir, but as I told your men, I don't know anything about the attack on your car. I'm sorry it happened, but —"

Mick held up a hand and the man stopped speaking. He walked over to Mira and whispered in her ear. "Stare at him, but don't say anything."

The goosebumps rippled down her neck again.

On the one hand, if this guy ran off and told everyone she could read thoughts, she'd end up in the same boat as Alice.

On the other hand, the terror on his face made her think it was unlikely he would talk. Also, Mick hadn't given her much of a choice.

Mick pulled a cigarette from his pocket and lit it before asking, "Do you want to try again?"

The man started babbling immediately. "I made the bomb, that was it, I swear that was it. I didn't know who it was for. We needed the tallies. If I had known it was for you, I never would have done it. Ask the Traveler. She knows I'm telling the truth."

Mira tried to keep the surprise off of her face. He'd folded so quickly.

"Your client?" Mick asked.

He let out a whimper, casting a glance at Mira.

Mick raised his eyebrows. "Go on."

"It was the Fidelity Officer."

"Gulliver?" Mick looked at Mira, forehead furrowed.

Mira kept her eyes on the man. He was still staring at her, between glances at his wife. He looked like he was in agony.

"Ignatius," Mira said softly.

The man nodded. "He was going to increase the rent on our home. We'd have nothing; we'd have to live on the streets. I had to do it. You don't understand."

"Right then." Mick took a puff of cigarette and tossed the aion into the man's hands. "Next time you come to me first, or you won't outlive whatever bomb you make."

With that, he turned and walked through the open door.

23

The boy and the mandocello

Once they were out of earshot of the home, Mira started. "Thanks a lot, Mickson."

He stopped. "How did you know it was Ignatius?"

"Just a guess." She crossed her arms. "You know I can't actually read thoughts, right? But by making them think I could, you might have – "

Mick waved a hand. "As far as they know, you're Alice."

"Until they see me at my spectacle tomorrow and I'm clearly not!"

"They have no way to get there." He turned, looking down the road. "They haven't two tallies to rub together."

That wasn't comforting.

He spoke again. "Do you know where I got that marking?"

"I'm guessing you stole it from the Hall of Magic."

"If I could get into the Hall of Magic, we'd be living in a very different world." He shook his head. "That was from your friend Samuel."

Mira turned to face him. "What? He doesn't even – how did you – "

"He came to me, and I paid a considerable price for five aions."

"That's impossible. Samuel doesn't even know what's going on."

Mick smiled. "Doesn't he? He had just been approved for integration and took off with his money."

Mira stood, mouth hanging open, feeling like a total dope.

He cleared his throat. "A carriage should come by here soon, and my favorite pub on Violet Island is in the next town."

"Is that an invitation? Or are you planning on using me again?" Mira wasn't interested in playing any more of Mick's games, intimidating a pub full of people by pretending to be Alice.

He kept his eyes fixed on the stretch of road in the distance. "An invitation. I have all I need now."

She looked out, shielding her eyes from the sun. He was infuriating, and yet she knew she wasn't going to tell him no.

It wasn't because she couldn't do it. She knew she could, and she could find her way back to the Traveler Center on her own, too.

It was more than that. It was the fact that despite her annoyance, Mira's heart was screaming for the chance to spend more time with him. She wanted to sit across from him, working out another of his riddles and feeling her heart race under his gaze. She wanted that flutter, that reminder of being so very alive.

"If there's food at this pub, then fine," she said.

He smiled, lighting another cigarette, and they stood in silence for the next five minutes until Mira spoke again.

"What are you going to do to Ignatius?"

He tossed the cigarette to the ground. "Kill him, I suppose."

"Come on. Really?"

Mick nodded. "Really."

"How about that." She looked down the road again, only to be greeted by the same blue sky. "I wonder why he did it."

"I assume to get ahead of his friend Gulliver." Mick shook his head. "Which reflects poorly on him."

"On Ignatius?"

"No. On Gulliver."

Mick raised a hand and waved, and Mira looked down the road to see a long black carriage approaching, pulled by four horses. It came to a halt in front of them.

"After you," Mick said, waving a hand to the open door.

Mira stepped up and into the carriage. There were seven other people on board, and only two open seats. She took one, next to an older woman, and Mick filed in behind her, paying the driver before taking a back seat.

It was nice to be out of the sun, but the carriage was still too warm for Mira's tastes. All of the windows were open, but the breeze was no match for the stifling heat. She sat back, shut her eyes, and sweated.

At the fourth stop, Mick tapped her on the shoulder and she got up, following him off of the carriage and onto the street.

They'd landed on the first cobblestone street she'd seen since Laurium, lopsided and uneven, but beautiful in its own way. Mira loved the sound of horse hooves on the stones, and there was more traffic here than near the Traveler Center in Tartarus.

Shops and pubs lined the street, their windows open, music pouring out. Mira felt like she was in a magical Nashville. There were bands and performers lining the sidewalks, with small crowds gathered around.

They walked on, side by side, passing pub after pub, until they reached one at the corner of a street. It had a white-barked tree growing next to the entrance, pink flowers hanging from its branches.

Mick opened the door for her and she walked inside. It was cool and dark, with tall ceilings and a band playing relaxing music in the center of the large room.

Mick led her to a table in the rear.

"What would you like?" he asked.

"Anything. All that intimidating made me hungry."

He nodded, getting up from his seat and walking to the bar. She watched him for a moment, then looked around at the other patrons. They were all Violets, it seemed, though no one was paying them any attention for looking different.

Mira had had enough attention for one day.

A minute later, Mick returned with two tall glasses filled with a pink, glowing liquid.

"Their specialty," he said. "Enchanted beer."

Mira reached for one of the glasses and took a sip. It was sweet and fruity, with a clean and crisp finish. "It's good. Thank you."

"I'll get the food when it's ready." He sat back, taking a sip of his own beer.

It was odd to see him drinking a pink drink. A guy like him wouldn't be drinking a pink drink on earth. Whatever a guy like him was, exactly. "Are you going to kill Gulliver, too? I don't think Leona would like that."

"Gulliver should be able to keep his house in order." Mick set the drink down. "The fact he didn't know about Ignatius makes me question his judgement."

The fact that his daughter was Leona made Mira question his judgement. "Not a good ally, then."

"No." He stared into space for a moment before fixing his eyes back on her. "Though he still has more credibility on Magnifico than I ever will, which may still justify the match."

The match. Of all those love letters, Leona was his best pick. That was sad.

He sat back, extending an arm across the chair next to him. "You don't look convinced."

Her face was too easy to read sometimes. "It's your life."

Mick raised an eyebrow, the slightest smile on his lips. "But?"

"Okay, well," she shrugged, "my cousin Sara always said if you're looking for reasons *to* marry someone, then you shouldn't do it. But if you're looking for reasons *not* to marry them, it means they're the right pick."

"Is that right?"

"It is."

He took another drink, eyes fixed on her. "Is that how you feel about your husband, the one you're in no hurry to marry?"

Her mouth popped open. "What are you talking about?"

Mick was grinning now, and he reached into his pocket to get a cigarette. "I've been through your memories. You dream about Sara all the time, but not Robbie. Hardly ever Robbie." He shrugged. "Sara didn't think you wanted to marry him."

"I didn't – we haven't had a – it's been long-distance for a few years, and we've both been happy with how things are." She trailed off. She didn't need to defend herself to Mick. "Sara rushed off to marry a guy she met three months ago. I don't think she's the authority on sensible marriages."

"Yet you gave me her advice."

Mira took a swig of her drink. The bus ride had left her parched, and her glass was nearly empty. "Take from it what you will. I'm just trying to be *helpful,* to pay my debts before I go."

"You still want to return?" He breathed out, the raspberry smoke floating between them.

Maybe she shouldn't have drunk that so fast. It didn't seem all that strong, though. More just refreshing. It shouldn't cause her to fall off of Dragon on the way home.

"Ever since I got here, this world has done nothing but try to control me or kill me." She hiccupped, putting a hand to her chest. "Excuse me. So yes, I want to return."

"And you have a good life to return to?"

"*Yes!*" She stopped and took a breath. He was making her feel defensive, which was silly. She forced herself to ease her tone. "A very good life."

"You could have a life here, you know. You have friends." His eyes drifted, settling on hers. "Admirers."

Mira snorted out a laugh. "Yeah, sure. I just need to make sure my uncle doesn't find out I'm alive. No problem."

She dropped her face into her hands and rubbed her forehead. The idea of staying was absurd. She couldn't even consider it.

"You could marry someone powerful. Someone who could protect you from him."

She lifted her head and shot back without thinking, "Someone like you?"

"Yes." He stared, his blue eyes zeroed in. "I could handle it."

There was that heart flutter.

Mira opened her mouth, but stopped herself before she spoke. He was either teasing her again, or this was his emotionally-stunted way of telling her how he felt.

She needed to know which one it was. "Now why would you do something like that when you have a perfectly disappointing Leona to marry?"

Another half-smile, this time wrinkling around his eyes. "Mainly because I can think of a dozen reasons not to marry you. By Sara's theory, that's all the reason I need."

Ah. So he was teasing her.

She rolled her eyes. "Rude. I already have someone who wants to marry me, thank you."

He was quiet for a moment before picking up his half-empty glass and gesturing toward her. "How is your bolt faring? Is it getting darker?"

"Nice try," she said, wagging a finger. "I'm not going to show you my chest."

"Not even if I tell you I'm an expert?"

If Mick was anything, he was a know-it-all. Mira let out a sigh. "Fine." She was wearing her favorite blue shirt, the one Alice had gifted her before she was swallowed by Magnifico. Mira pulled at the V in the front, exposing the edge of her bolt.

She peered down. "How does it look?"

"I have no idea." He sat back. "I'm not that sort of expert."

She would've thrown her drink at him, if she had any left. "Thanks."

He grinned. "I'm sorry. It does look like it's getting dimmer."

"It is?" She pulled her shirt over again, peering at the glow. She could convince herself it was darker, but she looked at it every day, so changes were easy to miss.

"You still have time. I'd imagine Ignatius will get you to Thunder Island in a few days."

She covered up her bolt. "Unless you kill him first."

He stood from his seat and straightened his suit jacket. "I can wait a few days. Would you like another drink?"

"How much are these? I need to pay you back."

"Half a tallie."

"Half a tallie! I didn't know I was drinking liquid gold."

He picked up both glasses. "Consider it a gift. A going away gift."

She shook her head. "Forget it."

"They have margaritas."

She paused. "How did you know I like margaritas?"

"Your memories."

Mira frowned. How much of her life had he watched before questioning if it was worth going back to?

"Do you want it or not?"

Mira scowled at him. "Of course I want it."

He disappeared, leaving her to stare at the pictures on the walls surrounding their table. The ones closest to her were of people sitting at this very table, faces smiling and arms outstretched. The pictures were in black and white, but Mira guessed every person was a Violet.

She looked across the table and spotted a picture of a group of musicians, all of them a touch blurry, apparently in the middle of a song.

Mira squinted and leaned closer. One of the of musicians looked like a young Mick. His hair was longer and his eyes were closed, playing a wonky-looking guitar, but it was definitely him.

She couldn't help but laugh. He looked so different, with a glee on his face she didn't think possible. The idea he had ever been young or carefree seemed absurd – everything about him was so rigid, so controlled.

When he returned with what looked like two half liters of margarita, she pointed the picture out. "Is this you?"

"I wondered if you'd notice." He set down her drink, along with a plate of biscuits and pies. "Me in another life, you could say."

"You play the guitar?"

"The mandocello. I planned to hide from my family and live my life playing music, pub to pub."

Mira turned back to the picture. He was skinnier then, runty even, in a loose white shirt and black pants.

The suits looked better on him, but he looked happier in that outfit. "From a carefree musician to a..." She paused.

"To a what?" he asked, blue eyes locked on her again.

"Trained killer? I don't know what you do."

He laughed, sitting back. "I'm not a trained killer."

"The killing is a hobby, then."

He shook his head. "Price of doing business."

"What business, exactly?"

He leaned in, the smell of his cologne wafting toward her again. "Selling magic."

"Oh." She leaned back. "You just gave an aion away today, though."

"That was for information. It wasn't a gift."

"You don't give anything away for free, do you?" She picked up her hefty margarita. "I wonder what this will cost me."

"Your company and your sage advice."

She didn't believe it, but at the same time, she'd be gone soon enough. It didn't matter. "Your grandma could make gold, and yet here you are selling off magic."

"She sold the marking not long after it became illegal to sell magic. It turned into her and my grandfather starting a sort of business."

"Which you've carried on."

He nodded. "Gold would've been much safer to sell. But my Granny, she had her own ideas. She wanted to spread magic. She thought it was important to define her life with loving acts."

"A life of loving acts," Mira grunted. "Here you are, two generations later, only in it for yourself. What happened to the boy in the picture?"

He smiled. "I met my wife at this pub. She'd worked here since she was a girl. You wouldn't approve – we married three months after we met."

Mira raised an eyebrow. Now she was getting some gossip.

"She was a Violet, my wife. Never had a family of her own, and she wanted to be close to mine."

"You didn't want that?"

He took a deep breath. "I was happy to stay here, playing music for the rest of my life. My father was training my older brother to take over the business. They didn't need me, at least not until my brother was killed."

"Oh." *Awkward.* "I'm sorry."

"He wrote a letter to a friend, bragging how he'd tamed Dragon. Got him to stop biting." Mick let out a long breath.

"The pillories had just started then. We didn't know our letters were being read."

"What happened?"

"He was swept off one day, accused of harboring magic. Dragon taming."

"Is that a thing?"

Mick shook his head. "They've been looking for that marking for centuries. There are legends, of course, but no one has ever tamed a dragon."

"Where would he even have gotten a dragon?"

Mick stared at her for a moment. "The Isle of Dragons. We'd gone there on an expedition."

Her eyes bulged. "You went there *on purpose?*"

"We went for fortune, looking for ambrosia."

Mira sat back, finishing the last of her margarita. "That seems extreme."

"Forty-three men landed on the island." He pulled a cigarette from his jacket and lit it. "Three of us returned."

She gaped.

After a moment, he spoke again. "I reported to the Council that I'd found a small flask of ambrosia, which they took and paid me a small fee. The rest of it I left to my family to do with as they pleased. It was enough to keep their business going for decades. Then I came here, planning never to return to Nordavia again."

Mira realized she was leaning towards him and forced herself to sit back. "But then the Council killed your brother?"

"Yes. He was taken, and my parents drove themselves to madness. They couldn't believe he'd be killed for such a foolish reason, especially when they had ambrosia the Council so badly needed."

"That's awful." Mira was glad he couldn't read her thoughts. She felt guilty for thinking he'd killed his own brother. Maybe it had just been his wife.

Or neither.

"I came back to Nordavia for Arianna. She was just a girl then. My parents got themselves killed in their search, leaving no one but the two of us to deal with what was left." He tapped the cigarette out. "That is what happened to the boy in the picture."

Mira told herself not to ask about his wife. If he wanted her to know, he would've told her. There was no point in asking.

But maybe he wanted to talk about her. "What was your wife's name?"

He kept his eyes staring down into his drink, the low lighting barely showing the scars on his face. "Ella." He finished his drink and stood. "You should prepare for your spectacle tomorrow."

Okay, he didn't want to talk about her. He wanted to go back to being well controlled, closed-off Mick. "Yes. Good idea."

Mira stood, tripping on the leg of her chair and catching herself against Mick. He reached out to stabilize her, hooking her arm into his.

Once she was righted, they walked out of the pub silently, listening to the music around them.

Halfway down the street, she decided if he wasn't going to break their grasp, she wasn't going to, either.

24

A spectacle

They flew back to Tartarus before the sun began to set. Mira no longer carried tension in her muscles – she felt relaxed and airy, enough so that she leaned back to pet Dragon's side as they flew. His fur was as soft as a chinchilla's, and as the haze of alcohol lifted, she thought it best to keep some distance between herself and Mick.

Dragon landed skillfully in the small lot behind the barn, and this time Mira accepted Mick's help in getting down. Once she was safely on the ground, she tried to pull her hand away, only for Mick to tighten his grip.

She looked up at him, his eyes fixed.

"I may not be at your spectacle tomorrow," he said.

"That's fine." Mira pulled her hand away, heart thundering in her chest. "Though if it goes well, and I'm integrated, I will need to see you afterward."

His eyes narrowed. "Why is that?"

"I'm not telling you yet." She smoothed her hair, tucking an unruly chunk behind her ear. "A lady must have her secrets."

"Are you a lady, then?"

She shrugged, turning and walking away. "As much as you're a musician."

. . .

The day of her spectacle started with a whirlwind – a team of five women appeared at her door waiting to bathe her, dress her, and attempt a sort of beautification mission.

Mira resisted their efforts to help her bathe, but she allowed them to do her hair and makeup. They chattered on excitedly, proud of what they had to offer in terms of skill and magic, and Mira went along with whatever they said.

She ended up with a braid around the crown of her head, while the rest of her hair was curled into loose spirals at the delicate touch of one of the women.

They presented her with two options for outfits, the first a floor-length red gown with glittering vines growing up the sides, or a silken purple jumpsuit with enchanted green leaves at the slim, sleeveless shoulders.

She selected the jumpsuit and was delighted when one of the women lengthened it for her. It was hard for a tall woman to find a jumpsuit, let alone one that was so pretty.

When no one was watching, she carefully slipped the Wesley memory into her pocket, and after a few dashes of makeup, she was ushered outside and into a carriage.

Mira's first stop was the town square, where people emerged from the shops to shake her hand and give her well wishes. From there, they stopped at the constable's office, where the staff was less excited to see her, but still insisted on snapping her picture.

A reporter was waiting for her, too, and under the watchful eye of the local constable, they completed a one-hour interview.

The topics jumped between her past life and her experiences on the island, and Mira was careful to keep her tone light and positive. She was smitten with the people on Violet Island, and she felt no guilt in heaping on the praise.

She felt a bit guilty glossing over the fact that the living standards on Violet Island were much lower than in Nordavia, between the shoeless children and the collapsing buildings, but what was the use? The Violets knew they had it bad, and there was nothing they could do about it. If she harped on about poverty, she'd end up like one of those churches.

After that was done, she was taken to the school and greeted by all of the children running outside at once. They rushed the carriage, pulling at her hands until she joined them in the court-yard.

It took all of three minutes for Mira's accompanying beauticians to chase the children off and curse them for touching the jumpsuit.

Mira tried not to laugh – they had worked so hard on making her look nice, after all – but when she caught sight of Cressida, she couldn't help it. She waved, bursting with laughter at the absurdity of it all as she was locked back into the carriage and carted off.

Cressida laughed too, forgetting herself in the excitement and waving wildly. She was disappointed that she didn't get to talk to the enigmatic Traveler again, but she hoped her role as episcope runner would give her an excuse to chat again.

Cressida comforted herself with this thought as the rest of the children cleared the courtyard and returned to their classrooms. Just as she was about to step inside, however, she found something interesting.

There in the dust was a small red vial. She stooped to pick it up and rolled it in her hand.

It was a memory, she was sure of it. She'd had two hours of training with an old episcope, and she'd even had a real memory to put inside of it.

This one had Mira's name on it!

Cressida smiled to herself. She'd get it back to Mira in time for the spectacle and get her chance to talk to her again after all.

• • •

The field for the spectacle could fit a thousand people, though Mira was told the turnout was expected to be closer to eight hundred. A stage was erected at the end of the field, along with a theater-sized screen.

A violet-eyed man introduced himself as the spectacle curator and showed Mira to her seat – a tall, throne-like chair next to the screen.

"I'll be peppering you with questions after each memory," he told her, "but don't worry! This is not a trial. We simply want to get to know you better."

Mira nodded. "No problem." A few more hours of performing and she'd be off the hook for good.

She sat in her chair as the field filled with families on picnic blankets to groups of rowdy drunken men and everything in between.

Mira sat, a smile frozen on her face, and chatted with the curator, and the beauticians who popped by to touch up her hair, and the constable who had volunteered to stand guard so "no one is tempted to rush the stage in excitement."

Mira scanned the crowd, hoping to spot a man with ice blue eyes smoking a cigarette and smirking at her, but he was nowhere to be seen.

She told herself he wasn't one to stick out, and perhaps he was tucked behind the drunken group, which was growing larger by the minute.

As soon as the sun set, the curator got in front of the crowd and talked into an empty jar, projecting his voice across the field.

"Ladies and gentleman, our guest Traveled all the way from Earth to be with us. She has agreed to share scenes from her world with us tonight, and I know you will find them as inspiring as I did. Without further ado, is my honor to introduce the magnificent life of Mira Meadows!"

She smiled and waved, relieved she didn't have to introduce herself. She still didn't know what she would say, though she knew it would be awkward.

The first memory played. Mira let out a breath when she realized what it was – her first meeting with Robbie.

She stared at his image on the screen, his half-crooked smile as cool as ever, and smiled.

Maybe they weren't super passionate anymore and maybe he didn't make her heart race, but he was still a wonderful person. It was hard to break up with someone like him without reason. They weren't unhappy, but they weren't terribly happy, either.

They were neutral. Neutral wasn't bad; some people would kill for neutral! Though Sara always seemed to think Mira should find someone who made her heart sing, or her blood boil, or whatever fanciful thing Sara had latched onto that day.

She and Robbie had grown apart over the years, that much was true. As she watched him on the screen, she realized she missed *this* Robbie. The Robbie he used to be, the couple they used to be.

Truth be told, she hadn't missed him much recently. Mick was right about one thing – she hardly dreamt of Robbie. She hardly thought about him.

So yes, maybe he wasn't The One. Maybe she'd break it off with him and find someone else when she got back from her near-death experience. Life was short, and she wasn't going to let it get away from her again.

The scene ended to the sound of applause, and the curator dragged the floating jar over to Mira.

"Can you tell us what you did in your past life?" he asked.

She nodded, reminding herself to smile. "I was a nurse."

"Did you manage to save the life of that poor man?"

"No, unfortunately we did not." She paused. "However, I did marry the other man."

The crowd let out a coo.

"A lucky fellow, was he not?"

She turned her head to look out at the audience and flashed a smile. "I suppose he was!"

Whoops and cheers rang out, and Mira was startled by how loud they were. Maybe Mick was right – she had some admirers.

Not him, of course. But some.

"Let's see another," the curator said, stepping away.

The second memory opened on a scene she didn't recognize. Mira was in the ER, working with Sara, as a panicked woman ran screaming, "My baby! My baby!"

Ah. She remembered. The woman's kid was having an asthma attack. Mira had run in, gave him a few puffs of albuterol, and he was right as rain. Not all that exciting, really.

Except the crowd loved it. They screamed her name, and the curator had to wait before he started with his questions.

"Was that magic you used there, Mira?"

"No sir, that was medication. It can work like magic, some-times."

Laughter, then applause.

"How many lives would you guess you had saved during your time in your world, Mira?"

"Oh, it's too hard to tell," she said, smiling.

He stared at her, raising his eyebrows. "Go on. Don't be shy."

Crap. What would Slava say? He would lie, and he'd make it sound good. "Hundreds, I suppose!"

Another eruption of cheers and chants from the crowd, and a few flashes went off.

Mira sat back into her throne, casually darting her eyes to the side of her jumpsuit to check if sweat was showing through yet.

Miraculously, it was not. Those beauticians must've done something to it. They'd pegged her as an anxious sweater from a mile away. They were pros.

"And now, Mira, a memory from the day of your death."

Her heart sank. Did Mick really think it was a good idea to show her getting flattened by a truck?

She sat back, jaw clenched, as the memory opened on a shot of her in the back of Sara's car.

Sara was being herself, ranting about the dog dirtying her backseat, and at that moment, it took everything for Mira not to burst into tears.

She missed everything about Sara – all of her ranting, her bad advice, her dismissive attitudes, her love of ice cream.

They'd be together again soon. She took a deep breath and managed a smile.

The memory went on, focusing in on Harold, her favorite homeless patient, and the crowd gasped.

Mira looked up, carefully dabbing at her eye and flicking away any escaped tears. She had no idea what they were surprised by until she looked and saw Harold's eyes.

They were the perfect shade of violet.

"I'm worried about you," he'd said. "You don't look long for this world."

The crowd gasped and the memory stopped.

"Mira," the curator said, his face creased with seriousness, "who was that man?"

"He was one of my patients. Whenever he ended up in the hospital, I would take care of his dog."

The crowd responded with a rolling *aww*.

"I didn't know there were Violets in your world."

She shook her head. "I didn't know either."

"Do you think he had the gift of sight? Did he know you were at the end of your life?"

If he had the gift of sight, he might've done himself a favor and won the lottery, but Mira didn't say that. Instead, she solemnly answered, "I think he must have."

Chaos in the crowd. They had to take a fifteen-minute inter-mission to get people to calm down.

Mira sat in her chair, her body relaxing. Integration was only a matter of time now. A few more memories, and she'd be back on Earth.

After the intermission, they saw another memory of her at work, one with her family, and one of hiking with Gonzo in the mountains. The curator announced it was time for the evening to end, much to the displeasure of the crowd.

He talked over them. "We thank you again, Mira, for sharing your lovely life with us. And we – "

He stopped, squinting into the crowd, shielding his eyes with his hand.

Mira looked out, trying to see what he saw. It was Cressida, standing on a chair near the episcope and waving her arms. "We have one more!" she yelled.

"One more?" The curator flashed a smile. "Well, then. Let's see it!"

An encore? That was clever of Mick. He was a master, it seemed, and he hadn't ended up embarrassing her in the least. He was true to his word. Maybe she could trust him with the Wesley memory after all.

The screen lit up, showing Mira walking to the front door inside her parents' house.

She sat up straight. What was this?

A moment later the door opened to show Wesley, his hair disheveled and his eyes wide, a hunting rifle slung over his shoul-der.

Oh no. This wasn't right. This couldn't possibly be right.

She slipped a hand into her pocket, frantically feeling around, finding nothing but a small hole at the bottom of the fabric.

"Where's your dad?" Wesley asked.

Eighteen-year-old Mira stared at him. "He's not home."

"You should invite me in for a beer. I just got done with a hunt, spent the day with the police commissioner. Great guy."

Mira stared at him. "You should go home."

"I've come back for my dog." He jutted his foot into the door, calling out, "Gonzo! Here, boy!"

Mira tried to shove the door shut, but it was no use. He pried the door open and stomped inside. Gonzo came running, barking full-force, his tail tucked.

"It's okay, Gonzo," she said. "Uncle Wesley was just leaving."

He paid her no attention, grabbing Gonzo's collar and dragging him to the back door.

"Stop it!" Mira screamed, running after him.

He opened the door and threw Gonzo into the backyard. It was open, totally deserted, with a wall of trees facing them.

"Hunting accidents can be so unpredictable," Wesley said, his voice calm as he raised his rifle, pointed at Gonzo. "One minute you go for a squirrel, and then, whoops!"

"No!" Mira screamed, sprinting past Wesley and jumping onto Gonzo, covering him with her body.

Wesley lowered his gun. "Aw, come on, Mira. You have to learn a lesson. You can't take things that aren't yours. If I don't teach you, who will?"

She glared at him, chest rising and falling with heavy breaths. "You've made your point. I'm taking Gonzo back inside."

Mira stood slowly, holding onto Gonzo's collar while still facing Wesley.

A smile spread across Wesley's face as he watched her walk past, and at the last moment, he reached for Mira's arm and threw her back.

Gonzo leapt into action, standing in front of Mira and barking at Wesley, saliva flying from his bared teeth.

Wesley had lifted his rifle again, taking aim, when Mira crashed into him, knocking him to the ground.

"What is the matter with you?" he screamed. "You're being crazy!"

They tussled in the grass as Gonzo barked a few feet away.

"He's vicious," Wesley said. "You're crazy to keep a dog like that around."

Mira kicked him away and grabbed the rifle, stumbling to her feet. She checked the safety – it was on.

Wesley lay on the ground, his lip split and freely bleeding.

Mira raised the rifle, pointing it at his chest. "If you ever come after me or my dog again, I will kill you."

He put his hands up. "Whoa, whoa. You're being crazy, Mira." He let out a little laugh, his composure returned, his professor voice back in full bloom. "Don't do something you'll regret."

"Get out of here!" she screamed.

He scrambled to his feet, almost tripping, and ran back to his car.

25

Have you ever lost someone you couldn't replace?

The memory cut out, and Mira realized she was gripping the armrests of her chair. She let go, afraid to look at the silent crowd.

So this was the memory she'd been carting around, just her threatening to kill a man with a rifle.

"Well, Mira. That was quite...something."

Someone here might recognize Wesley. But maybe they'd want to use the memory against him too?

She had to save this somehow. Mira rose from her chair and grabbed the jar. "That was one of the darkest days of my life."

"Who was that man?"

"My uncle. He had a habit of threatening my family."

The crowd murmured in low tones, and the curator asked, "Was that a rifle?"

"Yes."

"He was about to kill your dog, wasn't he?"

They didn't need to know about safeties on guns. "He was."

More murmurs in the crowd.

She took a breath. This was quite different than the image Mick had concocted of her as a gentle savior. How could she make this make sense?

She had no choice but to go with the truth. "I have many flaws, but one of them is not how much I loved my dog."

The audience laughed, and the curator cracked a smile. "He was a good dog then? How long did you have him?"

"He was the best." She bit her lip, fighting the tears that had sprung to her eyes. It wasn't often she had to talk about Gonzo. Most people didn't want to hear about a dog, which was just as well, because she could hardly talk about him without falling to pieces. "I had Gonzo for ten years before he got sick."

"Did you use some of that magic medicine to save him?" the curator asked, a twinkle in his eye.

"I did. I had to sell my car to afford it."

The curator took a step back. "Your car? For a dog?"

If there was anything Mira learned while sitting in that waiting room, counting the hours as Gonzo got his doses of chemo, it was that people would do anything to save a beloved pet.

Selling her car was nothing. Sara had driven her to work; she didn't even miss having it. She'd heard other people call and beg their family or bosses for loans, she talked to couples who had taken out second mortgages on their houses to pay for treatments.

She didn't claim to know much about love – her engagement had run so cold that even Mick picked up on it – but she knew this.

Mira cleared her throat. "So much of life is being alone, but dogs make it easier to be alone. They bring joy, and they bring endless love. Dogs make it easier to be alive." She paused, clearing the lump in her throat. "Gonzo was the light of my life."

The crowd erupted in a symphony of cheers.

Mira smiled, wiping the tears that had escaped onto her cheeks. The curator put one arm around her shoulders and pointed at her with his other hand. "Mira Meadows, everyone!"

She took a deep breath and waved. The moment of terror had passed, she had survived, and it was over.

Or so she thought.

At that instant, unbeknownst to Mira, two men rushed toward the stage. There was no one to stop them, as the celebrations had taken on a life of their own, and no one to notice their urgency amongst the cheers and outbreak of songs.

One had blue eyes, and one had green, each blasting through the crowd, stepping on picnics and ripping through the throngs that had crowded the stage.

The man who reached Mira first wasted no time – he grabbed her by the wrist and whisked her away.

"Congratulations," he said, dragging her behind the stage. "You've been approved for integration. Come with me."

26

Integration

Ignatius led her behind the stage, away from the crowd and to his waiting car.

Mira felt like she'd floated there. She'd made it. It was finally happening!

Ignatius opened the rear door of the car. "Take a seat. Go on."

"Thank you." Mira got in, careful not to let her jumpsuit get caught on anything. The women had worked so hard on it.

He slammed the door shut and jogged over to the driver's side. "We need to put together your application for Thunder Island. The sooner the better."

"Great!"

He started the car and took off, throwing Mira backward into her seat.

Mick had told her it would happen quickly, but she had no idea it would happen *this* quickly. She needed to talk to him before she left. She had to get him to take the memory and promise he would expose Wesley, not just on Violet Island, but on Magnifico, where people knew his face.

"Can we stop at the Traveler Center?"

He glanced back at her but said nothing, the car zipping down the dirt road. There was total darkness around them, and the headlights provided little warning of what was ahead.

"I have some things I need to – "

He cut her off. "You can't take anything with you. Nothing but your soul can pass between worlds. What else could you possibly need?"

She was quiet for a moment. He was right, and she didn't want to anger him, but... "I wanted to say goodbye to some people."

The car slammed to a halt, and her forehead smacked into the seat in front of her.

Ignatius spun around, his eyes round and intensely focused. "Show me your hands."

Mira pulled her hand from her throbbing head and slowly lowered it.

He smiled, his white teeth shining even in the darkness. "I need to check something before we go. Let me see your hands."

There was a moment where her mind tried to make sense of what was happening, trying to reconcile what she wanted to happen with what she could see happening in front of her eyes.

The mind, however, is slow in these situations. With the promise of Thunder Island in her thoughts, she was left immobile, a smile frozen on her face.

Mira's heart didn't need to ask questions, though. It had no agenda. It held no hopes, and clung to no fantasies.

Its only purpose in that moment was to scream for her to run.

She leaned to the side, searching for the tiny button that would let her out of the back seat, and Ignatius lunged, grabbing her other arm and locking it into a solid, wooden box.

"What are you doing?" she asked thickly, her mind still refusing to process the scene in front of it.

He reached, wrestling with her briefly until he got her other hand locked into the block. "Stop fighting," he snarled, teeth clenched. "You need this to get to Thunder Island."

The last time she'd seen a box like this, a man ended up in a flying sarcophagus. She tried to pry her wrist out of the block, but it only grew tighter.

Mira looked up at Ignatius. He was digging around in the front seat, and as soon as he turned around, she clocked him on the head with the block.

He grabbed her, pulling her forward and jamming a tiny, orange vial to her arm. She watched with horror as the orange liquid disappeared, and her eyes grew heavy and dark.

. . .

Mira came to and opened her eyes to a perfect, clear blue. She took a deep breath, stretched her neck, and yawned.

Her bed wobbled, jolting her into alertness, and she sat up. The blue above her was the perfect sky and the bed beneath her wasn't a bed at all. It was a canoe, made from the same waxen leaves as one of Slava's flasks.

What on Earth?

She steadied herself on the edges of the canoe and looked around. One end of the boat was stuck on land, the other in the water, lifting with each gentle wave rolling onto shore.

She looked out onto the water, crystal clear and turquoise blue as far as she could see. Mira had never been to a Caribbean beach, though she'd always dreamed of going, and for a moment she sat, mesmerized by the beauty.

There was nothing else – no boats, no people, not even a bird in the sky. Just endless water and the little rocky beach surrounded by trees.

Mira took a wobbly step out of the canoe and onto the beach, moving slowly. Her head was throbbing. She reached a hand and felt her braid – it had shoots of hair sticking out of it, and the bottom was knotted and rough.

Odd.

As soon as she cleared the canoe, it pushed itself off the beach with a pop.

"Wait!" she yelled, but it was no use. There was no one to hear her, and the boat certainly wasn't listening. She watched it cut through the waves and float off into the distance.

Mira was about to turn away when a large shadow rose in the water, growing rapidly and finally breaking the surface. It had a triangular head with black eyes, black scales, and a neck twice the size of the canoe.

In one splash, the boat disappeared.

Mira stumbled away from the water, barely slowing her pace when she fell backward over a rock. She picked herself up and ran into the dense forest lining the edge of the beach.

She struggled through thick undergrowth, branches cutting her face and tangling in her hair. She didn't dare stop, in case that *thing* from the water came after her.

When she was out of breath, which didn't take long in the humid air, she had to stop. She leaned against a tree, breathing heavily and listening.

There were some birds chirping, and maybe some scuttling in the branches above her, but nothing like what she imagined that creature would sound like crashing through the wooded forest.

Mira looked around, spotting what looked like a path a few feet to her left. She'd missed it entirely, running alongside it in her panic.

She untangled the leg of her jumpsuit from a jagged bush, ripping the delicate fabric, and toppled onto the trail. It was narrow, a strip of dirt as wide as her shoe, but it was enough. She walked along, peering up at the tall, leafy trees and back towards the direction of the beach.

Now she was awake. Something had clearly gone wrong. The last thing she remembered was fighting with Ignatius. He'd blocked her hands, and then...

And then what? Sent her to Thunder Island? It looked different than she'd imagined, though no one had told her much about it.

It could be Thunder Island, or it could be...a different island.

The path grew steeper, and Mira paused to rest her legs. Her muscles felt like they were on fire, starved for air and overtired. She hadn't felt this bad since she'd landed in Asphodavia the first time. She suspected it was Ignatius' magical orange juice lingering in her system.

Something cracked above her, and Mira dove under a tree, adrenaline pumping through her veins. When she looked up, peering through leaves, she saw that it was only a bird – an enormous bird whose body looked as big as hers, but a bird nevertheless.

Her heart slowed, and she sat down at the base of a knobbed tree.

This was too much. The edges of her mouth were cracking from dryness. Her throat was dry, too, from being left out on that banana boat.

Mira pulled the edge of the jumpsuit down to look at her bolt. Her heart dropped when she saw it. There was no denying it now – it looked faded. She could barely see the glow, even when she shielded it with her hand's shadow.

If this was Thunder Island, she needed to hurry up and find where lightning struck.

She got up, forcing herself to walk the trail. The edges were lined with thick ferns, and the trees were dense and towering above her. Once she got to the top of the hill, she thought she heard water.

Pressing on, the whisper of water turned to a trickle, then to the pounding of a waterfall. Mira rounded a corner and finally set eyes on it – a forty-foot-tall waterfall beneath her, water hitting rocks below and leaving a mist above the clear pool.

Though she had the urge to jump in and cool off, she suspected that was unwise, so instead she scrambled down to the water's edge and took a drink.

The water was crisp, cool, and fresh. It soothed her throat and somehow even soothed her muscles. There was a hint of kykeon in it, but she didn't care. It felt like she hadn't had water in days, so she drank until it felt like her stomach would rip.

She sat back against a rock, scanning the trees above her, when her eyes settled on a dark figure at the other end of the pool. At first she thought it was a tree, until it moved and looked up at her with yellow eyes.

Mira sat, staring straight ahead. It was no larger than a cocker spaniel, with a pointed face and brown and white feathers all over its body. It had two scrawny arms on the front of its chest, and it cocked its head to the side for a brief scratch.

If she didn't know any better, she would think that thing was a little baby dragon.

Mira stood and the creature jumped back, letting out a squawk before running off, its long, muscular tail disappearing into the ferns.

A wave of nausea crashed into her chest. Either that was a dragon, or she was hallucinating. She doubled over and hung her head between her knees, trying to stop the spinning.

Mira took a deep breath and raised her eyes, trying to recover. Her legs started to shake and she had to lower herself to the ground.

Perhaps it hadn't been such a great idea to drink all of that kykeon water, but now it was too late. Mira dragged herself under the cover of a rocky overhang just as she lost consciousness.

27

___

Run

A mist blew onto Mira's face as the waterfall pounded on. She pulled herself up slowly, expecting her entire body to ache after passing out on a pile of rocks, but other than some dizziness, she felt fine.

The trees cast what felt like an impenetrable darkness around her. The only clearing was above the waterfall, and the sky was black and twinkling with stars.

Mira could kick herself. She must've slept through the day, or possibly two. Why hadn't she slowed down on the kykeon water? It was like she enjoyed making the same mistakes over and over.

At least a dragon hadn't eaten her in her slumber. She'd been hard asleep, dreaming intensely, urgently, her mind filled with images of Alice and Mick and the faces she'd seen on Violet Island. It was as though her brain was trying to make sense of all that had happened in the last few weeks.

Despite the frantic dreaming, her mind had come up short. Mira had no solutions, and she was fresh out of schemes. The bolt on her chest was no brighter than the pale moonlight, sure to extinguish any day. All evidence pointed to her hapless attempt to help Alice being disastrous and landing her in exile on an island full of dragons.

She was the ultimate failure.

As much as she wanted to curl up into a ball and die, the sound of movement in the trees above sent panic through her chest and overpowered her vague feeling of despair.

Mira got up and quietly made her way back to the trail, getting to the top of the waterfall and crawling into a thicket of ferns.

She squatted quietly as a deer-sized dragon made its way down from the treetops, hopping from branch to branch until landing on the ground ten feet in front of her.

Mira stared, wide-eyed and afraid to breathe. It could probably kill her, though it didn't look particularly ferocious with its small, pointy head, green-blue fur, and absolutely dainty paws. It had dark, round eyes, and for a moment stood listening before heading toward the waterfall and taking a drink.

It was almost catlike, sleek and delicate, finishing its drink before bouncing back into the trees and out of her sight.

Perhaps staying by the watering hole wasn't the smartest idea. Though the dragons she'd seen so far were small – well, except for whatever that thing was in the water – there seemed to be an endless variety of them. Scaled, feathered, furry – who knew what else she'd walk into next?

She had to keep moving and find a safer place. It was going to be a long night.

. . .

When the sun rose, Mira was exhausted. She'd traveled seemingly in circles around the watering hole, unable to navigate in the dark, and the most frightening creatures she'd found were still the enormous birds.

She had yet to see another dragon much bigger than she was, catching more glimpses of cat-like dragons and the scaly little spaniel-types instead. There was a lizard who crossed her path, slow and plodding, but she wasn't sure if he was a dragon or just a strange, fat iguana.

The exhaustion convinced her she was safe enough to take a nap, and she drifted off under a small overhang of rocks and ferns. Mira awoke some time later with the groggy realization that something was touching her leg.

She sat up, screaming at the top of her lungs, before seeing it was nothing more than a brown slug the size of a paint brush roller trying to make its way up her leg.

Mira swatted it away, then realized her screams had silenced the forest around her.

Silence was not good. She ran off, back toward the watering hole, and was relieved when nothing seemed to have chased her there.

Her plan this time was to drink only enough to quench her thirst, but not enough to knock herself out. Hopefully her body would build a tolerance to the kykeon. Somehow the dragons were drinking it just fine, and she'd eaten so many dry nuts along the path that she needed to wash them down with something.

She'd just gotten to the base of the waterfall when she thought she heard something in the distance. Mira looked up, around, and behind her, but saw nothing.

She stood, silent and frozen, until she heard a cracking sound in the forest. It was getting closer quickly, and it sounded like tree branches snapping and crackling to the ground.

The sea monster?

Mira scrambled up the trail, the large rocks shifting underneath her feet and throwing her off balance. At the top of the waterfall, she briefly debated hiding in the ferns again, but the sound was too intense. She took off running down the trail.

Whatever was coming after her was much faster than she was. She turned around just as flames burst out of the trees, incinerating the leaves and leaving branches smoldering.

Running wasn't going to work.

Mira dove into the underbrush, crawling through mud and ferns, twigs snapping in her hair and ripping at her poor disheveled jumpsuit. She was desperate to find a rock, or cave, or anywhere she could hide.

There was a pile of rocks ahead of her, standing nearly twice her height and spanning as far as she could see. She looked over her shoulder before vaulting herself up as quickly as she could. On the other side, there was a few feet of rocky space that gave way to a jagged cliff.

Mira jumped down to the ledge, carefully landing on both her hands and feet as to not lose her grip, and peered over the edge of the cliff. There was nowhere for her to go but over a steep hundred-foot drop. At the bottom was more rocky terrain.

A deep cry rang out behind her. She froze as a powerful wind swept down, blasting leaves and dirt into her hair.

Mira pressed her body against the rock wall behind her. She wished she could disappear into the rocks. She wished she had a marking where she could fly or jump or do *anything*.

Instead, all she could do was quiet her breathing by covering her mouth and mute her terror by closing her eyes.

28

Maple syrup and honey

The beast's hot breath puffed onto her back. Mira sat perfectly still, eyes pinched shut as her heart pounded against her ribcage.

This was the end. She was going to die, and there was a chance she'd end up in an even more backwards world the next time. Was she going to keep falling down the wormhole of other worlds until she hit hell?

An idea hit her: play dead. Mira was lowering herself to the ground when the massive animal behind her bumped her shoulder, causing her to topple forward.

She flipped onto her back and opened her eyes, staring directly into the face of the towering dragon.

At first, all she could see was the bottom of his chin. His mouth was open, sniffing in deeply, and his fangs were exposed, each tooth longer than her arm.

She expected him to look reptilian, but he was covered in fur. His face had whiskers, and his nose looked wet and soft, twitching as he breathed her in.

He dropped his nose and Mira saw his eyes for the first time. They were enormous, larger than hubcaps, and the most magical shade of brown, like maple syrup touched with honey...

The air pressed out of her lungs. "Gonzo?"

The dragon's eyes brightened and he bowed down, arching his back and pointing his tail in the air. He nudged her again, gently, and Mira slowly reached out to touch his face.

He leaned into her touch. His silken fur felt cool against her fingers, and somehow he smelled the same, like dirt and corn chips.

Tears sprung to her eyes and Mira kissed him all over his furry snout, pulling his massive head in with both hands.

He let out a low whine and she picked herself up, wrapping her arms around his neck as best she could.

"I've missed you so much," she said, tears streaming down her face.

He stood still, stiff, like he always used to when she would hug him. Though he tolerated hugs, he never liked them – except from her.

After a moment, she pulled away and got a better look at him. He was at least four times the size of Dragon, if not bigger. He had immense wings, black and velvety, resting at his sides, and four immense paws. They weren't quite dog paws, but they weren't what she imagined dragon claws looked like, either. His fur was short and black with silvery patterns throughout, and on his chest and neck, he had tufts of long white fur.

He was *cute*. Terrifying at first, perhaps, and he looked different, but it was him.

"I can't believe this," she muttered, shaking her head.

His long tail swayed from side to side.

He was wagging his tail!

Mira choked out a laugh through her tears. "You're a good boy, Gonzo. Do you know that? Do you know how much I love you?"

He popped up, abruptly turning around and delicately picking up one of the downed trees. He turned and proudly presented it to her.

"That's a nice stick." Mira patted him on the leg. "Can you sit?"

He leaned, dropping the tree with a crash before planting his butt on the ground. Mira stroked his fluffy chest and repeated how good he was, and how pretty he was, and that he was the smartest dog dragon she'd ever seen.

If losing him was one of the worst moments of her life, then finding him again was one of the best moments of her death.

• • •

At least an hour went by where all she could do was cry, pet him, and repeatedly tell him how good he was. She searched his body for a bolt, but was unable to find one. Would a bolt still work on a dog? How had he ended up a dragon?

Mira wondered if all of the dragons on the island were animals from earth. She couldn't ask them, of course, but she wondered all the same. It would be helpful if all of the dragons were essentially enormous dogs, but the more she thought about it, the less sense it made. Dogs probably wouldn't have killed most of the men on Mick's expedition.

Maybe the mean ones were enormous cows. She grew up near a farmer who told her cows killed more people than sharks every year. He said, "When the cows do it, they mean to do it."

Mira had avoided cows ever since.

"Come here, boy!"

Gonzo came bounding over, his face in a familiar goofy expression. She patted him between the eyes before turning and climbing the rocks behind her.

He followed, easily clearing them and dropping to the other side. She thought he might flap his wings, show off how he flew, but he came crashing down, bushes and branches crunching beneath him.

It was like him not to fly. Gonzo had always been a lazy dog. When she'd tried to pick up jogging, it was Gonzo who flattened himself out on the sidewalk and refused to budge. Mira gave into him that time, and after that, stopped going on runs altogether. It wasn't fun to go by herself, and if it wasn't good enough for Gonzo, it wasn't good enough for her.

Yet if he could fly...surely he could fly. He must have been flying after her. Or had he just been running? He'd made a lot of mess, and a lot of noise.

If he could fly, that was something. Something huge. They could get away from this forsaken place and go anywhere they wanted. Thunder Island? Magnifico? Nordavia?

Before she could figure that out, she needed some water. Mira led Gonzo back to the waterfall and as soon as he got there, he balanced delicately at the top of the waterfall and drank.

Maybe there was less kykeon on top? She followed his lead and drank slowly. It was still cool and refreshing, but it seemed to have less of the kykeon flavor.

She stopped once her thirst was quenched and decided they had no time to waste. They needed to get down to business.

"Okay, Gonzo." She turned to him and he sat expectantly, the tip of his tail wagging slowly. "I need you to fly, and I need you to do it with me on your back. Can I get on your back, buddy?"

He looked at her, his butt wiggling with excitement. She gave him the signal to lay down, and he did as she asked.

"Okay. Don't freak out," she said, patting him gently before flinging herself onto his back.

Gonzo pulled away and Mira fell to the ground. He stood over her and licked her face with his giant black tongue.

"Okay, okay, thank you," she said, getting up with a laugh. "You're bigger than me now. Do you know that?"

He licked her again and she groaned, wiping it away.

This was going to be an adjustment for him. She looked around, spotting a rock that was about the height of his shoulder. Mira walked to it and called him over, then asked him to lay down again.

From the top of the rock, she carefully lowered herself onto his back, repeating herself in a low voice. "Stay, stay. Good, *stay*."

He wagged his tail, turning to look at her, and the sudden shift caused her to slip down his side and into the dirt below.

"Good boy. That was good." She scratched behind his ear and he tilted his head.

Same old Gonzo.

Mira kept trying, and after her fourth attempt with the rock, she managed to get onto his back and stay there. He was confused by it, but he enjoyed it when she leaned forward and scratched his neck.

"Okay. Just a few hundred more tries and maybe we can fly somewhere."

He turned to look at her and she clung to his neck, almost slipping off before he corrected himself, balancing her back to the center.

"Good boy! You're learning!"

She leaned forward, feeling the pull of sleep on her eyes. It wasn't as strong as the last time she'd chugged kykeon water, but it was enough that she thought it might be time to retire.

Mira slipped off of Gonzo's back and led him to a rocky overhang. "Come on, Gonzy. Bedtime."

He walked in, stooping low to fit, and turned three times before settling down into a nearly perfect ball shape. Mira nestled against his shoulder and he tucked his head next to her, closing his eyes and letting out a heavy sigh.

Tomorrow she could work on training him, and she could figure out what to do and how to do it. But today, Mira was allowing herself to bask in the illogical beauty of the moment.

Perhaps everything happened for a reason, and perhaps it didn't – but she'd managed to find Gonzo in not one, but two lives, and that meant something.

No, it proved something. The feeling she'd had after he passed – not the despair, but her ongoing attachment – that quiet, comforting steadfastness was real. The love between them was real, even after it seemed like he was gone.

Love is untouched by death. What is death, but a veil dancing over the illusion of time? Love cuts through our primitive understanding, defying laws of physics and rationality. It binds, crossing through worlds, invisible and unstoppable, the closest any soul can get to the divine.

Mira wasn't one to question such a powerful force. It was enough to feel it, and to recognize that it had brought her here.

She smiled and closed her eyes.

29

Start before you're ready

The way Mira saw it, she had to pick a plan. Plan A was to fly to Thunder Island, pray her bolt wouldn't run out, and return to Earth.

Plan B was to fly back to Nordavia, find a way to rid Pontos of Wesley, and somehow figure out how to save Alice, too.

There were a lot of unknowns with these plans. Mira would need help, and while Gonzo was an adorable start, he wasn't enough to fight Wesley and all of his political power. She'd have to fight fire with fire, so to speak, with a trove of support and resources she currently didn't have.

The Isle of Dragons had resources – ambrosia, at least. If she could get her hands on some before she flew back, she'd finally have a bargaining tool. She'd need to make a flask or hollow out a coconut or something, but she could figure that out later. Ambrosia was valuable and rare, and she could sell it and buy weapons, or political spies, or anything she needed.

Unfortunately, both Plan A and Plan B had complications – ones she was reluctant to think through. She didn't want to think about her bolt running out and her other body, her real body, dying. She didn't want to think about Wesley killing her, and Alice, *and* Gonzo with ease. She especially didn't want to think about leaving Gonzo behind, and deep in an ignored corner of her heart, a hole opened whenever she got too close to the idea of never seeing Mick again, too.

The idea of failure was too much to consider, so, like the flawed human being she was, Mira concocted a Plan C, the "It'll Be Fine" plan. It was something she couldn't allow herself to think through to its logical conclusion, because it didn't make sense, and it wasn't a plan she consciously knew she'd created. It was a comforting plan, a hopeful one, and that was all she could manage right now.

She would find ambrosia, fly back and save Alice, rid the world of Wesley, and somehow get herself and Gonzo back to Earth.

How she'd do that wasn't clear, but she was sure she'd figure it out. Now wasn't the time to overthink it. She'd jump first and build her wings on the way down.

Step one of the plan was teaching Gonzo to fly with her on his back. They'd done a lot of training when he was a dog – obedience, agility, even some bird fetching – but with flying, she had no idea where to start.

Day one began with Gonzo learning to accept her on his back. Her first attempts went much like they had the day before, but once she'd convinced him she was climbing onto him to scratch a particularly unreachable part of his neck, he changed his tune. By the end of the day, he would lower his head on command and make it easy for her to climb on.

The following two days were spent giving him commands for "go," "left" and "right." He'd learned those ages ago, and while she could navigate while walking, Mira didn't know how to get her lazy dog to use his wings. He was happiest plodding along, sniffing things, and snapping birds out of the trees for snacks.

That was something new, at least. He'd never been much of a hunter, but Pontos had changed him. Her gentle dog, so docile he'd once sat still as a litter of tiny kittens clambered over him, was now a menace to all creatures. He ate birds, he devoured lizards, and at one point, Mira watched as he chased a raccoon from a tree and ate it, too.

It wasn't a bloody affair, which she appreciated, and it had seemed like the raccoon had a chance of getting away. To Mira's astonishment, the fat little animal could fly, and he took off at one point, hovering twelve feet in the air before zipping off.

Mira hoped Gonzo would follow him and take off, too, but alas, he stretched his long neck and snapped the raccoon out of the sky like it was nothing.

His presence seemed to keep other dragons away. She hadn't seen even a small dragon in days. Yet the only time she'd seen him fly, or blow fire, or do anything dragon-like, was when he had been chasing after her.

So they walked. Gonzo was getting better about taking direction and balancing her on his back, which would all be important if he ever decided to fly again.

Mira decided they should cautiously explore more of the island in case she could find ambrosia. What would it look like in the wild? Would it be in a deposit? In a well? Would she need to go into a cave and hack it from a magical pool?

She wasn't sure, but she was confident she'd know it when she saw it. They moved east, away from the beach and the waterfall they knew, and through the jungle. The slim path, considerably expanded by Gonzo's paws, led them to a flat and expansive grassland.

It was peaceful, the grass swaying in the wind, but Mira was on high alert. They were far more exposed here than in the jungle, and any animal – or dragon – bigger than Gonzo would be hard to evade.

The further they went, the shorter the grasses became, until they gave way to sparse patches and rocks. In the distance, Mira could make out jagged mountains, gray and barren, a stark contrast against the blinding blue sky.

It made no sense to her. Weren't mountains supposed to have trees? Or grass? Or goats?

A goat would be nice. Goat milk sounded good. She'd been surviving on nuts and berries, but only ones she recognized, since she didn't want to poison herself. It wasn't much, but it kept her going.

Mira imagined herself chasing a goat down and trying to milk it. It would probably end with her tumbling down the mountain as Gonzo scooped up the goat and swallowed it whole.

Mountains could be good, though. Mountains might mean ambrosia, or caves, or something. They pressed on for the rest of the day, climbing the steep grade until they reached the top.

It wasn't the most comfortable travel. The sun was so bright it bounced off of the gray and white stone, blinding her at times. There were no clouds or breaks from the heat, and after they'd been going for a few hours, it dawned on her that it might be hard to find water the further they went.

That was her mistake, but she'd never expected the humid jungle to give way to such an arid wasteland.

Thankfully, Gonzo was able to easily traverse the shifting rocks beneath his paws and before long, they crested over the top of one of the mountain peaks.

This only led to more disappointment. Below them, all Mira could see were more rocks and what looked like sand. She squinted, unable to make out anything that might resemble water. In the distance, taller mountains stood in their way.

How big was this cursed island?

She was unsure if it was better to return to the jungle, or to press on and try to find water. It could be just around the corner. Or the rest of this island could be a desert full of giant dragons.

If only Gonzo would speed things up. Despite her pleas, he still didn't understand why she wanted him to "fly," or why he couldn't lay down for a nap.

When they reached the other side of the mountain, Mira took a gamble and directed Gonzo into the desert and toward a spot on the horizon that looked less scorched – or at least, less mountainous.

The sun began setting as they walked, which helped with the heat but made her worry about the creatures that might come out at night.

Luckily for Mira, she'd chosen the right direction. The sandy ground grew firmer, revealing scrub grass and eventually, real grass. Before dusk, they reached the green edge of a river, and both Mira and Gonzo drank heartily.

"Sorry about that, buddy," Mira said, patting him on the neck. "I took us a little too far."

They found shelter under a crop of trees and Gonzo curled up, satisfied to finally have a rest. Mira cozied under his tail and slept without fear of any sounds in the night.

. . .

The next morning, Mira decided to press a bit further into the island. The river was the first sign of life they'd seen since leaving the jungle, and she was convinced she would find something soon.

Past the river, they entered an evergreen forest. The trees' green needles alternated with purple and red, which Mira was fairly certain didn't happen on earth, but she couldn't be sure. The trees smelled the same at least, which was a comfort.

Life was bursting from every nook, with birds and rodents all around. Mira found a chestnut tree, much to her excitement, and loaded her pockets with nuts. She'd figure out how to get Gonzo to roast them for her later.

They marched on, and like she had in their previous life, Mira carried on a full conversation with Gonzo, out loud, and sometimes voiced his responses.

He loved it, looking back at her with his big eyes whenever she said his name, or when it sounded like she was asking him a question. She was just about to tell him how disappointed she was with the dragon population on this island when something enormous flew overhead.

Her arrogance never went unchecked. Mira, who had been picking berries, ducked down. She urged Gonzo to follow her, but his eyes were focused upwards. She followed his gaze and spotted what he was looking at – one of those enormous, terrifying birds she'd seen earlier, dive-bombing dangerously close to where they stood.

"Gonzo, let's go!" she yelled, running down the trail.

He looked at her and let out a whine, a moment later leaping and snapping the bird from the air with one swift movement. It made a sickening crunch in his jaws, and he shook it three times before dropping its car-sized body to the ground.

Mira took one look at it and gagged. It had flown threateningly close to her, yet seeing its brutal end filled her with pity.

Gonzo was unfazed, wagging his tail and happily trotting toward her. Mira tapped him on the neck and he lowered his head, allowing her to climb on.

"Not bad, Gonzy," she said, settling into her familiar spot. "But pretty cold-blooded."

Another shadow flashed overhead and Mira groaned. She didn't want a second giant dead bird on her watch, but Gonzo was already engaged.

She tried to call his attention away, but this time, he didn't whine. He let out a growl, deep and rumbling. Mira could feel the vibration in her legs.

This was different. She looked up, but couldn't see anything. "C'mon, boy. We need to –"

A cry rang out, something between a falcon and an angry cat. It reverberated in Mira's ears, and she threw her hands up to cover them.

"Ugh!" She scanned the skies frantically. "What is that?"

Gonzo dropped low, a moment later popping into the air. Mira had little time to react, managing only to catch onto his neck and hold on.

The next moments were chaos. Flames erupted to their left as Gonzo flew up and out of the tree cover. He spun gracefully, spitting his own blue fire behind them.

Mira gasped. She hadn't seen the flame last time, only the effect of it. He'd aimed it perfectly before, clearing trees in front of him, and now he fired it precisely at their attacker.

It was only then that Mira finally saw it. A dragon twice the size of Gonzo, with glistening, forest green scales. It had a mouth full of teeth and black, leathery wings.

It lacked everything that made Gonzo cute and looked like something from a biblical drawing of hell.

It fired its yellow flame at them again, narrowly missing, and Gonzo shot back, catching one of its wings.

The dragon let out another deafening cry and Mira screamed.

She didn't mean to, but she was scared, and useless, and terrified. Whatever that thing was, it had never been a dog. She couldn't tell it to sit or stay. It was a bona fide dragon, all fury and fire and death.

Gonzo didn't share her shock, and after his successful hit, he turned and flew furiously in the other direction. Mira clung to his neck, still reeling from the fight, and couldn't get herself to look back for a few moments.

Thankfully, the beast hadn't pursued them, and within minutes, Mira recognized the mountains they'd crossed the day before.

Gonzo flew on, and Mira shook off her terror and tried to check him for injuries. From what she could tell, he didn't seem hurt. That was a relief.

And they were flying! The wind ripped through her hair and she saw everything clearly laid out below them: the desert as a little patch of sand, the jungle ahead of them, and the ocean that went on far into the horizon.

Within an hour, Gonzo landed rather gracefully at their old waterfall and helped himself to a drink. Mira checked him over again, and satisfied he had no injuries, also had some water.

"I'm never going to complain about a lack of dragons again," she told him, shaking her head.

He cocked his head to the side, his black tongue rolling out of his mouth, and she laughed. "I'm glad you agree."

30

The distressing damsel

Following their brush with death, Mira felt much less cavalier about exploring the island. She still needed to find ambrosia, but she had to be smart about it.

Gonzo had reacted amazingly, but she couldn't count on him to save them every time, and she couldn't risk losing him. It was her job to keep him safe, not the other way around.

They spent the next day practicing flying with commands, and Mira kept Gonzo close to the areas they knew. Though they came across two smaller dragons, they weren't attacked, and there weren't any large hell dragons, either.

Mira was working on getting Gonzo to understand ascent and descent, flying above the waterfall, when she spotted something out in the ocean.

At first she thought it was driftwood, but as it got closer, she realized it was a small boat. Her heart sang at the idea that someone else had been exiled to the Isle of Dragons. A friend!

Could it be Slava, his episcope lies finally catching up to him? Or Alice, who had read the wrong thoughts? It could be someone entirely new, maybe someone who knew more about the island than she did.

Whoever it was, she was as excited to meet them, as any castaway would be. She directed Gonzo to land in the forest, and they then walked the path down to the beach to wait.

It took over an hour for the small boat to appear on the horizon, then another hour until it got into shore.

Mira watched from behind the trees, careful to keep Gonzo covered up. There was no need to scare the poor soul. As cute as he was, Gonzo was still a fire-breathing dragon, and he would require a gentle introduction.

She could see there was only one person on the ship, and they weren't unconscious as she had been when she arrived. It was a man, she was quite sure, in a crisp, bright white shirt, but she couldn't see his face.

When he pulled onto shore, Mira was still struggling to look at him from the bushes. It wasn't Slava – the man was far too trim to be Slava.

She needed to get closer. She told Gonzo to sit and stay, then turned to approach the beach. Gonzo wasn't happy about being left behind, but he did as he was told, albeit while whining a high-pitched complaint.

Mira quietly crept to the edge of the forest, peering through the trees and watching as the man covered the boat with leaves.

He turned around and Mira gasped. He wasn't in his customary three-piece suit, which threw her at first, but she recognized the man. It was Mick.

She felt like her heart would burst. Tears welled into her eyes and she hastily wiped them away, stumbling out of the forest, grinning like the fool she was.

Mick spun at the sound, pointing a rifle.

Mira put her hands in the air. "Don't shoot!"

His mouth popped open and he dropped the gun to his side. "Mira?"

"Mick!"

He walked to her and cupped her face in his hand. "You're alive."

His eyes swept over her face – up, then back again, side to side, finally lingering on her eyes.

The intensity of his gaze made her lose her breath for a second. "It's only been a few days."

"I should've known," he said, pulling his hand away. "If anyone could survive the dragons, it'd be you." He shook his head. "Have you been hiding?"

"Not exactly."

He stepped back to look at her. "Are you hurt?"

She shook her head.

He knelt down, pulling a brown-wrapped package from his bag. "I've got something for you."

She accepted the package, and as soon as she unwrapped the paper, the smell of fresh bread filled her nostrils. "Thank you." She took a bite of the bread, then of the hunk of smoked fish beside it.

"We can leave straight away," he said, pulling leaves off the little boat. "I have contacts on who can get us back to –"

"Wait," she said. Her mind was spinning with the sight of him. His eyes were the same hue as the water, bluer than blue. She didn't think them cold anymore, and all at once she realized they were perhaps her favorite eyes to stare into.

"I didn't mean for this to happen," he said softly. "If I had been at the spectacle – "

She held up a hand and he fell silent. "The spectacle was my fault."

"It wasn't." He started to drag the boat toward the water.

"It was." She walked after him, then stopped. What if he decided to leave her here when he heard what she'd done?

But lying wasn't an option. "I kept a memory – the one of my uncle. I was going to ask you to use it against him after I got to Thunder Island."

He stopped and turned to look at her. "You did it, then?"

"I didn't put it in the spectacle on purpose. I lost the memory, and somehow it ended up in the spectacle."

Mick shook his head. "It doesn't matter."

Whew. "So you're not going to kill me?"

His head was buried in the boat and he emerged a moment later. "No. I'd very much like it if you lived, Mira."

She flashed a smile. He did like her.

"Get in, then," he said. "We'll navigate around the island and
– "

Mira cut him off. "I need ambrosia."

"Ambrosia?" He reached a hand to wipe the sweat from his brow. "Why?"

"I'm going to sell it. I want to help Alice, and I want to get rid of Wesley."

"You're not going to get ambrosia."

She leaned closer. There was a lingering scent of his cologne, which she found slightly distracting. "Do you know where it is? You could help me."

"Mira, it's not going to work. You'll get eaten alive before you get near the ambrosia pools."

She stared at him, and he was about to speak again when his eyes grew wide and he drew his rifle.

"Get back!" he yelled, pulling Mira behind the boat.

Mira had never heard him raise his voice before and it startled her. It took her a moment to realize what he was reacting to – Gonzo, who was peeking his head out of the forest.

"No!" She yelled, running to him and spreading her arms across his massive, fluffy chest. "Don't hurt him. It's Gonzo."

Mick's eyes darted between them, rifle still aimed. "What?"

She turned and stroked his fur. "This is my dog. This is Gonzo."

"Mira, that's a *dragon*."

"I know, but look. Look at his eyes. Don't you recognize him? From my memories?"

"No!"

She glared at him, and he lowered his gun. Mira tapped Gonzo on the neck, then climbed onto his back. "See?"

Mick stared, his jaw clenched.

"He's friendly," Mira said. "We're getting better at flying."

"You're getting better at flying," he said, shaking his head. "Do you hear yourself?"

She shrugged. "What?"

Gonzo started walking and Mick stumbled backward.

"Hang on, buddy." She slid off of his back. "Stay here, okay?"

He pushed his snout into her and she gave him a kiss on the nose. When she turned back to Mick, he was upright again, staring with his mouth open.

"I don't believe this."

"I have a plan," she said. "We'll get some ambrosia, then fly back to Nordavia and – "

Mick finally broke away from staring at Gonzo and looked at her. "We can't fly to Nordavia. The dragon needs to stay here, Mira."

She put her arms on her hips. "He's coming with me."

"He can't."

"Then I'm not going," she said, crossing her arms.

"Then you'll die."

"Fine."

He let out a sigh. "You haven't thought this through."

"*You* haven't thought this through."

He turned back to the boat. "You're being a child."

She let out a huff. Mick didn't know what he was talking about.

"I've just found him again," she finally said, her voice stern. "I won't leave him behind. I won't."

Mick was silent, fussing with the boat. When he turned around, he addressed her again. "If you return to Asphodavia, you might be allowed to live. *Might*. We could try to get you to Thunder Island, or create a new identity and hide you in another city. You could marry a powerful Asphodavian for protection. One of these things may work to keep you alive. But if you bring along a dragon, you'll get us all killed."

She frowned. "It's not just any dragon. It's Gonzo."

"You can't keep a dragon, Mira!" He shook his head. "What do you think someone like your uncle will do when he hears there's a tame dragon within reach? Do you think he'll let you live your days in peace and harmony?"

She shook her head. "That's why we have to get to him first."

"Get to him first!" He scoffed. "A man who sees everything, owns everyone, and has unlimited resources? You're going to get to him first?"

"I have a dragon, and he doesn't."

He rubbed his face with his hands. "It doesn't matter. He'll take Gonzo and kill you. It'll be nothing for him."

"Gonzo won't go with Wesley."

"He'll still kill you, then. They've been trying to tame dragons for centuries. If the Council even caught wind of this – "

"They won't."

Mick let out a sigh and sat on the edge of the boat, head hanging low. "Thanks for coming to my rescue, Mick," he said, his voice high pitched. "You've risked life and limb. I'll listen to whatever you say."

She bit her lip to hide a smile. Mira had never considered the idea that someone would try to save her, let alone Mick. He must like her. He must feel *something* for her if he was willing to risk coming to her rescue.

"I'm sorry," she finally said. "I can't leave everything undone like this. I just can't."

Gonzo nudged Mira from behind, pushing her forward. She reached back and petted his head.

"I should've known you wouldn't be rescued easily," Mick said, looking up at her, a half-smile on his face.

Her heart let out a flutter. "Normally, I wouldn't allow anyone to rescue me."

"But you're willing to make an exception?"

She did a half-shrug, half-nod.

He let out a laugh. "All right then, Mira. Time for a new strategy, eh?"

31

Squirrel

On the walk to the kykeon waterfall, Mira rode atop Gonzo's back and Mick, having declined her invitation to join her, followed behind on foot.

"Does he breathe fire?" Mick asked.

"Sometimes."

"Has he breathed it on you?"

She turned around. "Of course not. He only used it when we were attacked by a dragon. And once when he needed to clear a path to get to me."

Mick raised an eyebrow. "Clear a path?"

"Yes." Mira turned back around. "Will that help us, do you think?"

"No. Nothing will help us."

Mira rolled her eyes. "You don't have to come, you know. Tell me where the ambrosia is and I'll get it myself."

"You'll get it yourself?" He laughed. "Quite useless, me coming here, wasn't it?"

She rode along quietly for a moment before answering. "I wouldn't say that."

"If I'd have known you had your dragon and your plans set –"

"I'm happy to see you," she said, turning and meeting his eyes. "I don't want to get you killed."

He was silent, and she turned back, stroking the fur on Gonzo's neck. He leaned into it, veering slightly off course.

"The Council drained the ambrosia wells on every island in Asphodavia. Even the islands they've vowed to liberate don't have much. They're getting desperate."

Mira laid back, propping her feet up, and Gonzo wiggled to balance her. "If I find some, could I bribe them with it?"

"You could. I've been doing it for years."

"From your last trip?" She sat up. "How much do you have left?"

"A few drops."

"Why didn't they 'liberate' it from you?"

He smiled. "My supply is hidden all around Nordavia. If they killed me, they'd never find the rest of it."

"Hm. Smart." They'd reached the top of the waterfall, so she slid off Gonzo's back and faced Mick. He was smiling. "They need ambrosia to extract magic from Travelers, right?"

"Yes."

"Don't they have enough magic at this point?"

"They have hundreds, maybe thousands, of aions hidden away in the Hall of Magic."

"Seems like a lot."

"They're greedy. It's never enough."

Of course. "All right. If I get ambrosia, I can negotiate to have Alice freed?"

He pulled a cigarette from his pocket and popped it into his mouth. "You might."

"What about Wesley? Can I trade ambrosia to kick him out of power?"

He lit the cigarette and took a deep puff before answering. "I don't know. It's never been done before."

"I'm sure Council members stab each other in the back all the time."

"That's true. With the ambrosia you have a chance, at least. They've been desperate the last few months, and after Alice's marking, it's only gotten worse."

Her heart sunk into her chest. "Why?"

"Being able to hear thoughts is an ultimate form of magic, up there with taming dragons. They will have total control."

"They already have total control."

He shook his head. "They are always looking for more. More excuses for surveillance, more ways to hold power. More reasons to be the purveyors of absolute truth."

A commotion broke out behind them, and Mira looked just as Gonzo tore a branch off a tree with his teeth and a squirrel came toppling to the ground.

It darted left, then right, running directly into Gonzo before getting away in the undergrowth.

"He hates squirrels," Mira said, dropping her voice so Gonzo wouldn't hear her say the word *squirrel*. "But even as a dragon, he hasn't managed to catch one."

Mick stared, watching Gonzo's frantic efforts, halfway jumping up a tree to look for the squirrel. After a moment, he said, "The Council will see you as a squirrel, even if you have ambrosia."

She let out a little laugh and turned to face him. "And like that squirrel, I'll still get away."

32

Walk, run, fly, die

I t only took a day of practicing for Gonzo to get used to having two people on his back. Mick was the one who had trouble getting used the idea.

He was nervous around Gonzo. He flinched whenever Gonzo got close, and while Mira thought he should take some time to get over his phobia, he insisted they needed to get moving. Though the west side of the island had fewer dragons, it still held danger, and the longer they lingered, the higher their risk of death.

Two days after Mick's arrival, they set out from the safety of the waterfall in search of ambrosia. Mick had brought a map of the island, and though the wells weren't marked, he remembered where they'd found a well years ago.

They took off in the early morning hours, and Gonzo's soft fur kept them warm despite the chill in the air. Mira sat up front and Mick wrapped his arms around her waist. She thought it might be awkward to be so close to him again, but strangely enough, it felt more comforting than anything. It was nice being able to turn around and see him there, his face scowling and focused except for when it broke to offer her a smile.

Per Mick's recommendation, they flew along the coastline toward the east side of the island. He explained that various expedition trips over the years had catalogued where dragons were most likely to be encountered, and the edges of the sea were the least dangerous – as long as they stayed out of the water.

"The largest expedition ever undertaken had three hundred men and women, split between two grand ships. Just as they neared the northern shores of the Isle, the larger of the ships disappeared. The survivors said all they could see was 'a great explosion of teeth.'"

Mira shuddered, remembering her first day on the island. "I've seen a sea dragon. Well – part of one."

Gonzo banked, curving gracefully, and Mick tightened his grip around Mira's waist. "The larger the ship, the larger the dragon it will attract. That much we now know."

"Where else do dragons live?'

"Anywhere with fresh water and prey. Once we get past the desert, the mountains will be full of dragons."

"And that's where the ambrosia is."

"Yes. It's said ambrosia comes from the remains of ancient dragons."

Mira turned to look at him. "Do dragons drink ambrosia?"

"Couldn't tell you. I know many lay their eggs in the mountains or near the ambrosia pools, and if you get near a nest, you're as good as dead."

She nodded and turned around. "Nice to know."

The island wasn't as big as it seemed when she had been on foot. Mira stayed on high alert as they flew over the first set of mountains, afraid they would encounter the same hell dragon from before, but it wasn't until they hit the second set of mountains that they even saw another dragon.

It was grey and lizard-like, smaller than Gonzo, with a rather puny set of wings. It flitted out from behind a mountain peak, abruptly turning when it spotted them.

"Look," Mira said, pointing to where the dragon had disappeared. "Gonzo is scaring the small ones off."

"Or he went to get his friends."

Mira frowned. She didn't think dragons had friends.

Thankfully, the grey dragon didn't return, and Mira directed Gonzo to land on a mountain ledge. It was a rocky spot a few hundred feet above the water, windswept and treeless.

Gonzo didn't seem tired – he beat his wings only when necessary, and glided along the rest of the time – but she thought it was prudent to give him a break before they reached a more dragon-infested area.

They took a seat looking over the sparkling turquoise sea, and Mick pulled the last of their food from his bag. He had eight flasks filled with water, which they planned to replace with ambrosia once they found it, as well as his rifle, slung over his shoulder.

"Do you remember where you found the ambrosia last time?" she asked.

Mick nodded and lit a cigarette. "At the edge of the forest, where the river joined the lake."

"Are there a lot of lakes?"

"Don't know," he said.

Helpful. "I can't believe you brought those cigarettes all the way here."

He pulled it from his mouth and offered it to her. "Would you like to try one before you die?"

Such a drama queen. "We're not going to die."

Mick cracked a smile, shrugging. "I don't like our odds."

"Then why did you come with me?"

"Because you stand a better chance of surviving if you're with me," he said. He cleared his throat. "Do you know what's in these cigarettes?"

"Smells like..." Mira leaned forward, "raspberries."

Mick blew out a puff of smoke. "Not raspberry leaves, but an herb that preserves markings."

She narrowed her eyes. "You have markings?"

"Of course." He let out a breath, squinting at the bright ocean in front of them. "I only wish I could hold more at once."

She sat back, studying him. "How many markings have you taken on?"

"Four, but one is weakened. If I take on another, I'll lose it."

"Four! What can you do? Can I get markings?"

"If you survive, sure." He smiled at her, his eyes clear and cool in the sunlight.

She was about to demand he tell her what his markings were when she heard a cry.

Mira shot up from where she was sitting. "What was that?"

"Bad news," he said, standing and pulling her behind him.

Mira looked over his shoulder, a feeling of panic flooding her. "Where's Gonzo?"

"Off starting a fight, it seems."

A blinding light blasted toward them and Mick jumped, taking Mira to the ground. A second blast of light hit a granite boulder near them, blowing it to pieces.

"It's a lighting dragon," Mick said. "Maybe more than one. We must be near a nest. We need to run."

Mira scrambled to get up. "Gonzo!" she screamed, frantically scanning the ten-foot rock wall ahead of them. Just behind it she could make out the green tops of trees, but there was no sight of whatever was attacking them.

A moment later, Gonzo came running, leaping from the rock face and landing in front of Mira.

"We have to get out of here, buddy." She tapped his neck, but at that moment another flash of light struck inches from Gonzo's back paws.

He lowered himself to the ground and growled.

Mira blinked, trying to clear the blind spots from her eyes, just as a birdlike dragon strutted in front of Gonzo. It was about Gonzo's height, without arms and much thinner. It had feathers around its head, puffed out like a fan, and a long, black beak that looked like it could snap a person in half.

"I've seen one of these dragons eat five men in under a minute," Mick said, staring ahead. "Don't take your eyes off of it."

Gonzo took two steps forward, still grumbling. The dragon did the same, beating its wings and prancing from side to side.

"Stay here," Mick said, slowly moving his rifle off of his shoulder.

"You're just going to make it angry!" Mira hissed.

Mick ignored her, taking aim and firing a shot, hitting a tree behind the bird dragon.

It spun, so quickly Mira almost missed it, before turning back at them.

Mick's eyes were locked on the beast. "You need to take Gonzo and fly out."

"No!" She was not going to leave Mick to be eaten by an electric bird dragon.

Mick took another two shots and the dragon spun around, screeching and sending its electric shocks into the trees behind them.

The trees burst into flames, and the dragon kept its back turned to them, doing its taunting dance at the perceived threat behind it.

Mira took her chance. "Gonzo, go get it!"

Gonzo leapt forward, taking flight and blasting a flame before crashing into the beast. Mira heard the crunch of bones and groaned.

A moment later, Gonzo dropped the dragon's limp carcass at her feet, tail wagging.

"Good boy," she said, trying not to look down.

Mick ran, throwing everything into their bag and grabbing her by the hand. "Let's not wait for the next one."

"Okay, okay." She tapped Gonzo and he lowered his neck.

They both hopped on and Gonzo jumped off the cliff, gracefully gliding down, floating above the jagged rocks being crushed by the waves.

Mick leaned forward at the same moment Mira turned around, their faces almost colliding. For a second, she thought he was going to kiss her. She was surprised by her disappointment when he didn't.

"We don't need ambrosia," he said. "We can go back to Nordavia now. I can protect you and Gonzo."

Mira's heart was still pounding, and with him so close, it only made it worse.

"I can't," she finally said. "I have to do this."

He said nothing more, and they flew on.

. . .

Past the mountains, they reached the edges of a thick, deciduous forest. More than once, a dragon emerged from the trees, all fire and fury, but Mira refused to engage in another fight. Whenever she heard or sensed any movement, she directed Gonzo to fly north, over the sea.

It slowed their progress, but each time the dragons withdrew into the treetops and left them alone. Mira could tell Gonzo was getting tired, though, and once they caught sight of the river, she directed him to land and gave him a break.

"Stay alert," Mick said, rifle at the ready.

Mira slipped off of Gonzo's back and gave him a quick hug before walking after Mick. "You're a terrible shot. Maybe I should carry the rifle."

"I wasn't trying to hit the dragon." He froze, motioning for her to stop.

She did, but Gonzo kept noisily bounding behind her. She put a hand in front of his face to stop him, too.

Mick listened for a moment, scanning the trees before waving her on. "I was aiming for the rocks behind the dragon to disorient it."

"Ah. I was going to say he looked too fast to be hit."

"He was, and his skin too thick."

Yikes. She hadn't thought of that.

They walked for another half hour, quiet and tense. Even Gonzo caught onto the change in mood. He followed closely behind Mira, nudging her every so often and letting out low whines.

"It's okay," she whispered. "We're going for a walk, okay?"

A half hour into their walk, Mick stopped and pointed at the scene ahead. "There, do you see it? Where the river opens."

She nodded. "Where's the ambrosia?"

"There were pools near the riverbed. Orange flowers grew at the edges. That's what I remember – the flowers."

Gonzo, who had been staring into the forest, crouched low and let out a deep grumble. Mira and Mick turned to look at him, trying to see what he saw, and a moment later, a brown furry beast the size of a grizzly bear charged from the forest, teeth bared.

Mira screamed and Mick pulled her back, taking aim with his rifle just as three more of the creatures ran from the forest. They had furry snouts, like Gonzo, but their limbs were short and stout, with thick paws and curved claws.

Two took off, their black wings pumping furiously as they hovered over Gonzo, shooting flames.

Without thinking, Mira ran forward, arm outstretched to grab Gonzo and pull him away. Mick caught her, forcing her back. "You can't fight them, Mira."

"I can't let Gonzo get hurt!"

Gonzo remained crouched low, looking up at his attackers before launching a stream of blue flame into the air. Both dragons fell back, and Gonzo leapt into the air, spreading his wings and letting out an earth-rumbling roar.

Mira felt Mick pulling at her arm and tried to wrestle away. "Let go of me!"

"We have to run," Mick said.

"No."

"He'll follow us, and they'll fall back. They're only protecting their young."

She tried to pull her arm away, but his grip was too firm. Mira looked back to Gonzo. He was on the ground now, wings outstretched and fire rolling in his mouth.

"Come on, boy!" she yelled before turning and running as fast as her legs could carry her.

The grass along the riverbed was soaked and swampy. Mud splattered and splashed as they ran, some reaching her face as they wildly tore through.

Mira stopped and looked back at Gonzo. He was still posturing, still growling. "Gonzo!"

Mick put two fingers in his mouth and let out a loud, sharp whistle. Gonzo turned his head, wagged his tail, and ran after them.

"Why doesn't he fly?" Mira muttered, but with each one of his enormous steps he got closer, and the panic in her chest receded.

One of the grizzly dragons pursued Gonzo by air, stopping not fifteen feet from the rest of the pack, spraying flames into the sky and roaring. It sounded more like an elephant than a bear or a dragon, but Mira was just glad it stayed away.

They jumped onto Gonzo's back and ran off, leaving the angry pack behind. Within a few minutes, they'd lost sight of the river entirely and had only the lake at their side.

It was so wide that Mira couldn't see the other shore. The water was a dark blue, almost black, with faint ripples at the surface. She didn't want to find out what lurked beneath.

Once it felt like the immediate danger had settled, she asked, "Did we miss the ambrosia?"

Mick let out a grunt. "I don't know. I didn't see any orange flowers."

She kept her eyes straight ahead as she mouthed a quiet *are you kidding me* to herself. They were going to die out here looking for these orange flowers.

Mira turned. "Should we take off and look from above?"

"It'll be too hard to see. If we keep going, we'll find something."

They continued on, with Gonzo slowing to more of a trot after he'd caught his breath and taken a drink from the lake.

They were wasting time, and every minute dragged. Mira could hear far too much activity from the forest – rustling, squealing, breaking branches. There was life all around them, and she didn't like it.

After an agonizing mile of straining to look for the orange flowers, Mira heard the sound of a roar. She didn't even turn to look at where it came from. She told Gonzo to fly, and off he went, jumping with one bound and getting them into the air above the lake.

Whatever beast had cried out didn't come after them, and they coasted above the water and across the lake.

"We shouldn't fly so low," Mick warned. "Something could jump out of the water and –"

"We're sitting ducks no matter where we go," Mira snapped.

He was right, though, and she leaned back, causing Gonzo to pull up higher before leveling out.

She was generally a poor judge of height, but she thought they were high enough to avoid being eaten by a jumping water beast.

Or at least that was what she told herself.

They flew in zigzags, staring down at the shores, looking hopefully at anything orange. Mira's heart leapt when she saw a small patch of orange on the distant bank, only to realize it was a flock of birds.

When they reached the edge of the lake, Mira was starting to feel panicked. "What else can we do? Where else can we go?"

"The pools may have dried up." Mick kept his eyes focused, constantly scanning the ground below.

Her panic only grew. What were they going to do? Fly around until something killed them? It seemed less and less likely they were going to find anything.

They needed the ambrosia, though. Nothing worked without it.

Mira let out a deep sigh, shielding her eyes and looking out at the southern shores of the lake. Tree-covered mountain peaks towered above the water there, jagged and steep. Would they have to cross those mountains, too? What was on the other side?

Mira leaned, causing Gonzo to bank and turn north again. Out of the corner of her eye, she spotted something.

"Hang on," she yelled, leaning in and getting Gonzo to turn. "There!"

Ahead of them sat a grassy plain, and touching the edge of the forest was a meadow covered in poppy-orange flowers.

"Do you see it?" she asked.

"That might be it."

Mira guided Gonzo to the field and he landed, panting slightly. "You need a break, huh, buddy?"

He leaned into her pets, closing his eyes for a moment before stretching his great paws and walking off. Mira followed him, eyes on the ground for puddles and pools.

The ambrosia ended up being impossible to miss. Gonzo came upon it first, a pond the size of a sedan, its golden yellow waters glistening in the sun. It paired beautifully with the flowers.

Unlike the forest on the other edge of the shore, the forest on this side was silent. Mira didn't even hear a bird; the only sound was the wind blowing through the knee-high flowers.

Gonzo stuck his nose down close, took a breath, and sneezed.

Mira laughed. "Not good, then?"

"This is it." Mick was already on his knees, dumping water from the flasks. Mira joined him, taking the empty flasks and submerging them in the shallow pool.

Gonzo bumped her in the shoulder and whined.

"Hang on," she said, pulling out her first ambrosia-filled flask.

He pushed her again, almost knocking her into the pool.

"Gonzo!" She turned to look at him and noticed he was holding his front paw up. Mira leaned in and reached a hand forward. There were shards of something on his paw, and Mira brushed off a large chunk. It was hard and smooth, covered in a gooey substance.

"Ew! What did you get into, Gonzy?" she muttered, wiping it away. "It looks like you stepped on a giant egg."

She froze and looked up. In the darkness of the trees, a pair of red eyes watched them, each one the size of a window.

Her heart dropped into her stomach. "Mick..."

He was on his third flask, tightening the cap and throwing it into his bag. "We should save one for water."

A thunderous roar drowned out her response, and a flurry of red scales and red flame came at them.

Gonzo leapt in front of Mira, the flames hitting his side. He let out a shriek, and the smell of burnt fur filled the air.

The dragon emerged from the trees, standing on its hind legs, nearly two stories tall. Its body was covered with red and black scales, and its claws were grabbing and swiping at Gonzo.

Gonzo leapt forward into the trees to escape, but the dragon was surprisingly fast, latching onto the tip of Gonzo's tail with its teeth. Gonzo cried out again, crashing into the ground at the base of the mountain lake.

Mira ran, legs on fire, to Gonzo's side as the attacking dragon landed and swiped a claw at her.

It got so close that Mira felt the air rush past her face. She leaned back, falling to the ground, and the dragon snapped its jaws at her.

Gonzo spat a blue flame at the dragon, forcing it back before he stepped over Mira, covering her with his body.

"Mira, get out of there!" Mick yelled, a hundred feet behind them. He fired a shot, and the round bounced off the dragon's scales like a pebble.

Gonzo was in a stare-off when the larger dragon lunged at him, mouth open. He avoided the attack, then threw his own flame back at the beast.

Mira felt a tug on her leg. It was Mick. "Come on now."

"I can't leave Gonzo," she yelled just as the dragon's tail whipped around, its spiked end hitting Mick in the chest.

He fell to the ground and the dragon moved on, snapping at Gonzo and taking swipes with its scythe-like claws. Gonzo shot his flame, but each time the beast danced around him, just out of reach. It leapt into the air, flapping its enormous wings, kicking up dirt and leaves, then landed behind them.

Gonzo turned, still covering Mira, and at that moment, the dragon took hold of Gonzo's neck.

"No!" Mira screamed, getting up and running at the dragon's flank.

There was a flutter of wings and a gust of air knocked her to the ground. The monster dragon screamed, releasing Gonzo and retreating backward.

Mira looked up from the ground to see flames roasting the dragon from above, the heat unbearable even from a distance.

She stumbled back, trying to get a better look. Flying above them were five other dragons, dragons who looked like Gonzo, with black, shining fur and blue flames.

The red dragon tried to shield itself with its wings, but the flames were too much, burning the skin of one wing entirely through. It dragged itself back into the forest, the dragons in hot pursuit.

In the silence, Mira heard Gonzo let out a whimper. She ran to him, and Mick wasn't far behind.

"He's hurt," Mira said, a sob escaping her throat. She ran her hands over the punctures in his neck, the blood streaming out in spurts.

"I can heal him." Mick dropped his bag and gun before placing both hands on Gonzo's neck. He shut his eyes as his hands glowed yellow, then orange.

Mira watched, tears streaming from her eyes, as the wounds slowly stopped bleeding, then pinched together, as if made of dough.

Gonzo's head was down, his eyes barely open. Mira ran to him, kissing his snout. "I'm so sorry, Gonzo. I'm so sorry."

He peeked open his eyes and licked her, his tongue like a slab of sandpaper dragging across her arm and face.

"Oh Gonzo..." she sobbed, arms wrapped around his head.

"He's not bleeding anymore," Mick said quietly. "We should go. I'll get on first. I can heal him as we fly."

"He can't fly," she whimpered, running her hands down his neck. The wounds were gone, but he was still laying there, weak.

"There's a string of islands nearby. It's not far." He patted Gonzo on the neck. "You're all right, eh boy?"

Gonzo lifted his head and let out a huff.

Mick patted him again before gingerly climbing onto his back. "He's alive, for now. We need to get away."

Mick lowered a bloody hand for Mira, and she reached up with her own shaking, bloodstained hands.

Gonzo stood, unsteadily at first, before taking a few limping steps forward. Mira gave the command, and they took off.

33

The market

They glided over the ocean, Mick at the helm, healing whatever wounds he could reach on Gonzo while directing him away from the setting sun.

Mira felt sick whenever she looked at Gonzo's side. His fur was singed off, the skin beneath blistered and red, and his left wing was ripped in spots.

He still managed to fly, and soon after they'd cleared the Isle of Dragons, another island appeared in the distance. It was no larger than a few city blocks, and though Mira couldn't see any dragons, she doubted she'd ever feel safe again. Mick assured her there were no known instances of dragons on this island, and he had Gonzo land on the sandy beach below.

Despite his injuries, Gonzo managed to touch down gracefully, his paws sinking into the wet, white sand. Mira slipped off his back and ran her hands over his sides, his legs, and his tail. The worst damage on his neck had been healed, but the burns on the left side of his body looked raw.

Mick walked down to the waterline and stooped to rinse his hands in the water. He returned a moment later and began working, first placing his hands on the burns, then onto Gonzo's wing.

His hands didn't look as bright as they had before, but they still glowed, healing the areas one small bit at a time. Mick himself had sustained a blow, a deep gash into his shoulder that had flowed freely and soaked his torn shirt with blood.

The blood was dried now, and when Mira asked if he was badly injured he just shook his head, eyes focused on the task in front of him.

Mira watched anxiously, less tearful now but still feeling shaky. Her only consolation was that Gonzo appeared not to be in pain. He slept through the healing, his ears and paws twitching with dreams.

It took over two hours for Mick to fully mend Gonzo. His burnt skin ended up pink and clean, the punctures on his neck scabbed over, and even his wing blossomed with patches of new dark skin.

Once Mira was done searching for any hidden wounds, she walked down the beach where Mick was splashing seawater onto his chest.

His wound had reopened, seeping into the water in a faint red haze. He raised his hand, barely flickering now, to his chest, and the edges of the gash slowly came together.

"Are you okay?" Mira asked.

He stood to face her, nodding. "Fine." The bags under his eyes had darkened to a deep plum, and his lips looked like pale rose petals, almost white in the center and pink only at the edges.

"I didn't know you could heal," she said.

He nodded. "It's a marking the Council fiercely controls."

"Why didn't you heal Arianna?"

"Childbirth is a different skill. The Council guards it even more intensely." Hand shaking, he pulled a cigarette from his pocket and lit it. "Are you hungry?"

She shook her head. "You don't look so good. How about you take a nap with Gonzo?"

"I'm all right."

"Mick, you need a break. You look like you're half dead."

He let out a puff of smoke. "I would be dead, if not for Gonzo. You would be, too."

She looked back at Gonzo, still snoozing, his tail now tucked under his snout, his white, fluffy chest stained with dried blood. "I know."

Mick took another drag of the cigarette, then turned, walking down the beach. "I'll be back."

She wanted to stop him, but the adrenaline was out of her veins and every muscle in her body felt weak. Instead she walked along the beach, collecting pieces of bone-white driftwood for a fire.

Mira didn't know how to start a fire, but it kept her busy. Every time she walked by Gonzo, she gave him a hug, or a kiss, and told him he was a good boy. He wagged his tail each time she passed, and after an hour or so, he started to wake up and lift his head.

She dropped her batch of sticks and stroked behind his ear. "No more dragons. Okay, bud?"

He stared, blinking slowly and concentrating on her. Even if he didn't know the words, he liked hearing her voice.

Sara used to laugh about it, asking, "Why do you talk to him so much? He doesn't understand what you're saying."

Mira refused to entertain Sara's doubts. "He gets the gist. That's all that matters."

That had been the hardest part of Gonzo having cancer. It wasn't the chemo – he'd spend an hour at the clinic every few weeks, then come bounding out from the treatment room, full of glee, as if it had never happened.

It wasn't the difficulty she had getting time off work, or the snide comments people made, or even the money. Mira didn't care about those things at all.

The hardest part was the last week, the last day, the last hour, when she knew the cancer had returned, when she knew he was in pain and he wouldn't be getting better.

It was when she had to say goodbye, but she couldn't say goodbye, because he didn't understand that word.

Instead she'd had to kneel, pressing her snotty face against his soft fur, whispering that they were going to go to the park soon, and that he'd get to see squirrels, that he was getting chicken for dinner and after that, they'd play with his favorite ball.

She repeated these things, over and over, stroking his silken fur and repeating how good he was until the vet made the last injection, and Gonzo closed his eyes for the final time. He drifted off, his head filled with all the ways she knew to tell him "I love you."

The memory of it rushed back to her now and she burst into tears, as she always did whenever she thought of him lying there, fighting to keep his eyes open.

Gonzo, all strength and fire now, leaned into her, nudging her for more pets.

She laughed, wiping away her tears, and raised her arm to scratch under his chin. He closed his eyes, savoring the moment, and she kissed him again.

It didn't matter if he couldn't understand everything she said. Gonzo had gotten her message that day, just as she'd gotten his message today.

She kept petting him until Mick returned with three large fish strung around his neck. "Do you think he's hungry?"

The skin on her face was tight and dry, streaked with tears and dirt, and her nose was completely stuffed. She hurriedly wiped it away, appreciating that Mick not called attention to it. "I'm sure he is."

"I'll get a fire going, then."

"Are you feeling any better?"

Mick pulled a lighter from his pocket. "Sure."

He didn't look better. Mira watched him, crouched low as he built a standing mound of wood. It was remarkable how he pushed past his physical limits, though she wondered if he had the ability to challenge any of his emotional limits.

Perhaps that had been locked away after the death of his brother, or his parents, or his wife, and now all he did was carry that flask around, and smoke cigarettes, and crack jokes.

No longer the boy in the picture indeed.

Mick built the fire quickly and roasted the fish before leaving to catch more. When he returned with an enormous three-foot fish, he cooked it and offered a filet to Gonzo.

"Little small for him," he said, "but it should help rebuild his strength."

Mira smiled. "It's nice of you to think of him."

She called Gonzo over and he stood, tail in a low wag, and walked over. He was no longer limping, which made Mira feel marginally better.

Mick tried to pass the fish off to Mira, but she shook her head. Gonzo leaned forward and delicately pinched the offering with his front teeth before pulling it away.

"He's gentle," Mick said in a quiet voice.

"Yes. Gonzo's always been a gentleman."

Mick returned, taking a seat next to Mira and offering her a hunk of fish.

She accepted, eating it and watching Gonzo closely until she was confident he was getting better.

She turned back to look at Mick, who had been silent this entire time – tending the fire, flipping the food. The sun was nearly set now, and the light from the flames danced on the high cheekbones of his face.

He really was handsome. The proposals made sense from that alone...

After some time, he returned and sat next to Mira, staring into the flames. "He saved me, too."

"He did, but I hope we never see anything like that dragon again." She paused. "And that pack of Gonzo dragons? Had you seen dragons like him before?"

He shook his head. "My last visit was not a long one."

Gonzo settled in behind Mira and she leaned against him. He kept his snout pointed toward Mick, waiting for more bites of fish, which Mick continued passing over.

"I'm sorry we almost died," Mira finally said.

Mick picked up his bag and tossed it over. "It's done. And now you have enough ambrosia to take over Pontos."

"Really?" She peered inside, counting four flasks filled with the amber liquid.

"Not really." For the first time that night, he smiled. "It'll help you, though, whatever you decide to do. My family lived the last fifteen years with less than half a flask of ambrosia. It only takes a drop to extract a marking."

She pulled a flask out and weighed it in her hand. "Huh. All this liquid gold."

He broke his gaze and turned to put more wood on the fire. "I suspect we can get back to Nordavia tomorrow, if Gonzo is strong enough. I'll put word onto the market we have ambrosia to sell."

"The market? Is this a black market?"

He let out a laugh before pulling out another cigarette.

Mira put the flask back into the bag and something caught her eye — a small golden ring.

"What's this?" she asked, pulling it out.

He tossed another treat to Gonzo. "It's nothing."

Mira sat up and slanted it toward the flames. Inside the ring was an intricate etching of a dog. "It's beautiful."

"I'm glad you think so."

She looked up at him. "Is it magic?"

"It's a ring." The flames danced on his face, his eyes locked on hers. "Made of gold."

She looked down at the ring, then back at him. Her heart took off again. "Oh."

"You were right," he added.

Should she slip it on? It looked like it would fit. "About what?"

He lit the cigarette over the fire. "About taking Gonzo with you. You need him, and I have a place for him where no one will find him."

She kept her eyes focused on the ring in her hand. The gold had the slightest hints of rose in it. "Thank you."

They sat in silence and Mira studied the ring in the firelight. After what they'd just been through, it should have been easier to talk to him about what it meant, or what he'd intended.

Yet he said nothing, and she didn't know what to say, so she also sat in silence for some time.

It seemed Mick would rather face another dragon than talk about it, though, so she forced herself to speak. "Did you bring this for me?"

He looked up at her and nodded once.

Her heart skipped a beat. He hadn't been joking, then. As much as she'd enjoyed flirting and joking around with him, she hadn't imagined what it would be like to actually have his affections. It was overwhelming, like finding out she'd just inherited a castle – one that was far from home.

Mira tore her eyes away from him and back to the ring. The dog inside looked so much like Gonzo. "I thought you were going to marry Leona."

Mick was quiet for a moment. He finished his cigarette and tossed the butt into the fire. "Marrying Leona would be an insult to Ella's memory."

Mira cleared her throat. "How did she die?"

"I killed her," he said, not skipping a beat. "For crossing me. No one gets away with crossing Mickson Kellet."

Mira leaned back, making sure to avoid Gonzo's recent burns. "I don't believe you."

He shot her a glance and smirked. "My parents became obsessed, almost mad, after my brother was killed. They were looking for clues, desperate for answers. Ella wanted to help them."

"What were your parents doing?"

He let out a heavy sigh. "Everything. Tramping through the forest at all hours of the night, threatening villagers, threatening officials. They stopped sleeping, they stopped eating. It was madness. Absolute madness."

"They blamed themselves."

He nodded. "No one could get through to them, and I refused to entertain it. When Ella got a tip that someone had information about my brother's death, she didn't tell me. She told my mother, who told my father, and they took off in the dead of night. It was in the middle of the forest that they were robbed, then killed."

Mira gasped. "That's awful."

He stood and removed the last fish from the flames, offering to Mira. She shook her head, and he turned, holding it up to Gonzo's snout. Gonzo moved quickly to snap up the food and this time, Mick didn't flinch.

"When Ella found out what had happened, she hung herself."

Mira stared at him, the flames highlighting every line in his face. "Mick. I'm so sorry."

He reached forward, petting Gonzo between the eyes. "I found the man who killed my parents. Got the information I needed. He'd been paid off by a Council member to make it look like a random attack."

"But why?"

Mick shrugged. "They asked too many questions and called too much attention to the pillories. The Council didn't want people questioning why their letters were being read. They didn't want people to know my brother lost his life over a joke about a pegasus named Dragon."

She didn't know what to say, so she sat, listening to the crackling of the fire.

"You don't have to marry me," he finally said. "It's an option. That's all."

If it weren't the worst proposal she'd ever heard, she would have kissed him. She might do it anyway.

"I appreciate the offer, Mick." She took a breath. Now wasn't the time to kiss him. There was no need for mixed messages. "My bolt is still glowing. Barely, but it's here. I might have a chance to go back."

"Good." He nodded, then shut his eyes. He looked so tired. "That's good for you."

Mira didn't know what else to say, or what to do. She was mentally exhausted, her mind still spinning around what they had to do to survive.

It seemed like Mick was done with the topic, so after a minute, she forced her way beneath Gonzo's paw. "I'll see you in the morning?"

"In the morning," he repeated, not opening his eyes.

34

An opportunity

The view from his Magnifico Island office was exquisite. Evander had suspected his career in academia had held him back on Earth, but now he had the evidence to prove it. He'd achieved much more in this new life, and the perks never ended.

Just outside of his window was the sprawling metropolis of Verity. It reminded him of a more manageable Manhattan – the buildings weren't as tall, but they were beautiful, all made with custom stone by the finest artists and architects. The streets were wide and always clean, now especially gleaming since he'd led the initiative to pave them with a magical type of gold a decade ago.

Unlike the rest of Asphodavia, the citizens of Verity drove cars, so there was no risk of horse manure lingering near the sidewalks. The shops were perfect, the department stores all at the level of Harrods, which he'd visited twice in his time on Earth, and the people dressed properly. It was paradise on Pontos.

The other side of the Council Building offered a sweeping view of the ocean, the white sand beaches only steps away. When he could tear himself away from his work, Evander walked the short trip to gaze upon the splendor.

It was as perfect as a society could be. Evander had made sure of it. He was the chess grandmaster of the world, moving the pieces into play, anticipating any downfalls and righting any wrongs.

That particular day he was contemplating another walk to the beach to clear his mind. The status of their ambrosia supplies was worrying the other Council members, but Evander knew better than to become emotional. He kept a cool head, no matter what, and the solutions always came to him.

He'd just changed into beach attire – a silken shirt and his favorite red speedo, a new fashion he'd introduced to the world last summer – when he heard a knock at his office door.

"Come in." It was important to never make his subordinates feel unwelcome, even if they rarely did anything useful.

"Apologies, sir," Ignatius said, tipping his hat. "I just now received a report I believed deserved your immediate attention."

Evander turned away from his view of the city. Ignatius was his newest deputy, still years away from understanding how things worked, but he had good instinct, and he was loyal. That was enough for now. "Yes?"

He handed him a stack of papers. "These are reports of increased ambrosia sales on Nordavia in the last two weeks, sir. Our sources believe a new well must have been discovered, based on the quantities."

Evander flipped through the pages, skimming. It wasn't his job to bother with details. "Any idea who is behind it?"

"Yes, sir. We believe Mickson Kellet is the supplier."

"Ah, such a thorn. He's hardly offered us any supply in the last few months. I thought we were close to eliminating him."

"We are, sir. It seemed his ambrosia had run out. But now – "

"Yes, things have changed," Evander snapped. "I'm not a fool."

"Sorry, sir."

Evander took a breath, striding to the window. "He has a sister, doesn't he? Perhaps it's time to make an example of them both."

"Good idea, sir."

"Let's put together a party. Bring along a battalion, remind the people of Nordavia what hiding ambrosia will do to them."

Ignatius made a curt nod. "Of course, sir. Should I round up a group of marked soldiers as well?"

"I can't see why we would need them," Evander said, his tone recovered from his outburst.

"Of course, sir."

He disappeared from the office and Evander smiled to himself. The walk had been a good idea after all.

35

Hello again

Life on Mick's farm wasn't all bad. Mira and Gonzo had a barn to themselves, complete with an underground cellar that housed many of Mick's most valuable aions. It was quiet there, with acres and acres of rolling fields, and at the border of the property was a dense forest. It was filled with squirrels and flying raccoons, and Mira and Gonzo were free to explore it undisturbed.

The calm allowed Gonzo to heal fully, which Mira appreciated, but she was starting to get stir-crazy. There were only so many pretty sunsets and late-night flights she could enjoy. She spent the rest of her time sitting in the tall blowing grasses and watching as her bolt grew dimmer by the day.

Mick stopped in whenever he could, leaving her food and updating her on his progress in selling off the ambrosia, as well as telling her about any new markings he was able to procure.

"This one is a favorite for hand-to-hand combat. Allows for speed and agility." He handed the glowing aion to her, then pulled another from his pocket. "I'm told this prevents bullets and arrows from piercing the skin, but we'll have to test it first."

"There's one I'd like to take back with me," Mira said with a smile. "Have you heard anything about Alice?"

Mick nodded. "She's alive."

That wasn't as comforting as she had hoped. "Nothing about where she's being kept?"

"No." He dropped a stack of papers on the ground in front of her. "It seems the Council doesn't have enough ambrosia to extract more than a few aions per Traveler, so they'll keep her alive for now."

Mira leaned down, picking up the top paper from the stack. It had a picture of her smiling broadly on stage in Tartarus. The headline beneath it read **The Traveler Spy.**

"That's a new one," she said before ripping it in two.

He stared at her, a half-smile on his face. "In case you start thinking about disguising yourself to go into town again."

She groaned. "I just wanted a little excitement."

"Your face is hung up all over Laurium. You going into town would be more than a little excitement."

He was right, and she knew it.

Still, despite Mick's scolding, Mira started pushing her luck. A few days after he'd dropped off the pile of propaganda, she took Gonzo on a night trip.

Under the cover of darkness, they explored the edges of the island, flying high above Laurium and as far as New Belgium, watching from the mountaintops as the townspeople slept.

On her way back to the barn, she spotted something unusual. One of the main roads into Laurium was filled with cars, their headlights illuminating the path in front of them in one continuous line.

Mira counted over eighty cars, and when she dipped lower to get a better look, she almost flew directly on top of a man on a pegasus.

Thankfully, he didn't notice a thing. He continued flying on, head focused on the parade below.

Mira flew back to the farm, telling herself she'd give Mick until the morning to report what was going on.

Unfortunately, he didn't show. He hadn't been by in days, and the coin he'd given her to communicate with him had been lost when she was sent to the Isle of Dragons.

It was too tempting for her to sit and wait. The parade of cars looked far too similar to when Alice had been taken – the open convertibles, the extravagant colors. It looked like visitors from Magnifico.

Either they were coming to take another Traveler, or they'd just brought one back. Mira wasn't going to miss the action.

After the sun rose, she secured Gonzo to a post with an enchanted leash Mick had gotten for her. It was supposed to be strong enough to pull a thousand ships, completely fireproof, and sealed to the earth with magic.

"Stay here. Okay, bud?" She walked away slowly, relieved to see Gonzo didn't struggle against the leash much. He pulled after her, then let out a sigh and laid down to wait.

Outside of the barn, she tied her hair back, donned a dark hooded cloak Mick had given her, and set out on her way.

• • •

The sun was past its midpoint when she reached Laurium. She wasn't used to traveling on foot anymore, and skulking under the cloak in the heat was exhausting.

Still, she declined three offers from farmers to give her a ride into town. It was too risky. Mick was right – her face was plastered everywhere. Her being sent to the Isle of Dragons had been treated like the greatest victory the Council had had in years.

Her walk revealed more than that, though. What Mick had failed to tell her was that there were other posters, ones that supported her. They were few and far between, but the message was consistent: why had this Traveler been sent to her death? How could one individual be a threat to such a powerful Council?

Mira knew whoever created those posters had risked their life to do it. The drawings of her were flattering, showing her with big, blue eyes and entirely tamed hair. On the lapel of her now famous purple jumpsuit was a small pendant of a three-faced woman.

The closer she got to the town square, the more crowded the streets became. Horses and carriages could no longer get through, and Mira had to push to catch sight of the fountain. She ended up standing behind a wall of people, and though she could see a number of officials, including Ferdinand, the scene in front of her was still unclear.

"What's going on?" she asked the person next to her, careful to keep her face obscured.

"The Council's come back into town," the woman said, not looking up at her.

"Did they bring a Traveler?" Mira asked, still straining to catch a glimpse of Alice, wherever they might be keeping her.

"No. They've caught Arianna Kellet. Took them long enough."

Mira forgot herself and turned towards the woman. "Arianna? Why? What has she done?"

"She caused the bloodshed on Violet Island," the woman said, shaking her head. "And she's been hiding an ambrosia well." She paused, her eyes scanning Mira's face.

Mira ducked her head and tried to move, only to find she was blocked from behind by the ever-growing crowd. She pushed her way through shoulders and chests, using her height to her advantage until her cloak got caught and her hood was pulled back, exposing her glorious auburn ponytail.

She struggled to put her hood back up, but the cries already started.

"Is that Mira Meadows?"

"Grab her! Grab the spy!"

She tried to escape, she tried to push her way through, but a gaggle of deputies rushed in, parting the crowd, and dragged her to the town square. They dumped her at Ferdinand's feet, his mouth hanging open in shock.

Now Mira had quite a view. The rear end of the square was boxed in by convertible Magnifico cars, all shining in the sun and loaded with deputies in green outfits. The deputies had rifles, lazily hanging at their sides or laid across the hoods of their cars. The cars went back as far as she could see, winding down the streets and around the corners.

Mira got up from her knees and cleared her throat. "Constable, I'm not a spy. I'm not – "

"How can this be?" He clapped a hand over his mouth and slowly shook his head.

Mira was trying to decide how best to respond when she heard a humming sound. She looked up and spotted a square, perfectly white box, so shiny in the sun that it was almost blinding. It was about the size of a ski lift seat, and she had the absurd thought that she'd see a pair of skis sticking out of the bottom.

Then the thought hit her that it may be another one of those flying sarcophaguses – prettier, but just as dangerous, and headed straight for her.

She turned, trying to run, but she tripped, and the next time she looked up, a tuft of white hair was just visible out of the top of the box.

Her chest felt heavy, and she stumbled to her feet as a pair of sickeningly green eyes came into view, then a small nose, followed by a pinched smile.

Wesley, hovering like a god on a cloud.

36

A shadow from above

Wesley snapped his fingers and two deputies rushed forward, grabbing Mira by the arms and forcing her to the ground.

She struggled against them, kicking and thrashing, as Wesley's box lowered itself directly on top of her leg. The weight was crushing, and she let out a scream.

"Oh dear." The front of the box popped open and Wesley stepped out, shaking his head at her. "My apologies." He smiled, low so only she could see it, before moving the box with a wave of his hand.

She let out a gasp. Her instinct was to run, but she came crashing down as soon as she tried to stand. Her leg couldn't support her weight, sending shockwaves of pain through her body.

Mira's mind went blank, and she felt like a mouse in front of a cat. Wesley maintained his calm demeanor and his vapid smile. It was worse than the dragon she'd faced at the ambrosia pools. He was an empty, soulless vessel with the practiced smile of a politician.

"Good people of Nordavia!" Wesley's voice boomed over the crowd, amplified by a floating gold ball. "I am Evander Kagan, sent by the Council just in time, it seems. Mira, the murderous Traveler who hid in your ranks for far too long, has returned."

A few boos came out of the crowd, and a man ten feet away spat at her. Mira glared at him as she struggled to drag herself further from Wesley.

There was nowhere to go. All the people surrounding them were glaring down at her. Some waved their fists and yelled, while others just shook their heads.

Mira recognized some of these people. They'd cheered at her spectacles, they'd patted her on the back. Now they'd transitioned seamlessly into the angry mob she'd once feared.

She changed course, dragging herself toward the fountain and away from their jeering faces. With each movement her leg blistered with pain, and when she finally reached the fountain, she laid back against it, panting.

From there, she caught sight of another familiar face – John from the Hecate Society.

He wasn't dressed in his usual loud colors, instead sporting a drab tan ensemble, but it was him. His face was creased in a frown, and he was whispering to the man next to him.

"The Council is here to protect you from these sorts of threats." He paused, looking down and shaking his head at her. "I can only imagine the extensive conspiracy it took to remove Mira from the Isle of Dragons."

"There wasn't any conspiracy," Mira yelled. "You're a liar."

Wesley laughed. "We have just caught Arianna Kellet stealing resources from the good people of Laurium. She's been hiding magic, stealing ambrosia and empowering dangerous Travelers to –"

Wesley's words were drowned out by a booming roar from above. Mira looked up, catching sight of a black tail disappearing into the clouds.

A woman shrieked and a stampede broke out. People rushed away from the square, spilling into the streets, even running on top of the deputies' cars as they tried to get away.

There was no way. It couldn't be Gonzo. It was impossible.

And yet it sounded like Gonzo!

She hoisted herself up on the stones surrounding the fountain. Amongst the cries, Mira could swear she heard people yelling the word *dragon*.

People ran past, one even knocking Wesley to the ground. He shouted, his voice full of rage, and commanded the deputies to do something.

Mira looked up again, scanning the sky and the buildings, desperate to see if it were true, but something struck her cheek and sent her toppling to the ground.

"I don't know what tricks you have," Wesley muttered, kneeling next to her. "But you're not getting away again."

The deputies encircled them, creating an area free of the stampede. Anyone who came close was shoved or beaten.

"I have half of the Magnifico forces behind me. It's over, Mira."

She picked her head up, wiping the blood from her eyes, trying to focus on the sky above. Just over Wesley's shoulder, she caught another glimpse of black fur.

"Over here!" she yelled, her heart feeling like it was going to burst in her chest.

Gonzo emerged from the clouds like a shadow.

The square was nearly cleared out, except for Wesley's deputies, who ran off in droves once they saw what was barreling toward them.

"What is that?" Wesley demanded. "Call it off!"

"I can't."

Gonzo touched down, clipping the roof of a nearby building with his tail and sending a few clay shingles crashing to the ground. The leash was still around his neck, the end of it frayed. He'd chewed through it.

"This isn't real," Wesley insisted, grabbing Mira by the arm and dragging her toward his white box. "Is this your marking? Making people see things?"

In a moment, Gonzo was behind Mira, growling his displeasure and crouching low.

Mira tugged her arm away. "Oh no, Uncle Wes. What you're seeing is real."

She dragged herself closer to Gonzo and watched as Wesley shut himself inside his little box.

"You're not going to do this," he snarled, lifting off swiftly. "You're not going to destroy what I've built."

Just over the side of the box, Mira spied the end of a rifle. She screamed, jumping for cover, and heat exploded from behind her. A dark blue flame hit the box, lighting it on fire just as it disappeared into the clouds.

37

A chance

An eerie stillness hung over the town square. Abandoned cars clogged the streets, some of them with their sputtering engines still running. There wasn't another soul in sight.

Water continued to babble out of the fountain, and Mira sat, trying to focus her mind away from the pain in her leg and onto figuring out what she needed to do.

Somehow she had to get onto Gonzo's back and get out of here. But how? She couldn't stand, and Gonzo was still agitated, panting and looking around, the fur on his neck bristled.

His reaction to Wesley was unreal. Never in his dog life had he tried to bite Wesley – or anyone, for that matter. Yet now, he'd flown in and blasted Wesley's hover box thing without hesitation. Perhaps he saw it as a threat? Or perhaps Pontos had changed him – fire first, ask questions later.

She sat for a moment, trying to absorb this. Wesley couldn't have survived it. Gonzo had engulfed the box in flame, and hit it with such a force that the entire thing had been blown away.

Wesley was dead. Gone. All of his scheming, all the power he'd amassed – erased in an instant.

Mira couldn't wrap her head around it. Would she be able to get Alice now? Arianna too?

Wesley being out of the picture was a good thing. At the same time, everyone had seen Gonzo. The Council could prepare. They could make a plan to hurt him, or to try to capture him.

Before, when Gonzo was still her own secret, she could have shown up and threatened to eat them. Used the element of surprise, flown in and out.

Now what?

It was too much to figure out at the moment, lying in the town square, her mind splintered between panic and pain.

She took a deep breath and forced herself to stand on her good leg. Gonzo leaned into her, and she grabbed two fistfuls of his fluffy white fur to steady herself. "I'm going to need some help. Okay, bud?"

He stood still, tail wagging, as she teetered to the side of the fountain and pulled herself on top of the bricks. With the two-and-a-half-foot boost, she was able to drag herself onto Gonzo's back. She gave the command and they flew off.

• • •

Mira took a shortcut to the barn, flying directly over Mick's house. She spotted his car out front and landed outside of his front door, sending one of the gardeners running in terror.

"Sorry!" she called out. "He's friendly!"

He was long gone, and she could hear screams from inside the house. At least Mick would know she was here.

He emerged from the house a minute later, followed closely by John, still dressed in his drab, non-fabulous, non-Hecate style clothing.

"Mira!" Mick threw his hands up. "What are you doing?"

John stood in the doorway, eyes wide.

"I need to talk to you," she said, shifting her weight and wincing. "And I need your help. Wesley crushed my leg."

The anger drained from Mick's face and he rushed over, hastily providing the head pat Gonzo demanded as he passed.

"Which leg?"

She pointed, and Mick placed one hand on her thigh and one hand on her calf. A chill ran up her spine, and as soon as his hand started glowing, the pain subsided.

No wonder Gonzo had slept through his healing. It was soothing, like getting a massage. Within two minutes, Mick was done, and Mira had to open her eyes.

"Thank you," she said.

He nodded. "Did you see Arianna?"

"No. What happened?"

He let out a sigh. "They've taken her for trial."

"Why?"

"They're claiming she was selling off an ambrosia well that belonged to the Nordavian people."

Mira swung her leg over and slipped down Gonzo's side. "That's ridiculous. She wasn't even involved."

"I know," he said. "They're trying to get to me. They want the rest of the ambrosia."

"Crap."

He looked over his shoulder and lowered his voice. "I was on my way back when something happened, Mira."

"What?"

He popped a cigarette into his mouth. "I heard you scream."

"You were in town?"

Mick held the cigarette at his side, eyes locked on hers. "No. I was miles away, but I knew you were in pain. I felt it."

Mira shifted her weight. It was impossible. Yet at the same time...

"Hang on." She held up a finger, her mind whirring away. "Felt it how?"

Mick putting a hand to his chest. "Here." He took a drag of the cigarette, then let out a puff. "It was like a punch, and it pulled me back to town."

"In your chest? Or..." She almost couldn't say it. Mick's inability to express how he felt had rubbed off on her.

At the same time, waiting around for him at the farm and pining after him for so many hours and nights emboldened her.

"Or was it in your heart?" she asked.

Mick looked up at her, then looked away. "Could've been."

She looked back at Gonzo, whose eyes were fixed on some trees in the distance. Was that how he'd found her, too? Was she marked to be connected to them both? Was it a marking, or love, or –

"Excuse me." John's voice rang out from the doorway. "I don't mean to interrupt, but I was hoping to talk to Mira."

She'd have to figure that out later.

Mira walked around Gonzo, her recently-broken leg feeling gummy and light. "What's up, John?"

"Mira," he said slowly, eyes stuck on Gonzo. "I came here to help Mickson free his sister, but it seems you have become the most powerful woman in Pontos."

"I don't know if that's true."

He nodded, pointing at Gonzo. "Yes, I think it is. Not even the Magnifican army dared face you. Do you know what this means?"

She smiled. "That I can get Alice back?"

"Mira, darling, you can get *everything*."

38

You'll own nothing, and you'll be happy

John went on, babbling about how the Hecate Society had been looking for a way to take back power from the Council for decades.

"With your help, Mira, we can finally do it."

"Do *what?*"

"Take control of the Hall of Magic. Once we have magic, they cannot control us anymore."

She let out a sigh and looked at Mick, but he was avoiding eye contact. "I don't know, John."

"You can unite everyone. With a dragon leading the charge, no one will be afraid. You'll be a hero."

"I'm not trying to be a hero."

"Don't do it for yourself. Do it for Alice, and Arianna, and all of the people who fear for their lives under the Council."

Mira frowned. If Sara were here, she would laugh in John's face. "Get your own dragon," she'd say, and not think twice about it.

John went on. "They keep us afraid, Mira, and that way, they keep everything – the magic, the land, the money, all of the goods and foods. We do all of the work, but reap none of the rewards. With you, we can rise up."

"You don't need me. Or Gonzo," she said. "You outnumber them. They can't fight all of you."

He shook his head. "If only it were that simple. The people don't see it that way. They've been beaten down for so long. They need inspiration. They need you."

Mira wasn't going to sign up to get Gonzo killed. She waved a hand. "Let me think about it."

"Of course." John's eyes lingered on Gonzo for a moment before turning to Mick. "We may be able to save Arianna, Mickson. I'll be back tomorrow."

"Thank you," Mick said.

They watched as he disappeared into a crop of trees at the edge of the property.

"How'd he get here so fast?" Mira asked.

"He flagged my car down. I was on my way into town to find you."

"Ah." Mira absentmindedly turned to stroke Gonzo's neck. To find her? Or to save her – again? "He thinks he can save Arianna?"

"She may not have left the island yet. He says they have a contact." He closed his eyes and leaned his head back. "They won't stop until they destroy us."

"I'll get Arianna," Mira said. "Where are they? I'll fly in and grab her."

"It won't be that easy."

"You didn't see how they scattered like chickens when Gonzo flew into the town square."

"They all saw you, then?"

"Yes, and – "

"Then you either need to fly to Thunder Island right now, or prepare for them to come and kill you."

Mira raised her eyebrows. "Why would they – "

"Evander – Wesley isn't going to let you live, and he's not going to let you keep a dragon."

She crossed her arms. "Wesley's dead. Gonzo turned him into a fireball."

He stared at her for a moment, then said, "Still. He's only one of the Council members. You are their biggest threat now, and they don't handle threats gently."

"You're sounding as dramatic as John."

"Only because I'm telling you something you don't want to hear."

She glared at him. How could he change his mind so quickly? One minute, he'd felt her pain in his *heart* and rushed to her rescue, and the next, he told her to fly off to Thunder Island forever.

It felt like he was pushing her away, and Mira reacted accordingly: full of fire, and without thinking. "So my choices are to run away, abandoning Alice, Arianna, and Gonzo, and go back to Earth right now, or I can try to take over the Hall of Magic?"

"I don't know if you can take the Hall of Magic, but your options disappeared the moment Gonzo came to your rescue."

"Why is the Council turning against you all of a sudden?"

He let out a breath, rubbing his face with his hand. "They know I have ambrosia and have decided to take it by force."

Ah, of course. Her flash of temper waned, and the flame in her chest receded. It was her fault they were coming after him for the ambrosia. It was her fault Arianna was taken.

She knew it, and he knew it. "I'm sorry."

"I am too." He took a seat on the ground against Gonzo and closed his eyes.

Mira sat down next to him. She was used to Mick having all the answers. Now he just looked tired.

"This is my fault."

"No, Mira." He turned to look at her, the bags under his eyes deep and creased. "This is the Council's fault. They believe they are the ultimate, and only, source of truth.

"They decide what we can and cannot say, and soon, what we can and cannot think. They pit us against one another and convince neighbors to report neighbors. They distract us with the dangers of Travelers, or insist our suffering comes from the fact that we're eye-ists in need of reform, or lazy, or weak.

"While people were busy trying to survive, the Council decided how it was best for us to live. They bought all of the land they could, all of the homes, and took control of all of the businesses. They ensured the people of Asphodavia were at their mercy and had to live by their rules. And now?" He shut his eyes and shook his head. "They are only tightening their grip."

Mira stared at him. He hadn't even looked this defeated on the Isle of Dragons.

"You want me to stay and help, then."

He looked up at her, the whites of his eyes red, and a tired smile broke his sullen expression. "I would never ask that of you. You have a life to get back to."

Mira sat back. "You asked me to marry you, sort of. Isn't that the same as asking me to stay?"

He took a breath, his eyes searching her face.

Mira's heart took off, pounding in her chest. She was sick of not knowing how he felt, not knowing what he was thinking. It drove her mad, and for the longest moment, he stared at her, silent as the smile faded from his face.

All she could hear was the wind blowing through the trees and the blood rushing in her ears.

"I wanted to protect you, not trap you," he said, his voice gentle and even. "I can't promise you protection now."

She shifted, and his hand grazed hers.

The heat returned to her chest. This time it wasn't fury or anger, but the overwhelming need to see him smile again, to make him laugh. "But maybe, I could protect you?"

He stood, breaking the trance and dusting off his pants. "It's best if you and Gonzo get back to the barn. We don't need anyone else finding you here."

As badly as she wanted to stay there, staring at him, she knew he was right. "Thanks for the healing."

"I'll stop by, maybe tomorrow. I need to talk to John's contact."

She pulled herself onto Gonzo's back. "I'll be waiting."

39

The Myth of Sisyphus

Mira tried to ignore the frantic feeling in her chest and fly carefully, avoiding roads or any prying eyes who could lead the Council to her door.

Even once they landed in the quiet, cricket-filled field outside of the barn, Mira was unsettled. It didn't feel safe anymore. The Council knew she was alive, and they knew about Gonzo.

What if they had someone who could locate her with magic? Mick had been looking for a Traveler he'd known with that marking to find Alice.

If anyone would have access to such a marking, it would be the Council. They could show up in the dead of night and surprise her, completely surrounding the barn. They could set fire to it if they wanted.

The image was too real in her mind. Mira decided they wouldn't be sleeping in the barn that night. Better to be out in the open, where they could escape quickly if needed.

She called Gonzo over to the edge of the field, a wall of trees at her back. There wouldn't be much sleeping that night, but that was okay. She could deal with that.

What about after tonight, though? She couldn't stay awake every day and every night. That would be a cool marking, but she didn't have it. She had something else – something tied to that petulant heart of hers.

Gonzo spotted a flying raccoon in the forest and took off, leaping into the air and snapping it into his mouth. He returned a moment later, licking his lips and looking quite pleased with himself, before turning three times and settling down with a sigh.

He had the right idea. Mira sat down, settling in against his side, and he wrapped his tail around her. If the Council was preparing to kill her, she at least had this hour to think. Perhaps two. She needed to slow her panicking mind and think through her options.

It all seemed so much easier on the Isle of Dragons. She thought she'd have more time to sort things out. She thought things would become clearer, or that more options would appear.

More options had appeared, in a way. They just happened to be options that resulted in her and Gonzo being killed.

She shifted, pulling Gonzo's fluffy tail closer, and he opened his eyes and focused on her.

That was one of the things that hadn't changed about him. When he was a dog, she used to look over and catch him staring at her. She'd smile, and say his name, and he'd thump his tail on the floor, as if he were bashful about getting caught.

Her dear, sweet mutt. He was her closest companion, he loved her unconditionally, and as Mira sat there, gazing at him, she got dangerously close to facing a truth she'd been avoiding for weeks: he could not come back with her.

Normally, such a harsh truth would evoke a destructive behavior in her, or an obsessive interest in a new hobby, or at the very least, a drastic haircut.

There wasn't time for any of that now. Gonzo's life was in danger, as was hers. Mira's bolt had nearly faded, and while no one could tell her how long she had, she could feel time was running out. She'd watched it fade, day by day, knowing precisely what it meant, even if she didn't dare say it out loud.

Mira had allowed herself to live in this fantasy long enough. It was time to face reality.

She took a deep breath and closed her eyes.

According to Mick, Thunder Island was only a few hours away by air. She and Gonzo could leave in the morning and she'd be back on Earth by dinnertime.

What about Gonzo, though?

She opened her eyes and looked at him. His eyes were firmly shut again, his face relaxed. He was taking deep, slow breaths as he slept, his ears twitching ever so slightly.

The thought of leaving him behind flooded her eyes with tears. Would she even remember finding him again? Would she remember anything about this world, this life?

A sob escaped from her mouth and he opened his eyes.

"It's okay, buddy. You keep sleeping. Good boy."

He nestled in closer, drifting off again, and Mira let out a slow breath.

She could entrust Gonzo to Mick. Maybe Gonzo and Mick could become best of friends, travelling the world, running from their enemies?

No. Gonzo would hate that. He didn't like to travel. He liked to sleep, and he wouldn't want to stay with Mick. He wanted to be with her, always, above all else.

All this time, it had never been a real option for Mira not to go back to Earth. She kept telling herself it was only a matter of time – if only she could get all the boxes checked, if only she could defeat Wesley and help Alice...if only everything worked out perfectly, then she'd go back as if nothing happened.

But things had happened. She'd made friends, and by some miracle, found Gonzo.

It wasn't just that. She'd met Mick.

He floated into her mind's eye and her heart fluttered.

He was so different from Robbie. There was the criminal aspect, of course, but it was more than that. Even when she and Robbie were new and things were exciting, her heart never jumped the way it did with Mick. Robbie had never looked at her the way Mick looked at her.

Despite being an easy plane ride away, Robbie couldn't find the time to visit her. They hadn't seen each other in months, and neither of them were much bothered by it.

Then she'd met Mick. First she was scared he would murder her, then she grew terrified he would shatter her heart, even if she couldn't admit it out loud. It was a different kind of love, and he was a different kind of man – one who rushed to a dragon-infested island to save her.

Still. It wasn't about Robbie. She could break up with him when she got back to her life and find a better match. She could still have the life she envisioned: getting married and having kids, all of that. Whomever she found, they'd grow old together, and they could hold hands in front of the TV watching a show that wasn't even that good, and it wouldn't matter because at least they were together.

That was how her parents had lived, and that was how she had planned to live. She just hadn't gotten to that part yet.

The panic quieted in her chest, and the tears slowed. Mira gently pushed Gonzo's tail off of her lap and stood.

She wasn't going to do this. She wasn't going to imagine a life here. It was *insane*. This entire world was insane! She could barely keep up with the rules, and she'd already been sentenced to exile once.

But, of course, she was already imagining it. Her mind had refused to acknowledge it, but her heart had known it was a possibility all along. It was quiet, of course, but her heart knew she would never leave Gonzo, it knew how she felt about Mick, and even how Mick felt about her.

What about Sara? Sara wouldn't be able to live without her. She'd be devastated, destroyed.

Yet even as Mira told herself that, pacing circles around a sleeping Gonzo, she knew it wasn't true. Sara had survived having Wesley as a father. She could survive anything.

It was more so Mira couldn't survive without Sara. They were more than friends, more than cousins. They were soulmates, traversing their lives together. How could Mira live without her? All this time, she could bear it only by telling herself she would be back soon, they'd be reunited, pick up right where they'd left off...

How could Mira live in this world at all? Forget never seeing Sara again, or her parents, or anyone else she'd ever cared about – the Council wanted her dead, and the Council always got what they wanted.

Unless...things changed.

She sat back down, so hard that a zing ran up her tailbone.

It was foolish to trust John. He said they had a plan, but how good of a plan could it be if he needed a dragon to tie it together?

It was madness. She couldn't stay in this world. How was she going to fix anything? Mira wasn't a fixer. Besides that, things couldn't be fixed. The rich and powerful had control of everything. There was no use fighting it. Like Sara had always told her, if she needed to save someone, she should save herself.

Except if everyone followed Sara's advice, the rich and powerful would always win. They'd be unopposed, and by virtue, unstoppable.

So who was right? Was it Sara, or was it kooky John? Was the Council all-powerful, or nothing more than a mass of weeds and pests?

A gust of wind pushed across the tall grasses and sent a shiver down her back. It was colder outside of the barn. Mira pulled Gonzo's tail in closer and wept, feeling the darkness of the night penetrate her very soul.

After a few hours, her wails faded into hiccupping sobs, until eventually she was nearly silent, except for bursts of tears when she thought about Sara and her parents.

Her heart had decided long ago, and now, as her eyes grew heavy, Mira knew her mind was made up, too. She drifted off to sleep, the stillness of the night finally matching the quiet within her.

40

I am Standing Upon the Seashore

Early the next morning, Mira returned to Mick's house. This time, there was no one outside for her to frighten, and when she knocked on the door, no answer.

She caught sight of faces peering down at her from the upstairs windows, but just as soon as she saw them, the curtains snapped shut. The only sound she could hear was the cry of a baby inside – probably Arianna's son.

The thought of him without his mother made her feel sick.

After fifteen minutes, she gave up. Mick clearly wasn't home, and it was no use terrifying his staff. She climbed onto Gonzo's back and flew on, this time in search of John's tent city.

She flew high, hoping the Magnifican army wouldn't spot her. There were no fancy cars on the roads, and no large weapons – she imagined a magical catapult would be their end – and after dipping low to check out three separate encampments, she finally found the one where she'd walked with John.

Mira circled the tent city and nearby neighborhood three times before disappearing into the clouds. She waited a few minutes before dropping down again, hoping to catch sight of any Magnifican officials or traps awaiting her.

All she found on her descent was a gaggle of children, staring up into the sky and bursting into cheers when they spotted Gonzo. They were quickly whisked away, by their sensible mothers no doubt, and Mira felt comfortable enough to land.

She had Gonzo touch down on one of the deserted streets in the neighborhood. Like before, there were no carts, shops, or people. The homes stood, perfect and empty, without even a single instance of curtains rapidly shutting as she went by.

Mira walked toward the garden slowly, as to not spook anyone, and Gonzo followed lazily behind.

"Don't run off and chase anything," she said to him, and he looked at her, eyes round and bright.

They reached the garden gate and Mira spotted a squirrel. She stepped in front of Gonzo. "*Don't*," she said softly. "Leave it."

He quickly saw what she was talking about and let out a whine.

"I said don't."

"Mira!"

She turned and saw John approaching, again dressed in drab attire. This time, he had on black pants and a dark green shirt. It looked like there was mud caked onto the fabric.

How very un-John-like. Some part of her had hoped to see another extravagant outfit.

"Hello, John."

He shot a smile at Gonzo. "Am I allowed to come closer?"

"Yes, of course." She waved a hand. "He won't hurt you. Though he might kill that squirrel."

Gonzo's eyes darted to her and he let out another whine.

"Leave it, Gonzo," she said sternly.

The squirrel sat on its hind legs, puffy tail at its back, chewing away at a berry and blissfully unaware of how close it was to being eaten.

"I have no regard for the rodent," John said.

Mira took Gonzo's head in both hands and dragged it away, breaking his focus on the squirrel. "Yes, but I don't want Gonzo stomping through your garden. He has big paws. Come on, bud."

Gonzo did as she asked, turning to face her. At the same moment, John bent down and picked up a small stone, whipping it at the squirrel and hitting it in the tail. It took off and disappeared.

"Wow." Mira dropped her hands. "You have great aim."

He smiled. "Thank you. You could call it a gift."

Ah. Right.

"What brings you here today, Mira? Have you thought about what I said?"

"I have." She paused. "I want to see what your plan is."

His face lit into a smile. "And I want to show you. Come with me."

He led her down the street, away from the tent city and past the eager eyes of a group of children. Gonzo followed behind her, the squirrel forgotten, his interest now focused on sniffing the edges of the street.

They reached the end of a row of houses and John opened one of the doors, then hesitated. "I'm afraid Gonzo won't fit inside, but we can keep the window open so he can see you."

The only time she'd tried to go somewhere without him was when she had gone into the town square. He seemed quite good at finding her, but it wouldn't hurt to keep the window open. "Sure."

He smiled, rushing in to open the large, bay window on the first floor before waving her inside.

"Stay here, Gonzy," Mira said, patting him on the snout.

Gonzo watched as she walked into the house. She settled into a table next to the window and he laid down, crossing his enormous paws and resting his head on them, staring.

Mira suppressed a smile. He was still a good boy.

"My apologies," John said, moving a large map aside and folding it. "We were working on locating Arianna earlier."

"Did you find her?"

"I think so." He paused before opening the map up again. It was detailed, showing every village and road in Nordavia. There were red O's and lines drawn on the southern tip of the island, where a river emptied to the sea. "Our source says she's being held here. They plan to take her to Magnifico tonight."

Mira leaned in and studied the map. "That doesn't look far."

"It isn't. We believe they're mobilizing to recover their vehicles and get off the island as soon as possible."

She smiled. "They're scared, aren't they?"

He looked up at her, his blue eyes brilliant in the sunlight. "I think so, yes."

"What kind of weapons do they have?"

He leaned back, intertwining his slim fingers in front of his chest. "It seems they didn't come to Nordavia with much, but we can't be sure. They have rifles, and perhaps some soldiers with markings."

She stared down. It was even closer than New Belgium. Gonzo could fly there in half an hour.

"We, too, have markings on our side," John added. He pointed to the river. "We have flame-throwers, men and women with great speed, and water shifters."

"Water shifters?"

He nodded. "They can create waves on the river and wash out their camps. Very effective."

Water shifters wouldn't have much effect against rifles, but Mira wasn't going to burst his bubble. "Do you have any weapons? Rifles?"

"Mick has supplied us with a dozen, and he's out securing more."

That was where he'd gone. He hadn't given up after all. "A dozen…"

"I know it doesn't seem like much," John said, letting out a breath. "But we don't intend to start a battle. The guns are a contingency."

Surely the Council would find that comforting. "Have you ever taken on the Magnifican army before?"

He shook his head. "There hasn't been the will to do it. People were too afraid. Now, however, things are changing. We've shared the knowledge of Alice's marking. Some didn't believe it, of course, but many have. After you were taken, much of Nordavia wanted to rally behind you."

She frowned. "Didn't seem that way in the town square."

"Those were Magnifican supporters. Trust me, Mira. You have many supporters, both here and on Violet Island."

She could at least believe that about Violet Island. "Are you going to rescue Arianna?"

He offered a weak smile, then pushed the map aside, revealing a larger map of Magnifico. It was a small island, with a desert in the west, a large forest in the east, and a mountain range splitting it down the middle. Verity was at the southern tip, just north of Thunder Island.

"I would like to, yes, but we don't have enough time to organize before she is moved tonight. Many in the Hecate Society believe we should focus on our raid of the Hall of Magic."

"Is that what you want my help with?"

"It is. We have ships – you can see we plan to arrive in Verity from the sea." He pointed at the map, where there were more X's and O's drawn. "The more people we can recruit, the more effective our campaign will be."

Mira nodded, taking in the map. It seemed like they would do fine without her. "Gonzo can't do much, you know. He could maybe scare some people off, but he's not a weapon."

"Could he clear the ground ahead of us?"

She shrugged. "If they're scared of him, maybe."

"I mean with flame."

She raised her eyebrows. "Oh. I don't know. He doesn't breathe fire on command."

John nodded, hand on his chin. "I see."

"He's not a fighter, John. I know that's disappointing for you, but it's the truth." She broke eye contact, looking back at the map. "I don't want him to be killed."

"He doesn't need to be a fighter," John said. "He will unite us. You can lead us. We're prepared, but we need a catalyst – "

"I'm not a leader." She sat back and crossed her arms. "My dragon isn't a fighter, and I don't know anything about the Hall of Magic or – "

He held raised a hand, eyes lighting up. "That is not your role, then, Mira Meadows. We each have a role to play, no matter how strange it may seem."

"You're going to launch into a riddle, aren't you."

He laughed, the curve of his smile making creases at the corner of his eyes. "I'm sorry. Whatever role you can play, we appreciate. I believe the sight of Gonzo will inspire people, just as you have."

She raised an eyebrow. "I'm inspiring?"

"Oh yes. You are the Traveler the Council sent to die." He leaned in. "But instead of dying, you returned with a dragon."

He made it sound cool. It wasn't really like that. "I guess." She let out a sigh and uncrossed her arms. "I do want to help."

He clapped his hands together and stood up. "Marvelous! That's all we ask."

"But I have my own terms."

He nodded so quickly that his ears shook. "Yes, of course. Anything."

She shot a look outside at Gonzo. He'd fallen asleep. *My fierce warrior.* "I need to get Arianna and Alice."

John nodded. "We have a friend on Violet Island who has a locater marking. We can find them."

She narrowed her eyes. "Really?"

"I believe we can recruit him, and I will personally assemble a team to recover them both."

"Okay." She paused. That was the extent of her terms, but there needed to be more to it than that. "Gonzo won't be fighting or killing people. He's just – he's not a fighter."

"I understand. We aren't planning on violence, Mira. This is not an attack. It's a raid."

"Something tells me they'll see it as violence. The Council sees name-calling as violence."

"Indeed, but for our purposes, it's enough that Gonzo appears fierce." He leaned over the table, pointing to the map of Nordavia. "Would you fly to New Belgium and Old York? To help us recruit more supporters?"

She shrugged. "Sure. That's easy enough. How soon will we go to Magnifico?"

"We need at least four days to organize and plan. We thought we would have longer, but if we wait – "

Mira cut him off. "We risk Magnifico finding a way to eliminate Gonzo and me, and crush this rebellion."

He stared at her, his face solemn and creased. "Yes."

Mira nodded. "I'll get ready, then."

41

The Dragon Queen of Nordavia

John introduced Mira to two dozen men and women in charge of organizing the raid, and she remembered exactly none of their names. Half of them gazed at her with awe, which made her uncomfortable, and the others were gruff and serious, paying her little attention, which she preferred.

One of the more pleasant surprises was finding Slava at the edge of the tent city.

"She lives!" he yelled, arms outstretched.

Mira ran to give him a hug. "You haven't been sent to prison yet?"

"Me?" He pursed his lips, blowing a raspberry. "Never. John has helped me with it."

"Has he?" Mira turned to look at John, who had disappeared back into his group of generals.

"Yes, I was going to be integrated. I thought I would stay here in Nordavia." He shrugged. "I like it here. I have friends."

"You have friends everywhere you go."

"Still," he wagged a finger, "I never take them for granted. John was the one who warned me about the island."

"What island?"

"The lightning island. All of the Travelers with no markings were being sent there."

"Thunder Island? Even if they didn't want to go?"

"Yes."

"But why?"

"Nobody knows, but John has helped me to go away! You know, to disappear. He has helped me to disappear."

"Looks like you didn't get far," she said with a smile.

The other people in the tent city were starting to gather nearby, keeping a respectful distance but still watching the exchange.

Mira shot a look back at Gonzo. He was still behind her, nose in the air and distracted.

"I came back to see you." He stared at her, shaking his head. "I cannot believe it."

"Now you can help me," she said. "Do it. Say you'll help me. Say it."

"Anything." He dropped his voice. "Unless you are going to feed me to your dragon."

She waved a hand. "No. You need to come with me, though. Help me recruit people for the raid on Magnifico."

"Of course! It would be my delight."

"You'll have to fly on my dragon."

His smile fell. "That will be difficult. Perhaps I can fly with something else?"

"You'll be fine." She turned, walking to Gonzo and waving for Slava to follow her. "His name is Gonzo. He's friendly."

"Most of the time," Slava muttered under his breath, but he did as she asked.

Gonzo perked up, eyes zeroing in on Slava.

"Offer him the back of your hand," Mira said.

Slava turned to her, his face pale. "To eat?"

Of all the people to be afraid of Gonzo!

She shot him a look, then grabbed his hand to pull forward. Slava only resisted a little, his face twisted into a frown. "Look Gonzy, this is Slava. Say hello."

Gonzo knelt down and took a sniff at Gonzo's hand. He then stood back and looked at Mira.

"Good boy!" she said, beaming. "See, Slava? Not dangerous at all. We'll fly to Old York tomorrow, then New Belgium."

Slava's face was still twisted. "I will need a lot of wine."

That afternoon, Mick stopped by the camp with a car full of weapons. Mira was busy supervising the children petting Gonzo one by one. Though he could get skittish around large groups of people, he'd always liked children, much to their delight.

After Mick had unloaded the car and spoken to some people, it looked like he was going to leave without saying hello. Mira ran over to him, Gonzo bounding behind.

"Hey! Hang on!"

He leaned an arm out of the car window, his eyes narrowed. "Does the famed Dragon Queen of Nordavia require my attention?"

"She does." Mira stopped, breathless, and stood next to his car. There was a cut on the bridge of his nose, and the bags under his eyes were still dark and shining. "Where are you going now?"

"To find more markings and more weapons."

"Oh." She cleared her throat. "I wanted you to know – I'm going to help get Arianna back."

He nodded. "John told me as much. You're doing a tour of the island?"

"Do you want to join?"

He cracked a small smile, turning away to face straight ahead. "It could hardly top our last tour."

"True."

He turned back to her, eyes lingering for a moment before taking a breath and speaking again. "I can't."

Her heart sunk. Until that moment, she hadn't realized how much she'd been hoping to have him to herself again. "Okay."

"I have a marking for you." He reached over to the passenger seat and grabbed a small brown bag. "Take the ambrosia, then smash the aion into your chest."

She accepted the bag, peering inside as the aion flashed. "What's the marking?"

"It's armor. You'll be able to resist stabbing, arrows, and bullets. Not entirely, but it will help."

"This has got to be more valuable for someone else," she said. "Someone who – "

"It's for you. Take it."

She lowered the bag to her side. "Thank you."

Mick opened his mouth to respond, but hesitated before adding. "I may not see you before the raid. I'm going with the team to find Arianna."

"I'll help however I can."

He nodded, starting the car. "Thank you, Mira."

She wanted to say something poignant, to tell him how she felt. Mira wanted him to know she was staying. For Gonzo. For *him*.

But she seemed to be suffering from the same disease he had. "Take care," was all she managed to get out.

Mira watched as he drove off, clutching the bag in her hand. An ache started in her chest and peaked just as he disappeared from her view.

It was only temporary, she told herself. He would be back soon. She could tell him everything – as long as they both survived.

That was too heavy to think about now. She hopped onto Gonzo's back and took off to find a quiet spot in the forest.

They didn't have to go far, and the silence was a soothing balm to her overstimulated mind. Gonzo went after a raccoon while she removed the aion and small glass ampule of ambrosia from the bag.

She popped the cork lid off of the ampule and downed the ambrosia. The tiny drop tingled on her tongue. She then took the aion in her hand and stared at it, watching the flashing for a moment before closing her eyes and slamming it into an exposed spot on her chest.

The glass shattered, and at the same moment, a zing ran through her. Her hands and legs flashed numb, as though she'd fallen asleep on them, but quickly morphed, growing hot.

Mira looked down at her chest. The skin was irritated, with a few scrapes from the glass, but it had been far less damaging than she'd expected.

Once her limbs cooled down, it was as if nothing had happened. Hopefully, it had worked, but she was flying out no matter what.

• • •

Bringing Slava on her tour was brilliant. During their first flight – which he found a way to enjoy, despite his fear of Gonzo – he came up with talking points.

"You know, Mira," he told as they flew north, "the Council does nothing new."

"What do you mean?"

"In my country, they had the same tricks. The rich have their corruption, and they divide, divide, divide. It is always about how we are different, so we do not realize we are the same. This speech I will give, it is from my heart."

She was just relieved she didn't have to speak. "Glad to hear it."

Slava practiced his recruitment spiel, mumbling it to himself as they traveled, then honing it once he gauged the reaction of the crowds.

His final speech, given in a small village south of New Belgium, was a masterpiece.

"We are not Travelers, or blue-eyes, or brown-eyes. We are not Violets against Nordavians. We are one. It is them who keep all of the money, all of the power, and all of the magic. The rich know they must distract us to keep it for themselves. Together we can take back magic. Together we can take back our life!"

His English still wasn't perfect, but the effect was there, sending goosebumps down Mira's arms.

Mira hardly had to say anything. She added a few comments about the help they needed and hundreds pledged to join the raid. Others donated their cars and wagons, and still others what little food or supplies they could spare.

A few people approached Mira and Slava after their speeches, saying they had a member of the family or a friend with a useful marking, hidden all this time, but they were willing to come out to help now.

When they returned to Laurium, there were thousands of people prepared to travel to Magnifico. The Hecate Society had arranged for ships to carry them to the shores of Verity, but as more people came, it seemed they'd be unable to transport everyone.

That was when a few train engineers stepped forward, offering to commandeer flying trains from both Nordavia and Violet Island to deliver people directly to the heart of Verity. There wasn't a soul on Magnifico who knew how to run a train, as those jobs were considered too lowly, so the Council would have no way of stopping them.

Still, The Council was aware people were organizing. Their pegasus-riding spies hovered above the tents in the night and watched the ships as they moved up the river.

It made Mira nervous, but there was nothing to be done. She spent the remaining time in the forest, hiding from prying eyes.

On the eve of the raid, Mira couldn't sleep. She was sick of waiting. All of her nerves had been focused on preparing, and there was nothing she wanted more than to begin.

As Gonzo slept, she kept herself busy by pouring over the maps John had given her. One was of Magnifico, and another showed all of the roads and landmarks in Verity. She was engrossed in her studies when she heard the sound of footsteps on the forest floor.

"Hello?" she called out, dropping the maps.

"It's only me," said a gruff voice.

Mira gasped, catching sight of Mick under the moonlight. Her heart leapt.

He'd come back.

"I see they've gotten you a uniform." He was smoking a cigarette, still dressed in a three-piece suit.

Mira laughed and looked down at her outfit. Two of the Violet women had made her a new purple jumpsuit, this one out of durable linen. It was sleeveless and came down in a deep V, showing off what remained of her bolt. They'd added a cooling enchantment to the fabric that felt heavenly. "Is it too much?"

He stared at her, the slightest smile on his lips, and shook his head. "No."

She resisted the urge to run up and hug him. It would only startle him. "Have you changed your mind about flying with me?"

"I would go anywhere with you." He stepped closer. "But for now, I've come to say goodbye."

Mick tossed the cigarette away and closed the distance between them, taking her hand in his. His touch was surprisingly gentle.

A breath caught in her throat. Surely he didn't think they wouldn't see each other again?

"I would ask you not to go to Magnifico, but I know you won't listen," he said, voice low.

"I could ask you the same." She squeezed his hand. The warmth of his touch slowed her heart rate, calming her. "But I have to go. I've decided I'm not going back to my world. I'm staying here, and I have to help."

Mick looked at her, his long eyelashes swooping as he scanned her face. "That's what you want? To stay?"

"Yes."

"Well then." He planted a soft kiss on the back of her hand. "I could stand losing you to your world, but I can't stand losing you in this world. Come back to me, eh?"

Mira nodded, and he raised his hand, delicately brushing his fingers against her cheek. She shut her eyes, heart rate picking up again, her mind spinning.

A moment later, she felt his lips on hers and she leaned in, kissing and taking him in.

He broke free of her hand, and when she opened her eyes, he was gone.

42

A day at the beach

Armed with her maps, Mira and Gonzo took off hours before the sun rose to survey the Council's forces. They reached the northern shores of Magnifico quickly, passing over in the darkness and flying high above the forest.

It was a cloudy day, perfect for them to remain concealed, and she made the decision to fly over Verity for the first time, staying high until she saw the light from the city.

It started small at first, with glowing, expansive neighborhoods weaving and winding their way toward the tall, twinkling buildings of the city's center.

Mira pulled Gonzo up, back into the safety, as she studied the map. The Hall of Magic was located in the center of the city, several blocks from the beach where they were landing. The train station was much closer – only a block away.

There was still no word as to where Alice was being kept, but Arianna was located in a prison overlooking the sea. According to the map, it was just outside of the city, near the landing point for their ships.

Mira steered east, and Gonzo lazily coasted along. The clouds broke over the beach and Mira had no choice but to expose herself in the rising sun. Ships were stationed all along the shore – she counted twelve – and at the northern end of the beach, built into a rocky cliff, stood what looked like a fortress.

According to the map, that was the prison. It was built entirely of stone, with five raised walls in the shape of a pentagon, and bastions pointing from each corner. Mira could see the tiny outline of guards walking atop the walls, the ocean crashing beneath them unnoticed.

In the center there was a lush, green courtyard filled with soldiers. A single flagpole stood in the center, built from wood and flying a flag Mira didn't recognize.

It was time to start showing herself – and Gonzo – to gauge their reaction. She dipped out of the clouds and flew over the courtyard.

The sight of Gonzo was met with cries. At least half of the soldiers scattered and ran, and the other half were knocked over in the confusion. Mira heard a few gunshots as she flew off, but she'd made sure to keep her distance so none of them hit. John had showed her the range of the rifles in Asphodavia. It was, thankfully, quite poor.

Mira spotted a ledge in the nearby forest overlooking the prison and guided Gonzo to land. She hopped off, checking him over to ensure he hadn't been grazed.

"Talk about fire first and ask questions later..." she muttered. She'd had some hope that if she remained peaceful, they would too, but that had proved to be naive. When people saw Gonzo, they panicked. And when they panicked, they became erratic and violent.

The forest seemed treacherous enough that it would take the soldiers some time to reach her on foot, and she set her mind to giving Gonzo at least a half hour of rest. Over the horizon, she could just see the first ship coming in from Nordavia.

She sat there, muscles tense, as she watched Magnifico's ships. The Nordavian ships didn't stand a chance if they came under fire. They were small and flat, made to transport people and cars, not to go to battle.

Magnifico had warships with gleaming, polished wood and cascading green sails. Each ship had between six and ten cannons peeking out of each side, and according to John, they were loaded with magic cannonballs that tracked their targets.

They were meant to destroy.

He'd assured her that most of the cannons were too slow to even hit pegasi, let along Gonzo, but Mira hadn't taken much comfort from this. They knew she was coming this time – surely they were prepared.

She looked at her watch and gritted her teeth. The Nordavian ships were supposed to appear at any moment. Hopefully nothing had gone wrong...

Her eyes were locked on the horizon when she heard a horse's scream. She thought it had come from the forest, so she jumped onto Gonzo's back and they launched from the rocky ledge into the sky.

The moment they were in the air, they nearly collided with a white pegasus, ridden by a man dressed in black. The animal reared, narrowly missing a collision and nearly throwing its rider, before reversing and plunging straight down and away.

Mira pulled back on Gonzo's mane and he stopped, hovering in place, as a calvary of nearly a hundred pegasi charged at them, three rows high and moving fast.

"Crap." Mira pressed down and Gonzo dropped, following the first horse. "We'll see how fast they are, Gonzy."

Gonzo was excited by the commotion. The pegasi were not a match for his size, and he easily picked up his speed and dropped below them.

The pegasi flew overhead, their riders barking orders and trying to remain in formation, and Mira turned Gonzo before launching him up and over the hooved flock.

Though the riders seemed fearless, the pegasi in the back caught sight of Gonzo and panicked, shrieking and falling out of formation. Mira pressed Gonzo forward – even at his slowest, he was proving faster than they were – and once she overtook the herd, stopped and hovered in their line of sight.

Another third of the horses fell out of formation, scattering in all directions. Mira smiled to herself, calling on Gonzo to pull up. A few gunshots rang out and she ducked, but she was too slow. One grazed her arm.

She screamed, and in that moment, Gonzo opened his jaws and released a torrent of blue flame.

Mira gasped and Gonzo stopped, hovering in place. "It's okay, buddy. Please don't burn these poor horses alive."

She turned back and saw the remaining calvary had fallen back, all of them frantically pumping their wings toward the shore.

Well. That had been effective, and no one was hurt.

Except for Mira. She touched a hand to her arm – it seemed the bullet had only managed to make a gash in her jumpsuit. Her skin was unbroken, though slightly irritated and red.

She leaned forward, checking Gonzo's fur for any signs of injury. He seemed unharmed, and he wasn't bleeding.

The Nordavian ships were now visible, and Mira was behind schedule. She was supposed to be distracting the Magnifican fleet.

They dove low, gliding over the water and out of what John said was in-range for the cannons. If he was wrong and they ended up dead, she would kill him, of course.

Gonzo was untroubled, dangling one of his paws to break the surface of the water below, and Mira smiled to herself. At least he was having fun.

A shot rang out, and a cannonball launched into the open water. Mira held her breath, bracing for an impact, but the cannonball got nowhere near them. It plopped into the water with hardly a splash.

"Ha!" She looped around, circling the ships.

Within moments, the entire fleet erupted in cannonball fire. The air filled, dense with smoke, but the firing didn't stop.

Gonzo let out a whimper, tossing a glance over his shoulder. Mira thought he was hurt at first, but then she realized he was probably scared of the loud noises. She pulled up, still circling the ships, but high enough that the sound of cannonball fire faded.

Mira was looking down at the ships when something whizzed past her head.

She turned at the last moment, catching sight of it as it flew into the clouds. It was an arrow, and it had banked rather aggressively to get so close to her.

Great.

She leaned left, then right, getting Gonzo to zigzag. He managed it with glee, and she reached forward to scratch his neck. He tilted his head into it, sending them off balance for a moment.

The sky had cleared to a perfect blue. There were no clouds to disappear into anymore, and Mira didn't want to send Gonzo back down to face the barrage, so she pulled him back, hovering high above the ships. They continued to fire, the grey smoke so thick that she could barely see the lead ship.

That was good. That meant they couldn't see her either.

The Nordavian ships were only a few hundred feet out from shore, waiting. The plan had been to try to exhaust the warships into using all of their ammunitions, but Mira didn't like that plan anymore. It was too dangerous, and it felt like it would take forever.

She had a hunch and decided to follow it. "We're going to go back down, but just for a minute, okay buddy?"

They dropped, slowly, into the edge of the smoke. Mira made sure to circle wide before bracing herself and letting out a scream.

In an instant, Gonzo's blue flame lit the darkness around them.

It worked!

They kept on it, circling wide as to not hit the floating tinder boxes, blasting flame through the smoke.

They banked three turns, Gonzo blazing all the while, as the sound of cannon fire died down. It was replaced with something else – splashing and yelling.

Mira couldn't see, as she was too deep in the smoke, so she had Gonzo raise himself up, high above the ships. The smoke was more spread out now, but still too opaque to see through.

She flew on toward the larger of the two Nordavian ships that had saved a small clearing for her to land. Gonzo had never had to aim so precisely before, but she pointed him toward it, and he hovered and landed at the last moment.

The ship gave a small lurch with his added weight, but nothing drastic, and the people on the deck cheered.

"Mira, that was brilliant."

John was beaming at her.

She nodded. "Thanks. I'm just going to check Gonzo over."

His sides were heaving with each breath, and she ran her hands over his fur, checking for marks or bleeds. Miraculously, he didn't have a scratch on him.

One of the grumpy generals dropped a bucket of water in front of Gonzo. "Back up. Give them space," he barked at the group of eager faces that had gathered. The ship was quite tightly packed, so they couldn't go far, but they squished backward so Gonzo had a few empty feet around him.

He dropped his head to the bucket and drank nearly all of the water before looking at Mira, mouth hanging open and dripping.

"Good boy, Gonzy." She patted him on the snout and he wagged his tail before laying down.

Hopefully he wasn't getting too tired. There was still work to be done.

John stood next to her, staring straight ahead into a pair of copper and gold binoculars. "We were going to deploy the water shifters, but I don't know that we need to make waves. They're swimming for shore – look at that. Abandoning their posts."

She stepped forward. "Let me see."

He handed her the binoculars. The smoke was clearing now, and all the ships had stopped firing.

She scanned the smooth water until she spotted splashing. It was the escaping sailors.

Mira smiled and handed the binoculars back. "Not bad."

John was grinning from ear to ear. "Not bad? This is wonderful. I think we're ready to press on."

Mira looked around at the excited faces around her. "Where's Mick?"

"Already on land," John said. "They'll be breaching the walls of the prison any time now."

She looked at Gonzo. He'd shut his eyes and his breath was heavy, already into a nap.

No one knew how to rest like a dog.

"How long before you approach the shore?" Mira asked.

The grumpy general stepped forward. "I say no more than half an hour. We should start our approach now, and if anyone comes after us, we'll need you again."

"I'll see you to shore," Mira said. "But then I'm going to help Mick."

He nodded. "That should be all we need."

Someone offered her water, and Mira accepted. They'd survived part one. They just needed the rest to go smoothly.

43

A perfect world

It took an hour to get the ships to shore. Mira let Gonzo sleep as long as possible, but she grew restless as they got closer. It wasn't smart for them to sit on the ship as a target. Dragons were safest in the air.

Before they got into the Magnifican ships' firing range, they took off, circling in the now-clear air.

Not a single ship fired on the Nordavians, and while there were some soldiers waiting on the sandy beach, a single fiery fly-by with Gonzo sent them running, too.

Once that was cleared, Mira flew Gonzo over the proposed route into Verity. She was careful to cast flame only when they were high enough to not catch the buildings on fire. She had no interest in burning anyone alive.

There were soldiers and cars lining the street, some firing at her, but they were quickly overwhelmed by the stampede of people running from Gonzo.

It was too easy.

She circled back and landed on the beach just long enough to tell John that the pathway was cleared.

"I'll be back soon. I'm going to check on Mick," she added.

John smiled and waved. The second ship had landed and dropped open, with Nordavians and cars pouring onto the beach.

She couldn't wait any longer. She needed to know Mick was safe. Being away from him made her heart feel like it was torn in two. If something happened to him...

Mira couldn't even think of it. Gonzo took off, beating his wings a few times before getting them into the air. She kept pushing him higher, well above the prison, before turning and flying over it.

The courtyard was in chaos, with soldiers running in every direction. At first she thought it was because they'd seen her, but then she realized it was something else – a group of people firing from behind a stone wall in the courtyard.

Mira had Gonzo fly lower, and she strained to see if she could figure out what was happening. It looked like one set of soldiers was firing on the other. What was going on?

She circled, getting lower, and was finally spotted. Orders rang out, and a group of soldiers arranged themselves in a line, facing her.

Mira let out a scream, and on command, Gonzo blasted his flame into the air. When he stopped, the line still stood strong, rifles aimed at her.

Whoops. So not everyone was afraid of her anymore.

She pulled Gonzo up just as the gunshots blasted behind them. He was as agile as ever, flying so nearly vertical that Mira had to cling to his neck so she wouldn't lose her grip.

Once they'd gained some altitude, she guided Gonzo to spin and return. The firing line was now distracted, being attacked by the soldiers behind the stone wall.

Mira scanned the scene below her. She didn't want to trap a bunch of prisoners in flame, yet at the same time, the prison itself was made of stone. It wouldn't catch on fire...right?

She dipped down, having Gonzo blast the flagpole with fire. It lit like a candle, flame dancing at the top, and she pulled away, gunshots at her back.

They all missed – or perhaps her new marking was working – and Mira banked, circling the prison. The only soldiers not running and not trying to kill her were behind the stones. She pressed on, trying to get closer. Only then did she recognize one of the soldiers – Mick!

He was alive! And he'd finally changed his outfit.

Mira grinned, catching his eye for the briefest of seconds and waving at him. She looped behind them, dropping low to blast flame just as she passed over their hideout, sending the remaining soldiers running for cover.

She pulled up and looked back. Mick and his fake soldiers were running up the stairs to one of the far walls overlooking the water. There were no soldiers nearby, all having retreated to the other end of the courtyard. Mira took a chance and landed Gonzo on the elevated walkway.

Mick came running, slowing only when he saw her. "Go, go, go!" he bellowed, waving the rest of his group past Mira and over the stone wall.

His face was bloodied, his hair disheveled. "You're not injured?"

"We're fine. Do you have a way to get out of here?"

Arianna ran past, a man on either side of her. She yelled Mira's name as she went, but the men didn't let her slow down.

"We do," Mick said. "Pegasi, just in the forest."

"I'll try to hold them back."

"Come with us."

She shook her head. "I can't. They're just entering Verity."

"Mick!" a voice called from below. "They're mobilizing down here."

He stared at her for a beat. "Hurry back." He planted a kiss on her cheek before taking off and launching over the wall.

He was alive.

That was all she needed for now. She'd cover their escape, help with the raid, and be back in no time.

Mira got back onto Gonzo and turned to face the courtyard below. There wasn't a single soldier in sight. It was possible they could be moving through the prison to chase after Mick, but –

A shock ran through her body. Mira opened her mouth to cry out, but nothing came. Her muscles went rigid and she fell off Gonzo, hitting the stone beneath them with a thud.

Gonzo turned, his face filling her field of vision as he pressed into her with his nose.

Mira wanted to reassure him, she wanted to reach out and pet him, but she couldn't move. He whined, nudging at her again.

"If it isn't the hero of Nordavia."

The paralysis broke, and at once Mira's rigid limbs collapsed to the ground. She staggered to her knees, looking up to see Wesley standing over her in a floating white box.

Her breath caught in her throat.

The box lowered, stopping on the ground fifteen feet from her. He walked out of it dressed in an all-purple suit, a white cape draping from his shoulders.

"Don't waste your dragon's flame on me again," he said evenly, walking toward her. "It won't work."

"Why don't you ever die?" Mira finally managed to spit out.

He laughed, waving at the four soldiers at his back. "I could say the same to you."

The soldiers rushed forward, throwing ropes around Gonzo's mouth that shut almost instantly, before he could react, and then more around his neck.

She screamed, but it was too late. Gonzo's mouth was tied and no flame could escape.

Wesley held up a hand. "Please, Mira. You look awful. You should save your strength."

Gonzo let out a growl as Mira was knocked down by one of the soldiers. Wesley stepped closer and smiled down at her before grabbing her by the arm and dragging her away.

Gonzo cried and whimpered, but though he struggled against the ropes, he was unable to move.

Wesley waved a hand and the soldiers walked away, disappearing into the prison.

"Being fireproof is one of my favorite markings," Wesley said, dumping her onto the stone. He untied the string around his neck and his cape fell to the ground. "People thought I was foolish for keeping it so long, but I knew. I *knew* the time would come when dragons would be tamed, and I wanted to be the first."

He had that crazy look in his eye, like he had the day he'd showed up at her door with a hunting rifle. It was a look of glee. It was, Mira had learned, how a sociopath looked when he was about to win.

"Congratulations," she said.

He put a hand to his chest, then used his other hand to pull a shining, silver gun from his pocket. "Thank you, Mira. It means so much to me that you brought me this dragon."

One of the soldiers returned, holding a small, white marble box. Wesley took it, placing it on the ground and shooing the soldier away. "This is for you."

He opened it, revealing an aion and what looked like a studded strap of leather. There was a quiet humming from the box.

"I'm afraid this will hurt." He grabbed her arm, securing the strap around her wrist. He then took the aion and held it up to her throat.

Mira remained still, staring down the gun barrel. Her heart raced and her mind darted between absolute panic and frantic ideas. Could she cut Gonzo out of his restraints? Could she pull the gun from Wesley? Where had he even gotten that?

Wesley pressed a golden button on the strap and fire blazed into her chest, down her back and out through her legs. Mira collapsed to the ground with a yelp, and Wesley pulled the aion away.

"Hm. Looks like it didn't take."

He knelt, hitting the button again, and the jolt ran through her body, pulsating and setting every nerve on fire.

"Ah, there we are."

Mira laid on the ground, gasping for air. She heard the sound of glass breaking and looked up. The aion was missing from Wesley's hand, and there was a dash of blood on the grey hairs coating his now exposed chest.

"Excellent." He re-buttoned his shirt and jacket before looking down at her and wiggling the gun. "I'll be right back. Don't go running off on me."

Mira's arms shook as she lifted her head to see what he was doing.

Wesley walked to Gonzo and tapped him on the nose with his hand. "Dragon, come."

Gonzo turned away, eyes downcast, and Wesley let out a sigh.

"I was hoping to extract a few more aions, but oh well." He walked back, gun pointed at Mira. "It seems the marking isn't enough."

"It's enough," Mira said, her voice hoarse.

"Is it?" He let out a tsk. "Scholars have said for years that dragons are pack animals. Do you know what pack animals need?"

"They're not pack animals."

Wesley went on, louder. "They need a leader. An alpha." He cocked the gun. "The dragon won't respect me until he knows I've defeated you."

Mira dragged herself up. Her legs were shaking, but she could stand. "That's not true. Not at all. You have no idea what you're talking about."

He snapped his head toward her. "How dare you." His voice was almost a whisper. "You know nothing about this world, but you're going to tell me how it runs? Do you know what I've done in Asphodavia?"

"Yeah. Made life a living hell for everyone."

He blinked at her once, twice, three times. "I've made a perfect world."

"Perfect for you, maybe." Mira could feel the blood returning to her muscles. Her legs and arms felt hot, and she was no longer shaking.

"People don't know what they need. I've given it to them."

She took a step toward him. "You think they want you to tell them what they need?"

"Asphodavia is a paradise," he continued. "Every year, every day, we get closer to perfection. We keep people from being *agitated*. Like you. Always so angry, Mira."

"They're angry because they're hungry and have no place to live."

He scoffed. "They're not hungry. There's food aplenty. They're angry because they have too *much*. Without guidance, they don't know how to think. People turn to their basest desires."

Like food and housing, and not having to give birth in a barn. Mira held her tongue.

"Because of me, regular people learn how to apply philosophy to their lives."

She wanted to grab the gun and bash him over his philosophical head with it, but she didn't think she could move quickly enough. Gun grabbing probably only worked in movies. "You can't control people into being happy."

He tilted his head and smiled. "Oh, Mira, of course I can. I already have. In this world, we train them to think productive thoughts. None of this hatred, and discontent, and anger."

If she couldn't grab the gun, what else could she do? He'd always had such an explosive temper. She needed to get under his skin. He might make a mistake.

"You've always been nuts," Mira said, "and grandiose and all of that. But now you've really lost it."

He grinned. "Mira! You've never understood anything. You did your little nursing job and patted yourself on the back for being a hero."

"You sat in your tenured professorship and congratulated yourself on being a genius because you knew a little physics."

"I am a genius." His smile fell away. "Do you know what dark matter is, Mira?" He waved his free hand, gun still fixed on her head. "Of course you don't. It makes up eighty-five percent of the universe. We can't see it, we can't taste it, we can't even measure it. But we know it's there, moving galaxies."

"Cool." She could run at his knees. He might shoot her, but she'd take him down.

"It is 'cool.' Dark matter flows through us. It connects us all. It's a miracle and a mystery, just like how we got to this world. Haven't you ever wondered how we got here?"

"Never crossed my mind."

He scoffed.

Comments like that bothered him, and she knew it. She pretended to stagger forward, feigning weakness, getting closer to him.

He kicked her in the knee and Mira fell to the ground, breaking her fall with her arms. Her reflexes felt about right, and now that she was closer to him...

"You never had any intellectual curiosity." He thrust the gun at her. "Get up. Put your hands up."

She stood, hands raised above her head. She was close enough to take him.

"There's a force connecting every soul, every universe and every star. A universal force, a universal dark matter." A smile spread across his face. "*I* am dark matter. I make the universe spin. My ideas are enough to change a world."

"You didn't get a single paper published after getting tenure, but now you make a universe spin?"

"That was bureaucracy," he snapped. "Do you know how I've sped things up here? It was me who discovered that reinserting Travelers back onto Earth pulled in more Travelers. In the last twenty years, I've found more markings than were found in the last two *hundred* years."

Mira gritted her teeth. That was why the Travelers were being sacrificed on Thunder Island. Wesley churned their lives like it meant nothing. He was proud of it.

He straightened a tuft of hair that had fallen out of place, regaining his composure. "I've changed the very relationship of time between our worlds. So don't you try to tell me how anything works."

"But," she said slowly, "if you're changing time – " Mira lunged forward, but she was too far to reach him. She'd barely moved when a bullet hit her in the chest and stopped her in her tracks.

"You shouldn't have done that," he said, shaking his head.

Mira lay on the ground, flat on her back and gasping for air. Wesley leisurely walked over, peering down at her. "Oh," he muttered, "you have to be kidding me."

Mira sat up and put a hand to her chest. There was blood, and it ached horribly, but there didn't seem to be a hole going through her.

"You're marked to bounce bullets?" He let out a sigh. "We'll have to do this the old-fashioned way."

Wesley leapt forward, his hands reaching for her neck as Mira ducked, escaping his grasp and tackling him to the ground.

He let out a yell and punched her, but it was worthless. Mira had six inches and at least thirty pounds on him. She leapt to her feet and ran to Gonzo, ripping at the rope around his snout. She could lift it, just barely, and saw he was bleeding beneath.

Wesley scrambled, chasing after her and striking her from behind.

The blow knocked the air out of her – he was surprisingly strong – and she spun, shoving him to the ground.

Four soldiers rushed over, and Wesley bellowed at them from the ground. "No! She's *mine*. I must do it."

The alpha dragon. *Right*.

The soldiers retreated to the center of the courtyard and Wesley got to his feet.

Mira turned back, frantically tugging at the knot on Gonzo's snout. It felt like her fingernails were going to rip off, but finally, the knot loosened and the rope fell away.

"Good boy, Gonzo. You know what to do."

Gonzo didn't need instruction; he turned to gnaw at the ropes tying him to the ground.

Wesley stopped, shoulders hunched and blood running from his nose. "Gonzo?"

Mira dropped a cold gaze onto Wesley. "Do you remember him?"

He opened his mouth, then shut it, staring blankly ahead.

"You tried to kill him before," Mira said, slowly walking toward him. "My dog, Gonzo."

"He was my dog," Wesley said in a low voice.

She broke into a sprint and Wesley braced himself, firing another round that missed her entirely. She collided with him and they fell to the ground, kicking and elbowing like children.

The gun had fallen from Wesley's hand and Mira kicked it away, clear to the far wall overlooking the water.

Wesley got up, running for the gun, and Mira ran after him. He got there first, whipping around wildly.

"Your marking can't beat everything," he said coolly, the gun aimed at her head. "As soon as I – "

Gonzo let out a roar and Wesley paused, looking over her shoulder with wide eyes. In a split second his aim shifted, away from Mira and above her head, pointed high and tight.

He was aiming for Gonzo. She wasn't going to allow that. Mira reacted without thinking, leaping forward and shoving him as hard as she could. A shot rang out just as Wesley went over the barrier, head over heels, straight onto the rocks fifty feet below.

44

The Laughing Heart

The round moved out of the chamber, past the impossibly soft loft of Gonzo's fur, and directly into his neck.

Gonzo, unlike Mira, was not bulletproof. The bullet went through his skin and exploded, exactly as it was designed to, blowing a gaping hole in his neck.

Mira ran to him. "Are you okay, buddy?" She applied pressure to the wound with her hands, unable to contain the bleeding, as she frantically looked for something to use as a bandage.

Gonzo didn't make a sound. He turned his head to look at her, breathing softly, steadily, as if trying to take in her scent.

The soldiers charged closer, yelling commands as they stomped through the courtyard. When they reached the first step, Gonzo whipped his head around and released a roar and a burst of flame.

They stopped, the lead soldier falling backward.

"Just hang on, okay, buddy?" she said shakily, removing her hands and running for Wesley's cape.

She tore at it, fashioning a makeshift bandage from the fabric and leftover rope, tying it around Gonzo's wound.

He tolerated it reasonably well, and only tried to scratch at it once before he was scolded.

When she released her grip, it seemed like the bleeding was contained. The soldiers had run off, too, disappearing into the prison and leaving them with only the sound of waves below.

Mira couldn't shake her fear of Wesley reappearing in one of those white hover boxes. She ran back to the rocky wall and peered over, cringing at she saw – Wesley's body, unnaturally bent and broken on the rocks, his pale skin splattered with foam from the crashing waves. His eyes were fixed open, and his mouth was, too, as though he still had one insult to hurl.

He was silent, however, and forever would remain that way.

"Let's get out of here, bud," she said, gently climbing onto Gonzo's back and giving him the command to fly.

He took off with ease, and as much as Mira wanted to return to Verity, she needed to find Mick to heal the wound.

She flew north, away from the beach and over the forest. The plan had been for Mick and his team to catch boats at the north-ernmost point of Magnifico, and Mira hoped it hadn't changed.

They flew over the edge of the forest slowly, with still no sight of Mick or his team. It wasn't until she reached the shore that she saw a small black boat waiting at the beach.

Mira touched down, startling the group of men guarding the ship. "I come in peace," she said, hands up. "Has Mick gotten here yet?"

"See for yourself," one of the men said, pointing behind her.

A pack of five pegasi had just broken out of the forest, flying in a single line. Mick was on the last one, his green soldier jacket missing, instead wearing a blood-stained white shirt.

They landed, the first few paying her no attention as they rushed onto the ship. Mira was careful to keep Gonzo from making any sudden movements and spooking the animals.

"How did I beat you here?" Mira slid off of Gonzo and onto the sand.

Mick grinned at her. "We flew under cover, over the trails. It's not easy when you don't have a fire-breathing dragon."

"You should do something about that." She untied the rope from Gonzo's neck and carefully peeled away the white cape. "Wesley got Gonzo. Can you heal him?"

He shot a glance at the ship before walking over and studying the wound. Mick touched the seeping blood with one hand and gave it a whiff. "It's a poison bullet."

"What!"

"I can heal him, but I need to get it out." He waved one of the men over. "Get me a knife."

The man ran back to the ship and Mick stared at her. "You were hit too?"

She put a hand to her chest. It was still tender to the touch, but the trickle of blood had stopped. "The bullet bounced off of me. I'm fine."

Mick gently brushed her jumpsuit aside, his fingers cold but not unpleasant. He shut his eyes and his hand glowed bright yellow, soothing the sore spot on her chest.

The man returned a moment later with a ten-inch blade. "We need to get going, sir."

"We will." Mick took the knife and returned to Gonzo's wound. "Keep him still."

Mira ran around to hold Gonzo's face in her hands. "Stay, Gonzy."

Gonzo flinched when Mick made the first poke.

"It's okay," Mira said, stroking his snoot. "Stay here, buddy."

It took an agonizing two minutes, but after extracting several hunks of metal, Mick declared, "I got it all."

Mira walked back just as Mick finished sealing the wound.

"Thank you," she said.

He nodded. "Did they get into the Hall of Magic?"

"I don't know. I'm going back now."

"Does he have the strength?"

She turned to look at Gonzo. He was sound asleep, eyes pinched shut and paws in the sand.

"He's tired, but he'll make it. Naps help."

Mick took a deep breath and turned to leave. "I'll be waiting for you in Laurium tonight. Mira?"

"Yeah?"

"Don't disappoint me."

She let out a laugh. "I'll try not to."

• • •

She let Gonzo sleep until the ship disappeared from her sight, then woke him by scratching his ear.

He opened his eyes and yawned, stretching out his front legs with his butt thrust in the air. The wound on his neck was furless, but healed, the skin pink and fresh. The only reminder of the wound was the dried blood in his fur.

"Do you still have some flight in you?" she asked, and he looked at her, eyes full and content. "Just a bit longer."

He wagged his tail and she climbed onto his back before taking off, flying high over the forest, the rushing wind peaceful and serene. It had turned into a beautiful day, the sky blue except for a few wispy clouds, the sun shining, the air fresh. The sparkling sea was so enchanting that she could almost convince herself they weren't constantly under the threat of death.

They passed over the forest with ease, and Mira could make out the sandy beaches of Verity in the distance. Rising from the center of the city, she spotted a black plume of smoke.

Not good.

They flew toward it, Mira constantly scanning the ground below for threats. The streets were empty, even of soldiers.

She kept her eyes down as they flew over the heart of the city. Mira pulled the map from her pocket, trying to find where she was and where the smoke was coming from. It didn't take long for her to figure it out.

It was the Hall of Magic.

She had Gonzo bank a turn, circling the smoke. Finally, she had found people, though it was hard to tell if they were Nordavians, soldiers, or regular citizens of Verity.

The wind was blowing north, and Mira guided Gonzo to land on a flat rooftop due south of the Hall of Magic.

From there she had a better vantage point, and Gonzo got a break. The grand building was engulfed in flames, half of it already fallen to ash. She looked on, studying the map and the scene in front of her.

It appeared the Magnifico army had put a blockade around all of the streets, trapping the Nordavians and Violets near the blaze. People were being herded into large buses at the edges of the street, while others choked on the smoke, pressed against the barricades. The soldiers on the other side of the barriers didn't budge, their faces obscured in what looked like gas masks.

That wouldn't do.

Mira pulled out the map. The road running east to the Hall of Magic led back to the beach, and the one opposite of it connected to the train station. She squinted at the name of it. "Record Road."

Mira ran her finger along the map and realized the Hall of Records was only two blocks from the Hall of Magic.

Interesting.

Surely all of these people would end up with black marks on their records if they survived, further ensnaring them in the system. Would it be prison? Reeducation? Perhaps a mass banishment to the Isle of Dragons?

It seemed short-sighted for the Hecate Society to place all of their hopes on the Hall of Magic. Perhaps they had to keep a narrow focus, but to Mira, Magnifico's draconian records kept people living as much in fear as did magic.

A plan formed in her mind as she got onto Gonzo's back and guided him to fly over Record Road. Each barricade was manned by no less than thirty soldiers, milling about with their rifles, some asleep in their cars.

Mira no longer had to scream – the feeling built in her chest and Gonzo spewed flame onto the cars littering the street. They lit in unison, sending soldiers running.

She circled around once, twice, until the soldiers had cleared out. They touched down on Record Road and she ran to the barricade. It was fifteen feet tall, with slick, shining wood on both sides.

People rushed forward, calling her name, pounding on the barricade, and sticking their arms through the slats.

"Get back!" she yelled. "I'm going to burn this to the ground."

Mira ran and jumped back onto Gonzo. She managed to get him to fly, hovering, over the barricade.

"Step back!" she yelled, waving her hands.

The crowd retreated and she didn't wait – she pointed Gonzo and drenched the barricade with flame.

It didn't even catch on fire, instead melting under the intensity of the flame.

Mira pulled Gonzo up to hover above. "This way! Get back to the ships."

People poured through the gap in the barricade and ran down the street. Mira took Gonzo to the other side of the trapped bunch and repeated the process.

Once that was done, she retreated to a building overlooking the scene.

Half of the trapped had made it out before the soldiers realized what was going on. A handful of cars came around the corner, and Mira was there to meet them, Gonzo blasting flame and keeping them at bay.

The Nordavians and Violets continued their escape behind her, running down the street. Mira got back into the air and once she was satisfied the area had been cleared, she followed her map to the Hall of Records.

It wasn't quite as grand as the Hall of Magic, the front facade made from red brick instead of white marble, but it was still formidable in size: five stories tall, with great windows on every floor.

Mira hopped from Gonzo's back and ran to the far side of the roof. He ran after her, his weight shaking the building beneath.

They did this for a few minutes before Mira got back onto his back and had him hover in front of the windows. Shrieks erupted from inside and terrified faces peered out of the windows.

People began to run out of the building; at first only a few, then a constant stream. She flew back to the roof and watched anxiously, hoping the occupants would get out quickly.

Soldiers arrived in five cars, jumping out and rushing people away from the building.

Good. They were finally being useful.

Mira wasn't going to burn anyone, but she was going to going to set one more fire before she left. The records had to go.

She waited, watching from the roof for twenty minutes. The building cleared out and the soldiers were distracted with her instead of the people fleeing from the streets.

Shots rang out her, all missing, and one soldier tried to come after her on a pegasus, but the animal panicked when it saw a dragon five times its size.

When she was satisfied there was no one left in the building, she had Gonzo hover a few feet above the center of the roof.

She set him off one last time, and Gonzo blasted his flame down into the building, blowing a hole of fire straight through.

Then they took off, the fire raging behind them.

45

Return

High above the beach, Mira could see the ships waiting at the shore. People poured onboard, and it seemed only a few cars had made it back unscathed.

Mira and Gonzo touched down in the sand and John waved from the edge of the sea. "Mira!"

"You're alive!" she laughed, walking Gonzo toward him.

"Yes, yes. A little smokier than before, but no harm done." His face was smeared with soot and one of his eyebrows was missing.

"What happened?"

He put his hands on his hips and let out a breath. "They set the Hall of Magic on fire as soon as we got into the city."

"You're kidding."

"I am not. Then they kept us in there, funneling people onto buses and into cars."

"I saw." She shook her head. "I'm sorry I wasn't – "

He held up a hand. "Don't be. We still managed to recover a few hundred aions."

"Huh." Mira made a face. "Not bad."

He nodded. "The Council destroyed thousands of them, though. It was an awful sound – the aions explode in the heat."

"You went inside?"

He wiped a hand across his face, smearing more soot. "Of course! We have two Violets who are fire resistant, and I helped guide them. It was the smoke that forced us out."

"I see." Mira looked over her shoulder, scanning the skies for any signs of attack. It looked clear.

"Thank you for coming to our rescue."

She turned back and offered a weak smile. "Sorry I didn't make it sooner."

"And Mickson?"

"They made it off the island." She cleared her throat. "I might've also done something not in the plan."

"Oh?"

"I burned down the Hall of Records."

John's jovial smile returned, his teeth shining white against his dirty face. "That's better than a raid."

She shrugged. "I thought it might help."

"Stay here." He held up a hand, backing up. "I've got something to show you."

John ran onto the ship and disappeared into the crowd. The people on board were smiling and laughing, huddled together and passing flasks.

They were happy to be alive. Who wouldn't be?

Mira turned around. The line of people parading onto the ships was dwindling. Hopefully they could leave soon and regroup on Nordavia to discuss how to rescue those who had been captured.

She looked down at her jumpsuit. It had seen better days, stained with blood and torn in places, but it still looked cool. The glow on her chest was gone, the bolt now nothing more than a red scar.

Her world grew quiet for a moment. She touched a hand to the scar, and the familiar zing did not greet her. Her heart sunk. Though she had known this moment would come, it was still painful. It still caused her lungs to tighten and her eyes to fill with tears.

Yet because of Gonzo, she knew she would see the ones she loved again. She could *feel* the link between them, the love that would remain unbroken and reunite them in the end.

Still, they were separated for now, and a heavy stone of grief settled into her stomach. She would be living with it for the rest of this life.

"I like the new look."

Mira spun around – there stood Alice in a white linen jump-suit, a wide smile on her face.

Mira jumped from Gonzo's back and ran to her, arms outstretched, until they collided with a grunt.

"They found you," she said, squeezing Alice tight.

She nodded, pulling back to look at Mira's face. "They did."

"They keep the Travelers locked up across from the Hall of Magic," John said, beaming. "I had a tip. We were able to release all of the Travelers."

Mira realized her face was wet. She wiped away the tears. "I'm so happy to see you."

"I can't believe this." Alice shook her head. "The dragon, the raid – "

"It's been a little crazy, yeah." Mira turned around and called Gonzo. He trotted over, thrusting his nose into her shoulder. "Do you want to fly back with us?"

Alice's eyes widened. "Fly?"

"It's perfectly safe." She paused. "As long as there aren't other dragons around."

Alice let out a laugh. "Sure. Why not? I haven't been outside in months. Might as well get a good view."

Mira clapped her hands together. The grief wasn't gone, but it was quiet for now. She'd have to learn to live with it, and from experience, she knew that meant seizing joy whenever it appeared. "That's the spirit! Follow me."

The sun was beginning to set and the first ship had launched from shore. Mira climbed onto Gonzo's back and offered Alice a hand. They took off, the setting sun at their backs.

46

A ring of gold

From the air, the tent city looked like a little Vegas. There were beams of red and yellow light shooting into the sky, an illuminated fountain launching some sort of a synchronized water show, and bonfires roaring throughout.

They landed and were immediately greeted by Slava.

"What is this?" he asked, arms waving in the air. "Our little Alice!"

"Hello Slava." She slid off Gonzo's back and landed gracefully on the grass below.

He pulled her in, squeezing her tightly. "We have missed you."

"I've missed you, too."

"They didn't hurt you too much on that island?"

Alice shook her head. "I'll be okay."

He reached a hand out to Mira. "Come now, Mira. Give Gonzo his break."

Mira leaned down and wrapped her arms around Gonzo's neck. "You're a good boy, Gonzy."

He shook his head, flapping his ears, and she laughed, releasing her grip and jumping down.

"I know he likes the raccoons," Slava said, walking into the camp, "but we have instead a few fish for him."

"He would love that," Mira said.

"For you, dear Alice, we have a smaller fish."

She laughed. "Sounds perfect."

"Come!" He walked on, toward the bonfire, looking over his shoulder at Mira. "How are the rest?"

"They're on their way. We stayed with the ships until they reached the river," Mira said. "Is Mick back yet?"

He frowned. "I have not seen him."

She nodded, trying to keep her thoughts from spiraling. If they had gotten this far only to lose one another at the last moment...

Mira couldn't let her mind go there. Just the thought made her feel brittle enough to shatter, drop, and sink into the ground.

They arrived at the impressive bonfire, its flames fifteen feet in the air. All around it, people were eating, laughing, and dancing to music.

Slava ducked away for a moment, returning with two plates of food. "For our dragon, a few fish." He waved a hand and two men approached, dragging a six-by-six canvas absolutely covered in fish.

Gonzo stood behind Mira, sniffing the air over her shoulder and licking his lips. One of the men looked up at Gonzo and froze, dropping his hold on the canvas.

"Thank you," Mira said, and the man nearly tripped over his own feet as he retreated back.

She set her plate down and picked up one of the fish. It was the length of her arm and four times as thick. She held it up, offering it to Gonzo. "Go ahead! Time for dinner!"

He stepped forward and gently took it in his teeth, then turned around to gobble it down in private.

Mira picked up her plate and took a seat on the ground next to Alice. "Thank you, Slava."

"Of course."

They ate quietly, watching the celebrations around them. As much as Mira wanted to know about Alice's time on Magnifico, it felt better to sit shoulder to shoulder and laugh at the clumsy, intoxicated wrestling matches that had broken out near the wine tent.

Gonzo finished his fish quickly, circled around three times, and nestled in behind Mira. He was snoring within minutes, and Mira was relieved she wouldn't have to wake him this time.

She finished her plate of food and sat back against him. Her muscles were still tense, her mind still on alert. It shouldn't have taken Mick so long to get back. Their ships may have been intercepted, or sunk, or lit on fire. The Magnifican army may have been waiting for them on Nordavia, or –

"I wouldn't get so comfortable."

Mira popped up, frantically looking until her eyes settled on Mickson Kellet, standing above her in a bloody shirt like the day she met him.

Tears rushed to her eyes and she stood, throwing her arms around his neck. He let out a small grunt and hugged her back, his arms soft around her waist.

"You made it," she whispered.

"I'm hard to kill."

She laughed and pulled away. "Why shouldn't I get comfortable?"

He cleared his throat and nodded his head across the fire. A group of five men was staring at them, and they looked away as soon as Mira turned her head.

"You have suitors waiting for their chance," he said. "The big one said he'd have you in his bed by the end of the night."

Mira scowled, and in that moment, the man turned to look at her. He smiled and waved.

Gross. She crossed her arms and shook her head. The man's smile faded, and the other men erupted into laughter.

"How is your bolt?" Mick asked.

She turned back to him. "Gone."

Mick frowned. "I'm sorry, Mira."

"Thanks." She took a deep breath. "It's okay, though."

He tilted his head. "Your eyes aren't good at hiding sadness."

"I'm not sad. I feel..."

There was so much more to it than that. Gonzo had survived. She had survived. The Nordavians hadn't all been hauled off to prison. Alice was home.

Her old life was gone, yes, but her new life was here, within reach. Mick was here, his eyes searching hers in the firelight.

"It's a shame," she said, "that these suitors aren't as eloquent in their proposals as the letters you used to get."

He cracked a half smile. "You read my letters?"

"Oh yeah, all of them. It was my job, Mick." She grabbed his hand and led him behind Gonzo, where prying eyes couldn't watch them. "The poetry was wonderful."

"The poetry was awful."

"The pictures were fun, though."

"I'll give you that." Mick pulled a cigarette from his pocket and popped it into his mouth. "So you don't want me to introduce you?"

"Why would I want that when I've already had one bad proposal?"

He laughed, the cigarette hanging from his lips. "It was bad, was it?"

Mira reached a hand into her pocket and pulled out the golden ring. "It wasn't even a real proposal."

He stared at her. "Would you like a real proposal?"

"From you?" He was infuriating, but she couldn't live without him. She pushed the cigarette from his hand and slipped the ring into his palm. "Yes, I would."

"You kept it."

She let out a breath. It felt like her heart would burst. "Yes, you dolt. I kept the ring."

"You're not waiting to see what the other suitors have to offer?" he asked, looking down as he rolled it between his fingers.

Mira smiled. "Unless they volunteer to rescue me from the Isle of Dragons – "

"*Try* to rescue you," Mick corrected, grinning.

She nodded and continued. "Then I don't see the point."

A small smile crossed Mick's face, his eyes lingering on hers before he cleared his throat. "Mira Meadows, Dragon Queen, terror of the skies, and ruler of my heart, will you marry me?"

"Yes!" It felt like her knees would give out, and she thrust both hands forward – one to steady herself on his chest, the other with her ring finger extended.

He slipped the ring on and took her into his arms, pressing his lips to hers, bringing her back to life again.

Epilogue

The nights will flame with fire

The first national election in Asphodavia was held one year to the day after the Magnifico raid.

The build for change was slow, but Mira's instincts had been right about the records – once they were destroyed, people all across the country began rising up.

It started with the train conductors who, after seeing how powerful they were in the raid, refused to transport people or goods until their demands were met.

Then the farmers, and the field workers, and the wine makers and bakers followed suit – refusing to live in fear, refusing the brutal rule of the authorities by reclaiming the constable offices with their own, locally-instated deputies.

Laws were changed once magic was no longer a weapon. Change crept upward, and the Council was abolished. The election was to create a parliament of representatives from every corner of Asphodavia to better represent the needs of the common people.

Though the concept of an election was new, there was no shortage of enthusiasm or candidates. Slava, for example, ran a lively campaign, ending many nights face-down in pubs all across Nordavia.

Ultimately, he lost to a Violet woman from a tent city south of Laurium. He still retained his position as mayor, however, which he insisted he was quite happy with.

Mira had no interest in running for office, despite a few calls for her to consider it. She felt it was unneeded, as there were far better qualified candidates, and unwanted, as she was content to take her time exploring and building her new life.

After a brief engagement and a whirlwind wedding, she and Gonzo moved out of the hidden barn and onto Mick's estate. An addition was built onto the main house that allowed Gonzo to join them through most of the day, which he loved, along with the open fields, skies, and rolling forests at his disposal.

Mira enjoyed it, too. She spent her days trading markings, a newly lucrative and legal market across Asphodavia. In her free time, she walked the fields surrounding their home. Mick had gifted much of his outlying property to the previous occupants of the tent cities. In a year, they'd managed to clear most of the land and plant enough crops to sustain and support themselves as they started their newly-housed lives.

Mick had saved one field for Mira, turning it into a vast garden filled with flowers, fruit trees, and whatever shrubs and bushes reminded her most of Earth.

He claimed he'd been inspired by a rose bush that had appeared in the center of the field the after day he'd met her. It stood three feet wide and six feet tall, with fiery red and orange-petaled flowers that bloomed throughout the summer.

Whether she believed him or not, she tended to it as though it were true. The rose demanded her attention, constantly wrapped by vines or choked by weeds, and the quiet of her work allowed her time to think.

She thought about Sara, and her parents, and the life she'd left behind. She thought about Wesley and his dark matter, about the force that ultimately defeated him, the one he could never understand.

In the evenings, she and Mick sat at the fireplace in their dragon-sized addition, with Gonzo cozily asleep on the enormous bed Mick had gotten for him. They talked into the small hours of the night, and flames from the fire cast their laughing shadows onto the wall in a little space that was small, insignificant, and at the same time, absolutely everything.

Note from the Author

Andrzej,

light of my life and dragon of my soul,

I love you then, now, and always. Until we meet again –

A Final Word

Join Nadia's newsletter to keep up to date on new releases: https://www.subscribepage.com/mira

About the Author

Nadia Jovie is an author and first-generation American. At a young age, she found herself in a strange gap between cultures and has been writing her way out ever since. A hopeless sap, Nadia brings home too many dogs and throws touches of madness and magic into life and storytelling. She lives in Pittsburgh with her tolerant husband, angry dog, and a rotation of homeless animals.